PATHBOUND ENTERPRISES BOOK 1

KATE SHEERAN SWED

To Sara

Join my mailing list to read deleted scenes from *Bypass the Stars*—and gain access to my exclusive VIP reader library!

Sign up here: https://www.subscribepage.com/bypassthestars

Searching for inhabited worlds is like digging for a beach ball buried in a haystack the size of eternity. To happen upon even one of them is nothing more than pure luck.

Pathbound Enterprises has had enough luck to last us several generations.

-Fifty-Year-Old Diary of James Hartiger, Astrophysicist and First Interworld Explorer

ONE
FRANKIE

Three years ago

OF THE THIRTEEN methods Frankie Hartiger had perfected for breaking into Sublevel D of Pathbound Enterprises Tower, scrambling the facial recognition panel on the Warren-700 security bot was usually the simplest.

Tonight, Frankie had been hunched in front of the malfunctioning heap of junk for so long that her legs were going numb. The new interworld transport operator's disembodied face hung suspended in midair before her, like a ghost returned to avenge a bad ID photo.

It was a hologram—a decoy Frankie had created to fool the dunce cap of a guard into opening the doors. She'd been doing this for months, using the trick to explore forbidden areas whenever she pleased. But this time, the bot wasn't budging.

When the real Liz Han dropped to a crouch beside her digital double, Frankie jumped. She hadn't even heard the doors open.

It was an awkward way to meet someone for the first time. Even by Frankie's standards.

The real Liz had a green yoga mat tucked under one arm and cursive tattoos on the backs of her hands: *If You* on the left, *Build It* on the right. She wore her black hair longer than it was in the picture, her ponytail tied low and flipped over her shoulder.

"Every time I sit for an ID photo, I sneeze," Liz said.

Frankie deactivated the digital Liz. The best course of action, she decided, would be to act like she was supposed to be here.

"I'm Frankie Hartiger," she said. "You secured a patent on citywide driverless car systems when you were nineteen."

At fourteen, Frankie figured she had time to beat that milestone.

"You're the daughter?"

A rhetorical question, obviously. Frankie hadn't made newsworthy contributions to the Hartiger Family Legacy—not yet—but she'd watched herself grow up on celebrity-zine covers. Family time, faked. The product of a talented photo collagist and a non-disclosure agreement as strong as soldered iron.

Fake or not, people liked to read about the first family of interworld travel. The *only* family of interworld travel. In the decades since her grandparents had succeeded in hopping between universes, no one else had come close to figuring out how they did it.

Frankie didn't even know.

Liz might.

"You've been directing commercial space flights since you were twenty-six," Frankie said.

"Don't tell me you know about the burger-flipping gig I had in high school, too."

Frankie did. She could have listed even more stats. Liz was thirty-three, Chinese American, five-foot-six. She'd also won eleven semi-professional digi-bowl championships, until she'd given up the sport seven years ago. Perhaps after recognizing the game as a mind-numbing waste of her significant mental capacities.

"I research every new high-ranking employee," Frankie said. "You actually deserve to work here."

"I'm not sure that's a compliment."

"It is. You patched the software on the security bots. Right? I'm the only other person who ever caught that glitch."

Liz allowed the bot to scan her face, then straightened as the glass doors slid open. "You aiming to be a commercial space director by twenty-six?"

"I'd rather build the rockets."

Liz started through the doors. "Come on."

It almost felt like a trick, like Liz might change her mind and slam the door in Frankie's face. But Frankie wasn't about to waste an authorized visit to the transport floor. She scooped up her trusty toolkit and followed.

Mom and Dad didn't spend enough time on Earth to bother with interior decorating. They'd stuck with the grounded-spaceship aesthetic that must have seemed appropriate when Frankie's grandparents had built the place. Metal walls, metal floors. Blinking blue lights ringed the raised control deck in the center of the room that operated all transport functions via touch screens and augmented-reality models.

Twisted together like an over-stylized puzzle at the far end of the room, the doors to the interworld transport dock gleamed.

Liz shoved the chairs to the perimeter of the elevated console and unrolled her yoga mat. "You watch *Mars Colony*?"

Disappointing. Liz seemed smarter than reality vids. "I

don't watch any shows, and before you ask, I only do virtual reality immersion for school assignments or history lessons."

The murder of Caesar was particularly good.

Liz sat on the mat and leaned against the railing that encircled the platform. With a few touches to the console, she pulled up a screen in augmented reality. The opening sequence began with its familiar blast of red particles—anyone who'd ever glanced at a billboard in New York City had seen that part—and the miniature cast members paced into view, waving and posing. What did they do for screen tests, check to see how good these people looked in spacesuits?

Frankie had a feeling this was not what her parents had had in mind when they'd hired a genius to run the interworld transport.

"Good, then you're not caught up." Liz patted the mat. "There's a guy this season who wants colonies on every planet in the solar system. He keeps saying he's going to Venus next. It's hilarious."

In real life, and with an occasional exception, human interaction was an unavoidable nuisance. The only reason most people talked to her at all was to get to her parents. As soon as someone learned that Frankie's parents basically ignored her, they'd drop her like an overheated drone.

Why would Frankie want to spend more of her time watching fools stumble around on TV?

"They shouldn't be sending those people to Mars," she said. "If he thinks Venus is habitable, he might leave the dome without his suit or something."

"The show is in its eighth season, and no one's died. The producers keep an eye on them."

"It's a waste of resources."

"It's science for the masses. Come on, sit."

Frankie sat. She wished she'd brought a sweater.

After the first episode, Frankie feared for the future of humanity.

After the fourth, she started to see Liz's point. A little bit. The show did use people-slash-characters to show how the colonies worked.

"My parents should do this with Suhainn," Frankie said.

She could suggest it to them. The idea might be good enough to earn her way back to their good graces—and maybe earn a ticket to Suhainn, too. They'd never brought her to any of their other worlds.

Before Liz could answer, the com unit buzzed to life with a shower of static. "Pathbound, do you copy?"

Mom. She never called before 2300 hours. Once, and exactly once, Dad had reported thirty-nine seconds late. He'd never been trusted to call on his own again. She knew, because that was reason number one for her trespassing down here. She liked to hear her parents' voices as they radioed in from other worlds.

Something was wrong.

Liz was already leaping for the table. "Copy, Cindy. Go ahead."

A burst of static. "We've got a situation. Retrieve the box for Sunset Protocol."

In all her years of spying, Frankie had never heard her parents ask for a protocol box. The word 'box' was something of a misnomer, since they were actually metal cylinders that lined the walls of the storage room—an excellent hiding spot for daughters who wanted to listen to her parents as they called in at 2300 hours every night. She'd hide, and she'd stare at the protocol names, from Asteroid to Zenith, imagining the kinds of disasters Mom and Dad might have planned for with the protocols. What failsafes they'd designed. She'd never quite been able to talk herself into disturbing one of them, in case its retrieval might give her away.

Liz hopped off the console and ran for the supply room. Maybe Mom and Dad were testing their new T.O. with a drill.

Or maybe Frankie should pick up the com and speak to her mother. Just in case.

When Liz stepped out of the supply room, her face was pale.

"What does it say?" Frankie whispered.

Liz shook her head, held a finger to her lips.

Thunder roared into the operations center, a sustained vibration that rattled up through Frankie's feet. She always pictured the tower trembling when the transport arrived, the city pausing its business to watch the floors shake. A scientifically improbable daydream, given how carefully the tower was designed.

Still. It reached into her bones.

The transport was back, and it was early. Sunset Protocol, step one? But Liz shook her head as she scanned the box's contents, the transport's arrival clearly as baffling to her as it was to Frankie.

Liz stuffed the box into her pocket and grabbed Frankie by the shoulders, shoving her across the room and into the supply closet. "Stay here."

Frankie didn't need the panic on Liz's face to convince her. She had no excuse for her presence here. She stayed, peering out while Liz sprinted to the console and opened the doors to the transport dock. The puzzle spun open with a dramatic twirl, revealing Frankie's mother and father. Behind them, the transport shuddered.

Whatever had gone wrong, it was not enough to upset the

perfection of Mom's hair, a sleek waterfall that poured into a dark pool of curls. And Dad, so tall his sun-stained head nearly brushed the door frame.

"We agreed on Sunset," Mom said.

"Meteorite Protocol is more than sufficient," Dad replied. No trace of his usual humor, no hint of a smile. He wore his flip-flops, despite the many warnings Frankie had given him about the dangers of poor footwear.

Liz stood on the console, fingers whitening around the protocol box. She looked shocked, her lips parted, eyes wide.

For a second, Frankie didn't understand why. Yeah, her parents were arguing. A crack in their usually flawless performance, a slice of reality. Rare enough to warrant curiosity, but hardly worthy of the horrified look on the transport operator's face.

And then Frankie saw the shoe.

Behind her father, on the grated metal floor of the transport dock, was a brown shoe. And it was connected to a leg.

Frankie moved to the other side of the door and risked sticking her head past the frame.

A boy lay at her parents' feet, motionless, his skin paper white. As she watched, a spot of blood on his neck swelled to a bubble and burst, trailing across his throat like a slit.

No one checked on him. No one even looked at him— except maybe Liz—and he obviously needed help. Did her parents know he was bleeding?

Frankie abandoned her hiding place.

She made it all the way across the room before her parents noticed her and fell silent. She ignored their stares and bent over the boy, setting her toolkit on the floor to take his wrist between her fingers. His skin was cold, but his pulse rushed strong and even. She let out a breath.

"Did you know she was down here?"

Frankie tuned Mom out and replaced the boy's hand gently by his side. When she did, something tumbled out of his grasp.

It might have been her imagination, but she thought she felt him flinch when it skittered to the floor. It was a stone, flat and round, with a hole punched through the top. Frankie picked it up and turned it over in her hand, running her thumb along the smooth edges.

A stone from another world.

A *boy* from another world.

The stone had markings etched on one side, an intricate series of crisscrossing lines that reminded her of the Celtic knots her grandfather used to draw. The markings on the boy's stone might have been language or design. She couldn't tell.

Frankie tucked the stone into the boy's shirt pocket, so he'd have it when he woke.

He smelled like the sea.

Convinced for now of his safety, Frankie looked up to find her parents staring at her. "What's Sunset Protocol?" she said.

Mom peeled off her jacket. "All right. Meteorite. Take him up."

Dad scooped the still-unconscious boy into his arms and carried him off the transport dock.

"Who is that?" Frankie asked. "Is he from Suhainn? What happened?"

"What happened," Mom said, her voice clipped, "is that he nearly got himself killed. He's lucky we were there to save him."

Frankie tried to imagine what kind of scenario in supposedly safe Suhainn would have resulted in a need to bring the boy to Earth. Had he been acting as a spy? Betrayed the realm somehow? Committed a crime? Had he murdered someone?

As far as Frankie understood them—which admittedly

wasn't very far at all—it wasn't exactly like her parents to inter-vene in a situation like that. Though what did she know, really? She was their daughter, and she had to break into restricted areas just to hear their voices. It was hardly surprising that a Suhainnan would secure more of their concern than she did.

As if anticipating the stream of questions about to burst out of Frankie's mouth, Mom raised a hand. "That's all you need to know about it, Francesca."

Mom shoved her jacket at Liz, and Frankie bristled on her behalf. Liz was the transport operator, not a laundry bot, though now was perhaps not the time to point that out. "You're fired," Mom said.

"Liz didn't know I was here," Frankie said quickly. "I swear. She even closed my usual entry points."

Mom still didn't look at Frankie, instead keeping her atten-tion locked on Liz. "Fine. Francesca will provide you a list of her loopholes. You'll run security diagnostics on everything else."

As if that would keep Frankie out for long. Mom should know what she was capable of.

Liz nodded, and Frankie wondered why she'd accepted this job when she could be doing anything, anywhere. Pathbound might be prestigious, but working with her parents? Not worth it.

After eight months and eleven days spent off-world, Mom hooked slender thumbs through her belt loops and turned to face her daughter.

Funny how Frankie dreamed of Mom's attention, yet wanted to run when she finally obtained it.

"The Hartiger name is bestowed, Francesca," Mom said.

The refrain might as well have been tattooed on Frankie's heart, she'd heard it so many times. But there was nothing she could do to prevent her mother from finishing it.

Mom was already heading for the door. She cast the words over her shoulder, an afterthought. Just like her daughter. "You earn your place in this family."

Frankie hugged her toolkit to her chest as Mom left her again.

TWO
FRANKIE

Now

THE ORIGINAL INTERWORLD transport was an antique. The centerpiece of the Pathbound Enterprises Museum, an artifact that people from every country on Earth made pilgrimage to admire.

The original interworld transport was *not* a cocktail-party decoration.

Or at least, it shouldn't be. From what Frankie could see—which was admittedly not a lot, since she'd elbowed her way through the red-carpet throngs just to stand outside the doors—her parents' hack of an event planner had authorized use of the transport's hood as a table for champagne trays. They hadn't even bothered to give it a good polish.

Frankie could only imagine her parents' disappointment. They'd been away for eighteen months this time, one of their longer jaunts, and this was the welcome they received. Blatant disrespect for Pathbound's history. On the eve of the first guided tour to Suhainn, no less.

That, of course, was a problem in itself. Her parents were keepers of the greatest technology ever discovered. They held the keys to other universes.

Their plan? Bus tours.

Frankie respected her parents' genius, and the need to maintain fresh interest in Pathbound Enterprises and inter-world travel. But Mom and Dad should be convincing Earth's VIPs to invest in further scientific advancements. Not just dragging a bunch of celebrities on a glorified camping trip.

Frankie wanted to help. And finally, she had a plan. To win them over, prove her worth as a daughter and a scientist, and earn her place beside them. She'd have preferred a private audience over a public performance, but her parents' schedules rarely allowed for one-on-one time. Which meant she had a party to crash.

It had been a long eighteen months. And Frankie hadn't wasted a second.

The only problem was that, unfortunately, she wasn't on the list.

"I'm sorry, Ms. Hartiger," the bouncer told her, for the billionth time. "I was specifically instructed not to let you into the party."

Security bots flanked him like mean little dogs, stunners primed. Those glorified traffic cones. They weren't supposed to be programmed for thoughts, feelings, or vendettas, but Frankie knew better. Try to sneak past them, and they'd zap her high heels off.

It might have been her imagination, but she could have sworn one of them snarled.

"Colin," Frankie said, "would I be subjecting myself to this dress, and these shoes, if I wasn't supposed to be here? No. It's summer. I've got trashy zines to read."

It wasn't completely untrue. The last article she'd read in *The Planetary Review* had cited a former *Mars-Colony* star's memoir as a source. Surely that counted as trash.

The bouncer adjusted his cufflinks and glanced into the party, as if tempted to confirm with her parents. "That's what you said last time."

"Colin. Come on. We go way back. How's your niece doing in chemistry? Megan?"

Failed, if Frankie had to guess; the girl couldn't even stutter out the difference between a halogen and a noble gas, thus ending Frankie's attempt to tutor her within the first five minutes. Frankie's best friend, Audrey, had wanted her to try again, had nearly convinced Frankie she was capable of showing kindness to more than three trusted humans. Unfortunately, Frankie didn't share her friend's patience for hopeless cases.

Colin's attention flicked over her shoulder, all the tense little wrinkles around his eyes smoothing into an expression of pure relief. As if he were a damsel and Frankie a witch demanding he let down his hair.

Frankie didn't need to turn around. She knew who Colin's prince in shining armor had to be. She suppressed a groan, if not an eye roll.

"Francesca knows she's not on the list," Jord Mathison said, "because she accessed it this morning. Via my account."

Someday, she'd install a noise-cancelling device in her ear that would pinpoint the frequency of his voice and automatically cancel it out with pattering rain or city noise or swarms of bees. Anything. And yet she spent hours upon hours listening to him talk. Her own self-imposed torture. But he was the only person who could teach her the language of his home world, so Frankie endured his existence as best she could.

It was nearly impossible to remember Jord as the boy who'd lain crumpled at her parents' feet three years ago. He wore a suit and tie, his blond curls mostly tamed this evening, though one of his shoelaces was untied. And of course, no party would ever be fancy enough to separate him from his favorite accessory: a smoothie so red it looked like he was drinking a vat of paint.

And oh, goody, he'd discovered twisty straws.

"How do you say 'infestation' in Suhainnan?" Frankie asked.

"*Plagnaid.*"

He smiled. Frankie decided not to tell him about the shoelace. "Well, *you* are a *plagnaid*."

"Thank you, Francesca. I gathered as much from context. May I have a word?"

Frankie tipped her chin in the air. "No, you may not. I'm here to see my parents. Go sign more autographs, or whatever it is you do with your time."

Filming another Virtual-Reality-TV program, no doubt. Frankie could never understand why people wanted to watch Jord walk from the gym to the board room and back—'six months in the life of Earth's first interworld immigrant,' with a convenient Pathbound-Tower backdrop to remind everyone who was responsible for his arrival here—but Earth remained fascinated nonetheless.

Fan clubs and weekly zine interviews hardly counted as a qualification. And yet whenever Mom and Dad hopped off to Suhainn, they left him to manage the company. The only person on Earth to have immigrated from another universe, Jord had somehow positioned himself as her parents' most trusted... well, she didn't know what his title was supposed to be, exactly. Part assistant, part manager, part... mascot.

Whatever he was, he had way more pull at Pathbound than Frankie could hope for, even though—as she'd pointed out to him on more than one occasion—he had no obvious talents, and couldn't have been much older than she was.

Whatever he'd been doing in his world, and whatever crime he'd committed to have him banished to this one—it *had* to be a crime—it couldn't possibly have prepared him to preside over board meetings. Her parents needed to invest in higher quality cronies.

Or Frankie. They could invest in Frankie. After tonight, they would.

Jord sipped his smoothie, looping the drink through the straw like a blood draw. "I'm afraid to ask *why* you're seeking an audience with your parents."

"I need a reason to see my family?"

"You're a Hartiger, so yes."

Jord had a talent for transforming little truths into barbed insults. She could never work out how he did it, or how to fight back. Was she supposed to deny the fact that her parents spent virtually no time on Earth, rarely bothered to call, and refused to schedule a fifteen-minute appointment with her when they did show up? She had to crash cocktail parties to see them.

He threw it all in her face with constant passive-aggressive jabs, as if he hadn't abandoned his own family, his world, to stay here. He'd betrayed them all somehow; that much she knew, or her parents wouldn't have had to whip him off to Earth to save his life. But after three years, Frankie still hadn't managed to learn enough about him to turn his history into a weapon. "Suffice it to say I have a plan," she said.

It was a business proposal, a scientific endeavor packaged

in a solid, Hartiger-worthy presentation. It would win her a seat at the board table. Maybe even a slot on tomorrow's tour.

If a place card with her name on it should happen to become a fixture at her parents' dinner table, too, she wasn't going to complain.

Jord swirled the smoothie to shake the clumps loose. Frankie willed the top to fly off and spill all over his nicely pressed shirt. That shade of red had to contain something that would stain. "I didn't get a shipment this morning," he said.

Frankie blinked. "What?"

"The urban farm delivers my fruit on Monday, Wednesday, and Friday. Today is Friday, and it didn't come."

It was their deal. Jord tutored Frankie in the language and culture of Suhainn, and Frankie paid him in the freshest, sweetest fruit she could find from the Midtown Urban Farm, a massive glass sphere in Columbus Circle where they grew produce from every climate, all year long.

"I tightened security in anticipation of the party," Jord said. "Maybe they had trouble delivering."

Or maybe he'd conveniently forgotten to provide Frankie with the proper clearance in hopes of distracting her. "Sounds like something you could have figured out on your own."

"And yet, alas, that is not our arrangement."

He always sounded like he'd stepped out of a Victorian period drama. All... over-puffed. Suhainnan formality, maybe. Or overcompensation for his youth.

He might be a disgraced lordling, or a merchant's son. He might be anyone. Three years ago, he'd simply appeared in her life, acting for all the worlds like the rightful heir to the Path-bound regime. He'd parried every attempt at friendship, and she was forced to watch from the sidelines as he slid into the role she coveted. Her parents treated him like a golden son, while their daughter was effectively an outcast.

"Nice try," she said. "Not leaving."

Before she could stop him, Jord took hold of her wrist. Lightly, but still. His touch made her cringe. "You know they don't like surprises."

Frankie started to move past him, but he blocked her path. "I'm sorry, Francesca."

He wasn't. Sometimes she thought he'd moved to Earth for the singular purpose of getting in her way.

Luckily, Frankie was enough of a Hartiger to know the value of a backup plan. Reinforcements, in the form of her best friend.

And Audrey LaRoche knew exactly when to make her entrance.

No sound had ever been as beautiful as Audrey's heels, clicking on the museum's mosaic tiles. She stopped short of inserting herself between Frankie and Jord. While the bouncer pretended to keep his cool—the amateur, he was practically hopping out of his shoes at the sight of Audrey—Jord held Frankie's gaze.

Audrey had rich brown skin and black hair she'd smoothed out of her face with a pink headband. Rose-gold gems dusted her cheeks, echoing the color of her shoes. The first celebrity to secure her spot on the inaugural interworld tour, Audrey wanted to see what she could learn from Suhainnan music. Pick up an instrument or two. True cultural enrichment. Not Frankie's forte, maybe—she had enough trouble interacting with Earthens—but a worthy reason to travel to other worlds.

Not that Audrey LaRoche needed Earth's other-world mania to sell albums. She could write songs with binary code for lyrics, and she'd sell a billion copies on the first day.

"I know I don't see your hand on my friend," Audrey said.

Jord made a point of waiting a beat before letting go of Frankie. "It's my second-favorite Earthen. Hello, Audrey."

Funny. Audrey LaRoche was most people's first-favorite Earthen. "Isn't the party inside?" she said.

Frankie folded her arms. "Jord won't let me in."

Audrey eyed the doors. "She's with me."

When Audrey got back from Suhainn, Frankie fully intended to send her several hundred boxes of chocolate.

"Sorry," Jord said. "Hartiger orders."

Behind him, the bouncer stared at Audrey with open awe. And probably a certain amount of relief that he didn't have to be the one to tell her 'no.' Frankie was half tempted to help him reunite his jaw with the rest of his face.

"I wouldn't even be here without her," Audrey said.

Audrey hadn't needed Frankie's help to get a seat on the tour. Audrey's name opened its own doors.

In fact, Audrey handled her celebrity status with a maturity that Frankie could only wonderingly admire. Though Frankie had been born under the scrutiny of the cameras, and Audrey had written her way in, it was Audrey who shepherded Frankie through the reporter gauntlets that popped up after school whenever Path-bound made the news in a big way. Audrey knew to pull the shades to keep drones from peeking in the windows, and no one in the world could match the grace with which she presented her middle finger for review. When necessary.

"Can't do it," Jord said. "But I promise to stay out here and keep Francesca company."

Audrey gave her eyes an Oscar-worthy roll before stepping between the bots. Where she immediately stopped and looked down. "There's something wrong with my shoe."

Not a diva moment. A carefully choreographed signal.

The bouncer lunged to assist with the false shoe malfunction, and even Jord glanced Audrey's way—giving Frankie the distraction she needed. She activated her smart watch, where her bot-stalling program was ready to go.

One touch to a beautiful blue button, and the nasty little dunce-caps froze at Colin's side.

Of everything Frankie had designed for tonight, all the hours she'd spent honing her plans, that one button had taken the longest. She'd nearly broken down before finally latching onto a loophole for a temporary signal jam that forced the bots to request instructions from an incorrect source.

All that work, and more than one migraine, just to squeeze a measly two minutes out of the tech. After that, the bots would reset to their defaults.

Still assisting Audrey, the bouncer didn't notice as Frankie darted past Jord—also distracted, though that surely wouldn't last long—and into the party.

Success.

From the inside, she supposed she understood—theoretically—why it might have looked like a good idea to hold the party here. The antique transport's rocket-style portholes beckoned visitors to peek in, to gape at the ancient tech. Guests floated from corner to corner, tent-like dresses billowing, straw hats casting mottled shadows across their faces. A few of them wore what looked like burlap overalls.

Utopian chic. It was all the rage. Though the effect was somewhat hampered by all the golden embroidery and gem-crusted embellishments.

"Now what?" Audrey said, having escaped Colin's attentions to stand at Frankie's side.

"Now I wow my parents. For the good of science."

"And humanity. Right? Like your grandparents?"

"Sure. Humanity, too."

Though Audrey might need to help her hire someone to head up that part of the research. After Mom and Dad said yes.

Frankie had a foolproof method of locating her parents in almost any room. Unless Mom had whacked it out of him over the last year and a half, Dad would be entertaining his guests with amateur magic tricks—sleight of hand. Cards, hats, doves. The more cliche, the more Dad loved to do it.

All Frankie had to do was follow the bellow of fake laughter and applause.

Sure enough, beyond the transport and between two glass cases housing her great-grandparents' journals, a ripple of astonishment burst forth from a cluster of faux Utopians. A colorful scarf drifted above their heads, then snapped out of sight. Dad.

A few of the guests near him dove for champagne refills as the drones buzzed by. Frankie couldn't blame them. She was vaguely aware of raised voices behind her, a scuffle at the door. The bots should stay frozen for another few seconds, though Colin might still decide to come after her.

She picked up her pace, and Jord fell into step at her side. "Is there nothing I can say to dissuade you?" he asked.

"I haven't been subjecting myself to your presence for two-plus years out of masochism. I learned to speak Suhainnan for a reason."

"They won't be impressed."

"I think she gets it," Audrey said.

Two high top tables separated Frankie from her father. His bald head towered above the crowd, which meant her mother would be nearby, too. They were like a matched set that way, always together.

Jord grabbed her arm. "Francesca, please. Listen to me."

Frankie stepped on his untied shoelace.

Jord tried to keep moving, and tripped instead. As he hit the floor, Frankie bolted the rest of the way and threw herself into the circle of onlookers as her father produced a quarter from behind Mom's unimpressed ear.

Frankie's appearance disrupted the applause, and everyone turned to stare. Not at Audrey, who had unaccountably vanished from her side, but at Frankie. She scanned the circle and found Liz, who gave her a nod of encouragement.

Aside from Mom and Dad, the rest were strangers.

Eighteen months was a long time to be gone, even by Hartiger standards. A sixteenth birthday, and a seventeenth. Eight robotics ribbons, five college visits, two Christmases, a prom dress. One miserable summer of waiting for Audrey to finish touring. A first kiss, and a last. Botched haircuts, disastrous sleepovers, and roughly forty-three thousand cups of coffee.

What was she even supposed to say to them, after eighteen freaking months?

Mom answered the question by speaking first. "Francesca," she said. "Did you come to warn us about a fire?"

THREE

FRANKIE

Frankie's cheeks burned. The ultimate betrayal of her sympathetic nervous system. She forced her lips into the most gracious smile she could muster. Most of the advice she read on interpersonal communication tended to emphasize smiling. "Hi, Mom."

Frankie knew better than to hug her mother, unless she wanted a lecture about how easy it was to smear makeup and wrinkle silk. Even without it, her mother's perfume wafted across the circle. Roses and gardenias. Mom looked Chanel, but she smelled like a garden.

Dad, though, threw an arm around Frankie's shoulder with a grin, his cologne assaulting her with an oily musk. He'd buy the latest top-shelf anything, even if it meant smelling like fish. "You clean up nice, Francesca. Did you grow three inches? Or is it the heels?"

Nerves drumming in her chest, she swallowed a wave of nausea and managed not to lean into her father's hug. That would only show weakness. "I go by Frankie, Dad."

"We named you Francesca," Mom said.

A few people in the circle chuckled. Frankie wanted to tell them Mom wasn't kidding. "I have something to show you," she said.

Dad patted her arm. "We're about to sit down for dinner. How about later?"

Oh, no. In the Hartiger world, *later* was synonymous with *never*.

"I want to see it, too," Audrey said, reappearing with Jord a step behind. His lip was bleeding, and despite Audrey's supportive words, her eyebrow-led expression telegraphed disapproval at Frankie's methods. It occurred to Frankie that Audrey might have stopped to help Jord up.

Frankie refused to feel bad. He deserved it.

Still, Audrey hadn't given up on her yet. Forget boxes of chocolate. Frankie owed her friend a fleet of the stuff.

"Could be fun," Liz agreed, and Frankie mentally promised a second fleet of chocolate. The transport operator looked as comfortable in her silver gown as she did on the control floor in yoga pants and slippers. She cradled champagne in one hand, a red clutch in the other, showing off the cursive tattoos on the backs of her hands. She knew what was coming; she'd helped Frankie install the projector-controlling button in her necklace.

Mom waved a hand that might have meant, 'Go ahead' or 'Go away.' Frankie knew better than to wait for clarification. She stepped out of Dad's orbit and reached for the clasp on her necklace, where she'd installed the on-switch. "You'll like it," she said.

Frankie tapped her smartwatch and activated Liz's necklace projector with the touch of a button. Over her shoulder, Jord sucked in a breath as Frankie's miniature map of Suhainn sprang up in full-color augmented reality. The docks, the governor's mansion, everything so realistic that a child might try to place dolls inside. Every fifteen seconds, a boat zipped down one of the canals, careening gracefully between buildings.

She particularly liked that touch.

"Pathbound has a responsibility to expand scientific research in other worlds," she began. "This model shows my plan for Phase One: The Cosmos."

"How many phases are there?" Jord asked, so quietly that she wasn't sure anyone else could hear.

He could heckle her all he wanted. It wouldn't work. "In Phase One we'll build observatories, allowing us to study celestial objects around Suhainn."

"Which would teach us what, exactly?" Mom asked.

Frankie was ready for that question. As she talked, she grew more confident. Her hands even stopped shaking, mostly. "For example, there's a theory that Suhainn is an alternate version of Earth. Studying the stars could prove it."

She was working on a few other inventions that could help, too, things that could make comparisons on a planet-wide level. But she wasn't ready to unveil those yet.

Jord coughed. "Whose theory would that be?"

Not important, in the least. "It might be a version where the climate-change race never happened. Sea levels would have risen, flooding cities. We might not be looking at a primitive society at all. It could be a post-apocalyptic one."

She paused, half expecting Jord to comment on the primitive society thing. He didn't. "The observatories would be added to established buildings, to blend in," she said. "Hardly noticeable."

Jord leaned over her shoulder. This time, he spoke loudly enough for everyone to hear. "Balcony on the second floor of the smithy. Roof deck on the tannery."

Frankie shoved him away.

Everyone in the circle was staring at her, the celebrities

politely sipping their drinks—Frankie recognized a red-headed woman from Season 4 of *Mars Colony*—with her mother glancing pointedly at her watch.

Frankie took a deep breath.

A flurry of movement near the doors caught her attention, and she looked up to see Colin bolting through the room. He knocked over a table, sending a pair of chairs crashing behind it, before Frankie saw why.

A man she'd never seen before was diving head-first through the room, his arms restrained behind his back, his silver hair flying in every direction as he wove between clusters of startled guests. The red letters on his T-shirt proclaimed a familiar slogan: REGULATE INTERWORLD TRAVEL NOW!

An anti-Pathbound activist. Frankie had seen the protest signs hovering beyond the fans on her way in, of course, but that was a normal part of life at Pathbound. People protested everything, from the closed-off nature of interworld travel to the very fact of its existence; some claimed the bypass system ripped holes in the universe, while others, probably inspired by Jord's success, wanted to open immigration to the wider cosmos.

They usually didn't make it inside.

The man flung his body into the middle of Frankie's holograms, landing on his knees so that the water appeared to lap at his neck. He looked like he was about to go under.

Instead of throwing himself in Mom's face, or Dad's, the man swiveled to face Frankie. "No one should own interworld travel," he said. "Please. There are people in *this* world who need places to go, the resources other places could provide. If Pathbound would just open the doors. Please. You have to tell them."

Maybe she was the first Hartiger to fall within his line of

sight, or maybe he thought the younger generation would be more open minded. The truth was, she didn't disagree with him. She thought the interworld bypass should be open to everyone. But Frankie was the last person who could help, even if she wanted to. She had no power to influence her parents in anything they did—including their lobby against any hint of interworld regulation.

He'd be better off appealing to Jord.

The man tried to crawl toward her, arms extended. Frankie stepped back, unsure of what to do, what to say, though surely a Hartiger ought to know the right response. The political response. The diplomatic one.

She had no answer as he repeated his plea, or even as Colin caught up and tackled him to the floor with more force than was probably necessary, slamming the man's cheek to the tiles. He groaned, squeezing his eyes shut. Frankie looked away as the bouncer hauled him to his feet, the awakened bots scurrying to form a ring around him.

"How did *this*—" Mom waved a hand in the man's direction, as though pointing to a spider, "—get inside?"

"The bots," Colin said. "They froze up. Don't know what happened."

Mom narrowed her eyes. And then she looked directly at Frankie.

Frankie managed not to flinch. She glanced back at the defeated protester, his chin nearly brushing his chest as the bots herded him toward the door. He'd gone to nearly as much trouble to get in here tonight as Frankie had. And she'd been the one to let him in.

This was the sort of thing that always happened to her. She built solid plans, excellent tech, and yet she never managed to anticipate this type of scenario. But how could she have known that creating such a brief bot-free window would lead to this?

She couldn't. She turned back to her presentation, preparing to forge on.

Abruptly, her holograms disappeared. She lifted her smartwatch. It still detected a working model. No error report. No instructions.

Useless. She gave it a shake, which obviously did nothing.

"Your technology appears to have failed," Mom said. She gave the group such a charming smile that Frankie wondered whether she'd taken acting classes. "Let's not allow this unpleasantness to spoil a nice party."

Mom hooked her arm through Liz's, stealing away one of Frankie's only allies. All Frankie could do was watch as they walked away, her wrist still half raised.

A lifetime of enduring Mom's disinterest on this Earth, and it still felt like a winter blast in the middle of July.

But her mother's reaction was perfectly understandable. It was exactly how Frankie would have reacted to a subpar presentation—not to mention a daughter whose recklessness resulted in dramatic party crashers. But Frankie's tech was supposed to be flawless, her science exhaustive. There was no reason the presentation should have cut off.

Audrey stood beside Frankie, staring after the protester. "I hope he's OK."

Dad clapped a hand on Frankie's shoulder, as if she'd lost a baseball game. He still occasionally remembered to treat Frankie like his daughter. A corner of bright yellow fabric peeked out from his sleeve, evidence of some trick he planned to perform later. Frankie wondered what Mom would do to him if his boutonniere squirted one of their guests with water. Probably kick him out, just like the protester. "It was a good effort."

"Let me come," Frankie blurted out, in Suhainnan.

Language was the last card she had to play. "I'm ready. I'm even packed."

For a moment, she thought Dad might say yes. "You speak Suhainnan," he said, and laughed. He twisted to face Jord, who hovered a few feet away. "How'd she trap you into that?"

Jord slipped his hands into his pockets. "Your daughter is very convincing, Mr. Hartiger."

Dad turned to Frankie. "Why are you so set on leaving Earth? Bad breakup?"

Of course. She couldn't possibly take science as seriously as romance. She hadn't dated anyone since her lab-partner-slash-boyfriend had dumped her right before prom when he'd realized she wouldn't be able to provide him with an easy route to an internship at Pathbound. Or a seat at the first interworld launch, or even an interview with her parents. All facts he had eagerly spread throughout the school.

Audrey had offered to eviscerate his social life—a threat she was fully capable of fulfilling—but Frankie just wanted to be done with the whole mess. And besides, Audrey's powers were meant to be used for good. Even Frankie knew that.

So instead, they'd focused their energy on tonight's presentation. With Liz on the team, it should have been perfect.

"I have ideas," Frankie told her father, still in Suhainnan. "Contributions. You'd already been to four different worlds by the time you turned seventeen."

"Yes, well... This might not be the best time, with the VIPs..."

"I'll behave."

Dad lifted an eyebrow. "Like you did with Althea Weathers?"

Frankie threw up her hands. "If the CEO of America's biggest software company can't handle a few suggestions, she's in the wrong field. You're welcome, Althea. What a drama queen."

"There's a time and place for constructive criticism," Dad said. "White House dinners are not on the list."

They had to bring her out occasionally, if only to avoid gossip. Instead of making the most of that particular chance, which had been among the last—and over two *years* ago—she'd once again invited their disappointment.

"Grandma and Grandpa found other worlds, Dad," Frankie said. Not to mention that, in the decades since her grandparents had succeeded in hopping between universes, no one else had come close to figuring out how they did it. "You have a legacy to uphold. You're coasting on their discoveries, leading a bunch of spoiled celebrities on a tour of the highlights. We can do better. Pathbound can do better."

"I'm sorry, Francesca," Dad said. "Maybe next time."

Frankie couldn't bear to watch him walk away. She pushed down her disappointment and focused on her smartwatch. No errors, no red lights, no indication of what the problem might be.

They'd be gone for two weeks. In Hartiger land, that was nothing. She'd get past their rabid, calendar-guarding assistants. She'd try again.

And then Audrey said, "Spoiled?"

Frankie frowned, still focused on the watch. "What?"

Audrey waved a hand in front of Frankie's face, forcing her to look up. "You think I'm spoiled?"

She didn't think that. No one worked harder than Audrey. But that *Mars Colony* star, milking her Red Planet stint for all she could get? The celebrity chef and his cheeseball catch phrases? They didn't deserve seats on the interworld transport, yet here they were. Ready to head off on safari. "You know I didn't mean you," Frankie said.

"Which one of us remembers hoarding spare change to buy yogurt?" Audrey said, her voice quiet. Frankie almost wished she would yell. "And which one of us trips people to get what she wants?"

Taken objectively, Audrey's points made sense. Frankie replayed the evening in her mind, searching for signs of her friend's waning patience. She didn't mean to disregard other people's feelings. She just didn't always know how to... regard them.

"You think your parents should do better," Audrey continued, without giving Frankie a chance to work her thoughts into words. "Well, I think *you* should. Have you thought twice about the protester who just left here? What those bots are going to do to him?"

"I—"

"You don't need to answer. I already know. I'll see you later, Frankie."

Frankie stared after her friend as the crowd closed around her, admirers eager for a moment of Audrey LaRoche's attention. "What just happened?" Frankie muttered.

"I'd say you alienated the only ally you had. Nicely done."

Of course Jord hadn't left. He witnessed every misstep she ever made. She glared at him. "Why are you still here?"

"For the record, you also called me primitive."

"Yeah, well, that I meant."

The swollen part of his lip was starting to turn purple, but he smiled at her anyway. "Thank you, Francesca. I'd say that about wraps up the evening, wouldn't you?"

She was almost sorry when he walked away, too.

FOUR
JORD

No matter where Jord stood in Pathbound Tower, he felt as if he were about to fall or be crushed, or perhaps one followed closely by the other.

On the lower floors, layer upon layer of glass and steel teetered above him like a threat. And yet any floor above the sixth induced staggering vertigo, which meant titanium shades on his apartment windows and a sad waste of his balcony space. It was too unnerving, to stand equal with the sky.

Humans were fragile. Towers could fall.

But the Hartigers had summoned him to the penthouse after sunrise. And one did not refuse them an audience, no matter how fervently one might wish to avoid it. So here he was, at the top of the tower, trying not to imagine how it would feel to have the floors collapse beneath him.

Jord found Frankie asleep on the doormat when he stepped out of the elevator. She wore her dress from last night, her curls a tangled mess around her face. Of all the things he expected from her, a split lip was long overdue. A miniature replica of his home world, though. That required a moment of recovery.

She had access to enough video that stealing the precise azure tint of the water in Suhainn wouldn't have been an issue. But she'd included the gliding swoop of the butterfly-winged *feilean* bird, the lace of the moss that drooped over the tree branches, even the ring of mountains glowing emerald in the distance.

Strangely, it had been the round sails on the fishing vessels that had snagged his breath in his throat. He'd been half tempted to reach for the stone he kept in his pocket, to give it a toss and test the minuscule difference in gravity.

If he didn't know any better—and if she didn't make an enormous fuss out of the fact that she'd never traveled between worlds—he'd think Frankie had been sneaking to Suhainn to take notes.

The only thing she'd missed was a sky stuffed with stars.

Jord leaned over Frankie to swipe in. He had access. She didn't. That was... Well. That was the Hartiger way. Everything they cared about was in Suhainn, anyway. What did it matter who could get in?

Cindy and Michael kept their shades wide open, and New York glinted beyond the windows as the sun chased its reflection from tower to tower. This city was as garish as its inhabitants.

Jord told himself firmly that the windows were only screens. Background. He deliberately turned his back to the view and focused on Frankie's parents. Their apartment was pleasant, in a synthetic kind of way. Hints of floral smells from scented candles and perfume rather than flowers, the blinding white upholstery signaling infrequent use of the furniture.

And of course, the Hartigers themselves. Rarely seen. Rarely missed. Michael flipped pancakes at the stove, while Cindy sat perched on a stool beside the counter, sorting a stack of papers. "I can give you something for the vertigo," she said, licking her finger and swiping a page to the side as if it were a digital document on a tablet.

As usual, she spoke like she knew everything about him. When it came to the Hartigers, Jord had no secrets. He was just one of their many commodities, and he was only that because he'd forced himself into the limelight to prevent them from making him disappear.

He had reason to believe they'd taken such action before, in his own world.

Jord slipped his hands into his pockets. "That won't be necessary."

She blinked at her papers. "Your own accommodations must be uncomfortable, if you can't stand to look out the window."

"I manage."

"You're being stubborn."

As if she cared. No doubt she'd have preferred a more pliable Suhainnan to act as her personal specimen for study. Too bad. She was stuck with him.

"Give the boy some space," Michael said, tossing a pancake toward a plate on the counter. He missed, and the pancake landed on the floor with a wet smack. "We'll be back in two weeks. If he changes his mind, he knows where to find you."

Cindy folded the corner of a page and kept flipping. "It makes no difference to me."

Sometimes, Jord couldn't help but look for hints of Frankie in them. She had Michael's height, Cindy's scatter of freckles. In essence, though, she was quite different. Or so he continued to hope.

He shouldn't have agreed to teach her about Suhainn. But when she'd come to him, more than two years ago now, her face lit with that fiery determination as she laid out her plan to pay him—as if he needed Earthen money—he found, to his complete surprise, that he couldn't refuse her. No matter how ill-advised it might have been.

Every week, every day, he resolved to end it. To cut her off. Every week, he failed.

"Not homesick for a trip to Suhainn, I hope," Michael said.

Jord never let himself think about Suhainn. He spoke of it to Frankie, yes, but in the language of dry cultural studies and adjective arrangement. He was careful, dreadfully careful, to keep his lessons free from any mention of the salty rivers, the impossible blue of a sky that had never seen coal, and the inevitable silence that must now haunt his brother's rooms.

History and culture, the little he knew of it. And language. That was it.

Leave it to Frankie to dredge up his liabilities, with her holographic *feilean* birds and gliding boats.

Her parents already knew his liabilities, though he did his best to pretend otherwise. In truth, he wasn't sure what he'd find should he ever have the chance to return to Suhainn. He had reason to believe the Hartigers controlled everything there —the king included—though the people didn't know it.

He realized that Michael was still watching him, that friendly expression still locked on the man's face. He force himself to smile. "Not homesick at all, sir," he said. "Earth is much dryer."

Michael shook his head, grinning. "There are days when I think I'd kill for a fluffy towel." He slid the last pancake onto a plate and set the pile in front of Cindy, who stared at it like he'd offered her a vat of rat poison. "Breakfast, before the launch?"

Jord's stomach twisted at the thought of eating that. "Already ate. But thank you."

"I hope you're not neglecting protein," Cindy said. "Suhainnan fruit is much heartier than what we have here."

Of that, he was well aware. "I remember."

"You look thin. Have you been experiencing any syncopal episodes?"

"My English is good, Mrs. Hartiger, but I'm not sure—"

"She wants to know if you've fainted," Michael said.

How motherly of her. "Ah. No fainting, thankfully."

Cindy swiveled to study him. "You tripped last night. Are you having trouble keeping your balance?"

Jord sucked his swollen lip into his mouth before thinking better of it. "Only when your daughter is nearby."

Michael leaned on the counter. "Francesca did that?"

He looked impressed. Cindy didn't. How they'd managed to miss that entrance, Jord couldn't guess. "What about numbness? Heart palpitations, fatigue?"

None of that, he thought of telling her. *Only the crushing despair of living in a world that smells of smoke and asphalt.*

Jord had been a nobody in Suhainn, a servant-in-training who'd opened the wrong door at the wrong time. And because of that ill-timed shortcut, he was trapped here. Likely for good.

He couldn't do anything to help Suhainn from the fake king they'd propped up there. He couldn't even help himself.

"Did you summon me here for a physical," he said, "or is there something you need?"

Cindy slipped a paper out of her pile with a look that told him his attitude had been noted. "Make sure security has the final list for the VIP area that Michael insisted on setting up on the transport dock. I zipped it to them, but he keeps changing it."

"They're never going to keep track of a piece of paper," Michael said.

"When I give them paper, they know it's important. When you send a dozen different lists, it's a potential security breach."

Jord took the sheet and scanned the names. "I'll make sure

they reset the DNA access coding immediately after the launch. I'll watch them do it."

"See, Cindy? He's got it under control."

If the Hartigers dealt him responsibilities, even dribbles of power, it was only because Jord had been successful in shoring up a second fail-proof life insurance policy. In addition to the minor celebrity status he'd managed to attain, he made himself a truly capable addition to Pathbound, an indispensable asset. He used his notoriety to rake positive press toward the company—while also amassing a group of witnesses to his existence, who would inevitably ask after him in the event of his sudden disappearance.

At times, Frankie seemed determined to believe him an exile, guilty of some terrible crime. In reality, he was nothing more than a prisoner, leashed to Earth because of an accident of fortune he wished he could reverse.

So, yes. He had things under control. And he'd see to every last detail.

"If that's all, I'll get this to security and make sure everything else is ready to go," he said.

As he passed the counter, Cindy stopped him with a finger to the wrist. From anyone else, it might have been a pleasant touch. From Cindy, it was a warning that sent goosebumps buzzing up his arms. "If I need to perform an examination, I will."

It would certainly be problematic, if her prized interworld celebrity were to expire like a bug in a jar. Couldn't have that. At least, not unless she commanded it.

The back of his neck twinged. Cindy let go before favoring him with a rare smile. "We're still studying the effects of interworld travel, after all. You're our responsibility."

Responsibility, science experiment. All the same to Cindy Hartiger.

Jord couldn't trust his voice, so he just nodded. She almost sounded concerned. Almost. As though that were explanation enough to treat him as a specimen. A lower form of life. Every time they left, he forgot how much he hated it when they came home.

"Sure you don't mean an alternate version of Earth?" Michael said.

Cindy let out a breath that might have been a scoff. Never a laugh. "Of all the ridiculous theories."

He pretended not to hear. He didn't know if the Hartigers had their own reasons for their unkindness towards Frankie, but Jord did everything he could to keep that wedge in place.

If Frankie seemed prickly and impossible, well, he'd also watched her shield Audrey from paparazzi drones, and deliver coffee to lab techs working late into the night. He'd read the legislation she'd drafted on equal access to the multiverse. And he'd seen her tears after that undeserving weasel of an ex-boyfriend broke her heart a few months ago. Jord had hated the boy's smug, spiky hair, and the way those fingertips were always grazing her hips. Even more, he hated the way she'd cried through their lesson, which she'd refused to cancel, when the imbecile dumped her.

Jord had set a box of tissues on the counter, and otherwise pretended not to notice. He'd also doubled the length of their lesson, which *she* pretended not to notice until she brought candied almonds to their next meeting, and left the bag behind.

It was a gesture he didn't deserve. He showed her no more than the barest scraps of decency, and she responded with kindness.

Frankie was not meant for Hartiger ways. If her parents didn't break her, they'd mold her into a monster, and Jord was not at all certain which fate would be worse.

Better she should stay locked out.

Frankie was still asleep when he opened the door, her head pillowed in her hands. The dress made her look like she was drowning in a puddle of black ink.

He couldn't help it. He hesitated, watched for the rise and fall of her chest. She seemed healthy enough. Physically, anyway. Emotionally... Well, she had Hartigers for parents. No medicine would remedy that.

A more courageous person might wake her. Ensure she made it to the launch on time. Usher her inside to speak with her parents, consequences be scorched.

Jord stepped over her, and headed downstairs.

FIVE

FRANKIE

Frankie woke with her nose buried in her parents' doormat. Nothing like the sweet aroma of rubber to greet the day.

She hadn't changed out of her party dress, because she hadn't wanted to miss Mom and Dad. If standing upright in silk was uncomfortable, sleeping in it was worse. It felt like someone had rolled her in cellophane.

At least she'd had the sense to abandon her heels, though she was too groggy to remember where. She'd stopped in her apartment to grab her backpack, hadn't she? Maybe her shoes were there. Toe-pinching horrors. She should have tossed them out the window.

She glared at the cruel daylight streaming in from the window at the end of the hall. This would be embarrassing, if there were anyone here to see her. But the only sign of life was a cleaning bot waxing the floor.

They always missed the corners.

Maybe she should have gone to bed, spared herself the humiliation. She couldn't shake the thought that if she could get their attention for five minutes, without an audience, she might be able to convince them her plan was a good one. She had more than holographic maps. That had just been the sales pitch. She should have shown them the budget projections and the hiring schemes. She should have shown them blueprints.

Or maybe she should have ditched her parents to chase after Audrey, with a dozen apologies. She could find her friend now, ask for ideas on how to use Suhainnan knowledge to help humanity on Earth. That was what Audrey wanted, wasn't it?

Frankie had no idea what she'd do with that kind of data. Maybe she'd slip out to Teuscher for a box of Audrey's favorite champagne chocolates instead.

I'm-sorry chocolates. A great substitute for humanitarian deeds.

Where were Mom and Dad?

When the elevator doors slid open with a chime, Frankie thought her parents might have pulled an all-nighter.

It was Jord. Of course it was. Frankie was too unlucky to run across a friendly custodian while looking like she'd crawled out of the sewer. He strolled over to her holding two coffee mugs, his curls still damp from the shower. Frankie didn't want to contemplate what she smelled like right now.

"No," Frankie said. "Anyone but you."

Jord dropped down beside her and held out a cup of coffee. "So sweet. And here I came to supply you with caffeine."

It had to be early, if her alarm hadn't gone off yet. It was supposed to wake her for the launch, on the off chance she didn't rouse on her own. Her watch blinked 6:15. Plenty of time. "Did my parents come home last night?"

Jord leaned his head against the wall. "They did."

Which meant they'd stepped over her. Twice. "They could've at least brought me a blanket," Frankie said. She meant it to sound flippant, but couldn't keep the tremble out of her voice.

"Take the coffee, Francesca."

Frankie took it. "I hate you."

"Yes, yes. I'm aware."

Her persistence should *please* them. It was a family quality, wasn't it? Her great-grandfather had been the one to monetize the race for climate-change solutions, convincing corporations and governments alike to throw everything they had at the problem. Hence the reason Pathbound Tower wasn't half underwater.

Her grandparents had literally figured out the math necessary to visit other universes.

"My tech should have worked," she said. "I spent months on that presentation, and the projectors just... died."

Her mother would never forget this. Every time Frankie tried to pitch anything, for the rest of her life, Mom would point to this failure. And probably ask what kind of ruffians had been able to barge through the door because of her daughter's oversights.

Jord said, "Hold out your hand."

Frankie would spend the next year obsessing over what she'd screwed up, unless she could resolve the issue quickly. "Maybe the museum's system shut mine down."

Jord reached for her right hand and tugged it gently away from the coffee. "It wasn't your fault." He dropped the silver necklace into her palm. "It was mine."

Frankie looked at it, the chain curled in her hand like a snake. Her projector. She hadn't even checked for it. "You stole my necklace? How?"

"It wasn't difficult. Though I had to trick your smartwatch."

"But you suck at technology."

He lifted a shoulder. "Even I can dial up the brightness on a hologram and make it disappear."

Thus making her smartwatch think the projections were still working. Clever.

This was the kind of thing that made her think he'd been a criminal in Suhainn, that her parents had experienced a burst of uncharacteristic kindness and brought him here to save him from the gallows. What had Frankie ever done to him, that he had to make her life so impossible? "You sabotaged me."

He didn't bother to deny it. The worst part was that for a second there, she'd almost forgotten he wasn't a friend.

Frankie's watch buzzed to life, a miniature cube with Audrey's face blinking into the space above Frankie's wrist. "I hope you're not so petty you plan to skip the launch," Audrey said.

"The launch isn't for another two hours."

"The launch is in five minutes, Frankie. What's wrong with you?"

Audrey cut off the feed as Frankie leapt to her feet. All this coffee nonsense finally made sense. "You reset my watch. And then you brought me coffee? As an apology, or as a distraction?"

Jord pressed his palms to his knees. "An olive branch. But I won't pretend to be sorry. I'm not."

There was something supremely unsatisfying about stalking away from someone in order to wait for an elevator. Barefoot, no less. She pushed the button with as much dignity as she could muster and waited, arms crossed, as he followed her.

"Where are you going?"

"To the transport dock. To convince my parents to bring me to Suhainn."

At the very least, to see Audrey off. To make her see that Frankie didn't think she was spoiled, to explain what she'd been trying to say. Audrey had called her, right? That had to mean she was willing to forgive Frankie. Didn't it?

No time for chocolates. No time to rehearse that apology.

"Maybe you should change your clothes," Jord said.

"Maybe you should go back to where you came from."

"Excellent suggestion. Why don't you put it in the Path-bound comment box? I'm sure someone will see to it, in two to three light years."

Frankie's first instinct was to remind him that light years were units of distance, not time. It wasn't like him to snap at her —his weapons were sharper than that—but she didn't believe his wounded kitten act. Or his concern for her attire.

If he was so worried, he'd do the smart thing, and he'd get the hell out of her way.

SIX

FRANKIE

As soon as her bare feet touched the metal floor of the transport operations center, Frankie wished she'd followed Jord's advice and taken five minutes to change her clothes. Her dress wilted around her ankles, irreparably crumpled from her night spent on the floor, and she could only imagine what her hair looked like. The pack slung over her arm was a great accessory, too. Perfect.

The operations floor hadn't changed much since Frankie'd witnessed Jord's arrival three years ago, though her parents had added screens with travel vids on either side of the dock. Images of Suhainnans playacting cheerful lives for the camera, of epic mountains and lakes in the uninhabited worlds the Hartigers planned to treat as oversized national parks. Inter-universal parks? Dad would come up with a catchy term, no doubt.

Frankie hadn't thought this place could get any tackier. Whoever had designed those ads should be fired, along with the party planner. This was the interworld transportation center at Pathbound Enterprises Tower, not a Vegas casino.

In the center of the room, Liz stood on her raised control deck, where her team monitored transport functions via touch screens and augmented-reality modules. The operators were focused on a digital model of the transport, where tiny figures swarmed for last-minute checks. Liz wore a pants suit with a purple shirt underneath, way dressier than usual, though her hair was pulled into its signature ponytail. Her eyes widened at the sight of Frankie, but she quickly returned to her work.

And, too late, Frankie remembered the virtual reality viewers. Everyone on Earth had just witnessed her entrance, in what had to be the world's most public walk of shame. In fact, if she'd been watching it herself in VR, she might have suspected scripting. Especially with Jord striding in at her side, that smug grin on his face.

God, he was horrible.

Her parents had the tour group assembled in front of the transport dock in an arc that could only mean Frankie had missed photo-op time. In addition to Audrey, the tourists included a celebrity chef and his husband, both wearing forty-five liter backpacks, and the redhead from *Mars Colony* Frankie had recognized at the party. Her name was Wendy. She'd once climbed to the top of the colony dome, unsupported, to change a light bulb.

In comparison, Suhainn would be a beach vacation.

They all stared at Frankie like she was some kind of wild animal. Except Audrey, who—despite having called her down here—refused to catch Frankie's eye.

Mom looked like she was heading off on safari, with her hat artfully decorated in swaths of mosquito netting. Her expression was entirely unreadable.

Didn't matter. Frankie knew what she was thinking. Hapless daughter, no finesse, etcetera. Mom would die before making a mortifying entrance like this, in last night's wrinkled ball gown. She'd fire her assistant if she saw half as many creases in her expedition outfit.

Mom cast a single glance in Frankie's direction before returning to the people who didn't embarrass her at parties with their inferior technology. The people who mattered. As Frankie approached, Mom turned her back and led the tourists to the dock, leaving Frankie no chance of reversing last night's shame.

Only Audrey lingered. She rested her pack on the floor and bent to tighten her laces. Frankie wished she'd sent a drone out for the chocolates, after all.

She aimed for Dad. He let Mom take the lead while he adjusted his backpack and gave the camera one last wink, or whatever. His performative streak made him an easy mark. Dad was always aware of the cameras, a side effect of growing up Hartiger; if he walked away from his daughter, the audience would notice.

Frankie had no problem using that knowledge to her advantage.

"Let me come," she said. "I know what I'm doing."

Dad gave her his signature pat on the shoulder, windbreaker crinkling as he moved. Frankie couldn't help wondering if he had scarves hidden up his sleeves. He glanced at the ceiling. Cameras, cameras, cameras. The VR viewers could be standing right beside them. Listening in. No doubt some were delighting in a full 360-view of her dirty hair.

At least they couldn't smell her.

"Next time, sweetie," Dad said. He leaned into her ear. "Try thinking smaller next time. More specific. Remember that wildlife tracker you designed? Something like that. Fits the bill."

Sweetie. Right. A return to the days of designing wildlife trackers would certainly be thinking smaller. One of her more discardable inventions. She had no idea why they were so in love with it.

On the dock, Wendy flattened her hair under a helmet, while the chef loaded backpacks onto the luxury-style transport Frankie's parents had commissioned for the inaugural tour. This wasn't one of their usual, simple vehicles; this transport had cushy seats, a figurehead at the prow wearing a space helmet, and gold letters etched into the side: *Suhainn-Bound*. Cute. Gross.

Basically, it was a yacht. A waste, given that the trip took a total of thirty-four seconds. God forbid the VIPs should forgo lower back support for even one of those.

They *were* spoiled. Some of them. But definitely not Audrey. Audrey saved imperiled spiders from arachnophobic classmates. Audrey lent her driverless car to teachers recovering from knee surgery and never made billionaire lists because she gave so much of her money to charity.

Her friend waited a few feet away, watching the preparations. They wouldn't be diving into this adventure together, but that wasn't Audrey's fault. Frankie took a deep breath and went over to her. "I didn't mean it to come out like that," she said. "You're not spoiled."

Audrey clutched her backpack straps. "I know I'm not spoiled, and that's not an apology."

Maybe Audrey was too pissed off this time to be placated by sweets. "I'm sorry, OK? I'm sorry I said it. I was upset."

"Yeah. That's what makes me think there's a part of you that meant it. You want to help? Do something good? Find out what happened to that protester from last night. I had my people reach out to him. His daughter has no idea where he is."

Frankie blinked at her friend. "How am I supposed to find him? He's probably in a bar or something."

Audrey sighed. "That's what I thought. See you in a couple weeks, Frankie."

Only Audrey didn't start walking. She stood there and tugged at the locket she wore around her neck, her eyes pinned on the dock, where the chef and his husband were getting one of the security bots to take their picture.

"Hey," Frankie said. "You know all those commercial spaceflights you've been on?"

Audrey loved the view of Earth from space. She wrote songs about it. She painted it. She shot into orbit every chance she got, so she could see it again and again. But Audrey hated lift-off, and Frankie didn't blame her—all those rockets shimmying and shuddering.

"This is easier," Frankie said. "It bypasses the flying part. No atmosphere to outrun."

Frankie steeled herself, ready for a comment on how Frankie had no way of knowing how easy it was, since she'd never been.

Worse, Audrey didn't respond at all. She gave her head a shake, then walked straight through to the dock.

Of all the things Frankie had screwed up last night, insulting Audrey was the worst. She needed to find a way to make it up to her friend. Two weeks was plenty of time to consult Liz on the mechanics of a real apology. Surely she could whip up some innovative philanthropy that Audrey would appreciate. Something big. Groundbreaking.

Or she could look for the protester. Assure Audrey that he was safe and sound.

They were best friends. They had to be OK.

Ears ringing, Frankie stepped onto the platform to stand with Liz. She wrapped her fingers around the railing behind her, grounding herself with the cool metal. New plans always made her feel better. She definitely needed one to impress her way back into Audrey's good graces. She'd have to step up her game on the tech front, too, if she wanted to interest Mom and Dad in her work. Shedding the dramatics might help.

Right now, all she wanted to do was sleep. She dropped her backpack at her feet, hoping no one had noticed it.

"Five minutes and counting," Liz said. "You OK, Frankie?"

"Fine." She wished she'd thought to bring a jacket. The transport operators stared resolutely at their assigned points on the 3D transport projection, avoiding Frankie's gaze as Audrey's miniature figure slid into the front row.

Jord pulled himself up to sit on the rail beside her. "I guess you're wishing you'd made a bet about whether I'd get to go," she said in Suhainnan, more to distract herself than anything else.

"*Te-all*," Jord corrected. "*Uspil* means to gamble."

"Same thing."

"Not at all. *Téall* is betting, like slot machines. Card games. *Uspil* is chance."

Frankie glared at him. "Same. Thing."

"No, Francesca. *Uspil* means to take a chance on some-thing. Someone." He reached into his pocket and pulled out a pill bottle. "For example, I know better than to leave these at home when I anticipate a meeting with you. Not a chance I'm willing to take."

"What is that?"

He pressed the bottle into her hand. "Ibuprofen," he said, pointing to his swollen lip.

No way he was going to make her feel bad about that. She shoved the bottle into her backpack, annoyed. "I'm supposed to believe you knew I'd trip you?"

"The source of the pain might be unpredictable, but the point remains the same. And it wasn't a gift, Francesca, it was an example."

"Next time give me a chance, and you won't need it."

Yeah, right. That would be like asking him to give up smoothies.

"Two minutes," Liz said. "I don't know what you two are arguing about, but please remember we have company."

"I'm sure they're enjoying the entertainment," Frankie said.

Jord stared at the transport model as Mom and Dad got everyone settled, the digital lines flickering around them as the system finished its checks. "Suhainn isn't that great," he said, still in Suhainnan.

"Obviously. You came from there."

He swung his heels against the lower railing. "Earth has indoor plumbing. Pretzels. Those little sticks with cotton on the ends, so useful."

"You came to Earth for Q-Tips?"

"Suhainn is wet, all the time. You'll see. They'll come back looking like drowned cats."

"I don't want to go to Suhainn."

If he knew it was a lie, he didn't let on.

"And we're a go," Liz said, as the transport lit up in green. "Cut the chatter, you two."

The transport engines fired with a roar that vibrated in Frankie's sinuses. She set her jaw to keep her teeth from chattering, while Jord continued to drum his feet on the rail. Witnessing a transport launch was like living inside a thunderclap, brief but intense. Frankie wished she could see inside the model, make sure Audrey was doing OK. She pictured her friend clutching the locket, which contained a picture of Audrey with her parents and three brothers.

The transport model glowed, its intensity increasing for three seconds, two, one, before it winked out of sight.

"That's that," Jord said, brushing his hands together. "What will you do with your free time now, Francesca? I hear pinball is making a comeback."

"Wait," Liz said. "Shut up."

Without meaning to, Frankie exchanged a glance with Jord. His brown eyes held the same question. He shrugged.

Liz leaned in toward the table. "Michael? Cindy, do you read me?"

Frankie jumped as an alarm blared, a red light flashing to life above the transport dock. She'd never heard any alarm on the operations floor, and she spent more time down here than almost anyone.

The rest of the operators had stopped working to stare at Liz.

They looked scared.

"What's going on?" Frankie asked.

Liz tapped the screen. Off. On. Frankie had no idea what she was trying to do.

"The controls are dead," Liz said. "Communications are down."

SEVEN

FRANKIE

A lost com signal, on the day of a televised launch.

It had to be a ploy. A bit of drama, to keep people glued to their VR goggles. Dad thought in audiences and advertising dollars. He'd always been a better celebrity than he was a physicist. Frankie figured he'd married Mom mostly to keep some scientific genius in the family.

The obsession with spectacle was unhealthy. Really. He should get it checked out. After this, Mom would probably make him do that—if she didn't murder him before they got back to Earth. Mom liked things to go smoothly.

Frankie hoped he'd at least thought to warn his passengers before performing a stunt, so Audrey wouldn't be freaking out right now.

"It's an act," Frankie said. "Right? Some of Dad's nonsense."

He'd kill her for saying it out loud. She didn't care. Someone in the room would throw her a wink, a small smile. Reassurance, in any form.

No one looked at her.

Jord slid off the railing, his face pale. If they were faking, he clearly didn't know about it.

Not a good sign. "Abort the mission," Frankie said. "Return the transport."

Liz shoved the nearest operator out of his chair and bent over the console. "I can't. Everything's frozen."

"So is the problem on our end, or is there something wrong with the transport?"

Liz ignored her.

All right. If this was a spectacle, then Frankie was going to give the viewers a show. If it wasn't... Well, she could help. She grabbed her pack and ran for the transport dock.

It took one good hard shove of the shoulder to wedge the doors apart. Her parents were good that way. Always a failsafe. The alarm blared, a corkscrew burrowing into her skull. Her earplugs were easily accessible, in compartment F of her backpack, but there was no time.

As she started to squeeze between the doors, Jord grabbed hold of her arm. She hadn't even registered the fact that he'd followed her over here. "What are you doing?" he shouted, the alarm practically drowning him out.

"Manually opening the bypass."

"The cameras," Jord said into her ear. "People are watching."

He really was their creature, wasn't he? Frankie pulled away. "Then they can watch me save everyone."

The word 'dock' sounded picturesque, especially given Suhainn's watery environment, but it was more of a garage-slash-airplane hangar where concrete won out over metal. Rows of helmets to the left, lockers to the right, and the gate to the interworld bypass ahead.

It was the bypass that allowed them to skip between universes, not the transport itself. They could make the trip in a canoe, provided it had been outfitted with life support and a propulsion system. With the right math and the proper instruments, you could set up a bypass anywhere.

Only Pathbound Enterprises knew how.

Opening the gate from this end should trigger a radio signal to call the transport back. With the computers failing, Frankie would have to do it manually.

Failsafes.

Jord stepped on her trailing dress as she threw herself at the control panel in the corner of the dock. She wrenched it out from under his feet. He refused to leave her alone. Like a demon with a soul to collect.

Frankie dug into her backpack as she ran, rummaging for the toolkit she'd stowed in compartment A-2. By the time she reached the control box, her screwdriver was ready; she wedged the head under the panel and flipped the door open. She knew what she'd find: clusters of switches, bundles of multicolored wires. She toggled the top three switches, the most direct way to open the door.

Nothing happened. Of course not. That would have been too easy.

Normally, Frankie lived for a chance to coax badly behaving machinery into functioning the way it was supposed to. Right now, every breath mattered.

What was happening to the transport, out in the bypass? She'd promised Audrey they'd be safe.

The alarm screeched on, threatening her concentration. Frankie buried her hand in the tangle and sorted out the wires she needed. Blue. Orange. She'd studied.

Jord leaned in close, watching her work. "Are you sure this is a good idea?"

Too bad the alarm wasn't quite as loud in here. The doubt in his voice made her want to punch him. Lucky for him, there wasn't time. Frankie used her knife to slice the wires in half. "I know what I'm doing."

"That's not what I asked."

"Just hand me the strippers."

Surprisingly, he obeyed. "What happens when the bypass opens with us in here?"

Frankie gritted her teeth and squeezed the strippers. She'd almost left them behind—it was hard to imagine a Suhainnan scenario where she'd need wire strippers—but she hated the idea of splitting up her set, so she kept them in. She gave them a good tug, exposing that beautiful copper.

"Francesca?"

"I'll give you five seconds to get out. It's generous."

The truth was, Frankie didn't know the answer to his question. She knew gears, wires, and engines. She could work a few tricks with computers, and she dabbled in augmented reality—though that was more of a hobby. It wasn't like she could study everything in the world, not until they finally figured out how to upgrade a human brain without killing its subject.

She hadn't exactly anticipated that there might one day be a need to hot-wire the doors to the interworld bypass while standing unprotected on the dock. An astrophysicist might be able to predict what was about to happen. Reason told her that opening the gate couldn't possibly unleash the full effect of space on them. For starters, everything would have to be bolted down. They'd need stronger protection between the dock and the operations center, to shield them from radiation. Not doors she could bust through with her shoulder.

Jord stayed.

Frankie let out a breath, nice and calm. She brushed the wires together. The gate cracked open.

Lightning struck the transport dock. The reverberation slammed her against the wall, the wires slicing across her palms as the explosion wrenched them from her grasp. Jord landed beside her as smoke gushed out of the bypass.

She didn't need to be an astrophysicist to know *that* shouldn't be possible. What had she done wrong?

Frankie tried to inhale, and choked instead. Burning rubber assaulted her nostrils as the gate disappeared behind a wall of ash. She felt the vibration in her feet as it slammed shut. Still, more smoke poured in. From where?

Disoriented, she propped a hand on the wall. Her fingers smarted against the hot concrete, blood pouring out of her ripped palms. She tried to pull herself to her feet, but Jord shoved her to the floor.

For a second, she fought him. Until her sluggish brain recalled the fact that the best way to *not* die of smoke inhalation would be to stay low.

Her brain could stand an upgrade to its disaster response mechanism, too.

They crawled for the exit, sticking close to the wall. If they lost sight of it, they'd never find their way. As she moved, Frankie squinted across the hangar, slowing her progress to search for a shape, a light, a person. Anything—anyone—that might have been salvaged when she opened those doors. Every few feet, her dress caught on something behind her; she gathered the fabric in her fist as best she could, and she kept moving, her palms sticky with blood.

Through the gloom, a glint of metal.

The transport. It had come out of the bypass after all. The bypass wasn't smoking—the transport was.

Frankie stopped. Audrey was in there. Her parents.

She'd promised.

Jord slung his arm around Frankie's shoulders and dragged her toward the door. When she struggled, he shouted in her ear, "You can't!"

She could. She had to try.

Heat radiated off the transport in ripples, as though to physically push her away. She couldn't see it, but she knew it was there. She could reach it. As soon as Jord let go. He leaned into her ear, muscles shaking with the effort of holding her. "You're going to kill us."

"No one's making you stay."

Whether he heard her answer or not, he didn't let go. By inches, he forced her toward the exit.

She'd have fought him forever. But Pathbound mechanics were already storming the dock—how long had it been? Thirty seconds? Sixty?—hoses dragging at their feet. One of them pulled Frankie the rest of the way before disappearing into the smoke, a protective mask clamped around his face. She stumbled to her feet, sucking in deep breaths.

The floor was a tornado of chaos as transport operators dashed for the exits. Was there a protocol box for this scenario? Were they following instructions, or succumbing to panic? On either side of the doors, the travel vids advertised busy canals, otherworldly feasts, and people laughing above a tagline that read *Experience Suhainn.*

Protocol or not, Frankie didn't join the evacuation. She couldn't take her eyes off the transport dock.

The fire burned, a chemically orange rage that seared through the smoke, lighting the operations floor with a sunset glow. Frankie had yanked the interworld transport out of space. And it was on fire.

"The cameras," Jord said, from somewhere behind her. "Off."

This time, Frankie didn't argue.

EIGHT

FRANKIE

WHEN FRANKIE WAS TWELVE, she'd fallen into one of the elevator shafts and broken her leg.

She'd been on the roof, trying to intercept the elevator's binary output so she could trick it into stopping on Pathbound Tower's hidden floor. Which *definitely* existed. You didn't have to be a conspiracy theorist to notice how hard the freakishly polished gargoyles worked to lure the eye away from the exterior anomalies.

And conspiracy theorists didn't have access to Pathbound's elevators, where they'd immediately have noted the five extra seconds that elapsed between floors twelve and fourteen. Every time.

Frankie did have access, and unlike the chattering employees who were too busy gossiping and trying not to spill their overly foamed espresso drinks, she'd noticed the anomaly.

And she'd decided to explore.

The elevator circuits had turned out to be too complicated to manipulate, so she'd turned to plan B: jam the elevator one story below the roof—where security was light—and work out how to ride it from the fourteenth floor to the thirteenth. Without dying.

Plan B had ended with a slip, a fall, and a crack of a landing on top of the elevator. Her screams had drawn rooftop security, who'd had to call the Fire Department to rescue her. EMTs had whisked her to the hospital. Her leg had been set, a neon-green cast applied. And because she was Francesca Hartiger, no one had scolded or lectured. If eyebrows had lifted, they'd done so behind her back.

The doctors had assured her that her parents had been called.

Pathbound's doorman, Ernie, had helped her navigate her crutches up to her apartment. He, too, had promised that her parents had been called.

She'd waited.

Mom's assistant: *They must be on their way.*

Dad's assistant: *That's strange. Are you sure they've been called?*

Mom's other assistant: *Let me just... OK... should I have the cafeteria send you some soup...?*

They hadn't come.

It wasn't hard, after the Pathbound Disaster—or so the media dubbed the assumed deaths of six high-status celebrities, including the Hartigers—for Frankie to imagine that her parents were just away on another long trip. Weeks, months, years. Their daughter's harrowing fall, and badly hurt leg, had not called them away from their work. Frankie was used to their absence.

This time, it was Liz's withdrawal that hurt. After the Pathbound Disaster, the transport operator had retreated to the operations center and shut the door. She'd stayed there through the media frenzy, admitting no one who showed up without a warrant. She'd stayed there while Frankie hid beneath hats, sunglasses, and umbrellas in her attempts to avoid the reporters that chased her to school every day for the first six weeks.

Liz had even stayed there through Audrey's memorial service. The most excruciating hour of Frankie's life, and she'd had to endure it alone. Shunned by her classmates, who acted like she'd personally murdered her best friend, Frankie had even wished for Jord. Just to break the monotony.

He hadn't bothered to show up, either.

But Frankie couldn't be angry at Liz, because her transport-floor vigil could only mean that Liz believed what Frankie believed: Audrey was alive, and so were her parents.

And if they were alive, they could be rescued.

FRANKIE FOUND Liz alone on the operations platform, staring at the communication console and muttering to herself. She snapped her head up when Frankie came in, ponytail bobbing. Her eyes were rimmed in red, and Frankie couldn't help thinking her eyestrain would improve if she'd turn the lights on properly.

The travel posters by the dock were shut off now, thank god, though not much else had changed in terms of the physical layout of the place. A starburst of scorch marks marred the floor in front of the sealed transport dock, which—as far as anyone but Frankie knew—was still sealed for investigation.

Frankie steeled herself for questions about what new loop-hole she'd used to get in this time. She'd finally mastered the elevator trick—the recoding, not the riding—and she'd been using it to bring the service elevator to the transport storage hangar every day for the last six months.

She'd prefer not to explain that to Liz just now.

"You look nice," Liz said, and Frankie's chest expanded in relief. "Date?"

At ten AM on a Saturday. Right. "Um, no? Memorial service?"

Liz rubbed a hand across her face, scattering crumbs out of her sleeve. "Shit. That's today."

As outlined in the protocol. Down to the last lily. Without the protocol-box instructions, the world surely would have memorialized her parents much sooner, but last wishes were last wishes. No matter how they were delivered.

Needless to say, Frankie was not included on the list of personnel allowed to access the protocol instructions. The pieces she knew, she'd learned when she demanded search parties or tried to put a stop to anything resembling a funeral.

Interworld personnel manager: *Not in the protocol.*

Interworld security manager: *Not in the protocol.*

Interworld immigrant slash Hartiger crony: *Not in the protocol, Francesca. And watch your vowels.*

For a bunch of people who supposedly believed the Hartigers were dead, everyone sure was afraid of disobeying their orders.

"What are you working on?" Frankie asked Liz, still hesitating by the doors.

"Reviewing some calculations."

Frankie crossed the room and sat down beside her. Half-consumed mugs of coffee littered the console, a situation six-months-ago Liz never would have allowed. One of them was sprouting disks of green mold. "You mean you're obsessing."

"Can you blame me?"

Seeing as Frankie had been doing the same thing, no.

Yes, the transport had returned to Earth engulfed in flames, leaving everyone else in the world to assume the passengers were dead. That her parents and Audrey had evaporated into the middle of space, or melted into puddles, even though there had been no evidence of organic matter in the wreckage.

Pre-disaster Liz would have assembled a search party, and damn the stupid protocols.

"Need any help?" Frankie asked.

Liz gripped the edge of the table. "What are you doing down here, Frankie? I have work I need to—"

"Come to the service," she said. "I want you there."

Liz glanced at her coffee-stained shirt. "Didn't you file a cease-and-desist to try and stop this funeral?"

Pre-disaster Frankie had been different, too. Pre-disaster Frankie would have trusted Liz, would have shared her plans instead of trying to trick her friend. "That was denial talking," she said. "I'm ready now. Look, if you don't come, I'm going to have to spend the next hour with Jord."

"He's not all that bad, Frankie."

Frankie pressed her fingertips against the raised scars on her palms where the wires had sliced her flesh when she'd opened the bypass. She found herself doing that a lot these days.

She hadn't seen Jord much since the disaster, either, aside from that one humiliating request for support in her campaign for a search party. "Unless he's changed since the last time I saw him, I doubt it."

Liz sighed, and Frankie knew she'd won. "I'll need a change of clothes."

"Meet you in the lobby in ten minutes? It's—I could use a minute alone down here, if that's OK."

It was only half a lie. She did need a minute, but she wouldn't be meeting Liz upstairs.

The Liz who'd been a sister to Frankie for the last five years? That Liz wouldn't have bought it.

That Liz would have noticed regular activity on the service elevator since the week after the Pathbound Disaster. She'd have caught Frankie in the vehicle hangar before Frankie could unzip her tool kit. And even though Frankie hadn't wanted to attract notice by rotating the floor—an action that would have triggered activity reports across several departments—Liz should have noticed that her protege had spent the last few months painstakingly dismantling a ten-seater in the hangar.

And then reassembling it on the dock. With the help of her smartwatch and her tools, it hadn't been a problem. It had just…. taken a while.

If no one else would bother to look for Audrey and her parents in Suhainn, then Frankie would do it herself.

Post-Pathbound-Disaster Liz never even checked the dock. She was distracted by grief, and the weight of self-blame. Frankie felt a twinge of guilt for taking advantage of that.

But only until Liz nodded, got up, and left her alone.

As soon as she was gone, Frankie sprang into action. She jumped off the platform and ran for the supply room, where she'd stashed her gear.

Frankie wasn't usually a fan of poetics. The chance to save her parents' lives on the day of their memorial service? That was too good to miss.

NINE

JORD

New York's rhythm was nothing but a jarring, jangled mess.

From the main entrance, it was easy for Jord to take in the comings and goings, not only of Pathbound Tower, but of Pathbound Center beyond the doors. So many people, packed together out of grief for the Hartigers. Or curiosity. Whatever the reason, the cold snap wasn't deterring them. People had abandoned the bizarre Utopian fashion trend quickly enough once winter arrived, which was unfortunate. The muted colors hadn't attacked his senses like the fur-lined parkas that flashed by now in every shade of neon. And the polka-dotted galoshes tromping along beneath them.

The whole garish parade was topped by the constant whir of technology—ID chips pinging and smartwatches vibrating— not to mention the high-pitched whine of the driverless cars that Earthens claimed were silent, yet buzzed in Jord's ears like a swarm. Funeral or no funeral, the salty smell of hot dogs wafted over from the vendor across the street.

The swirl of activity made him dizzy.

Instead of retreating to the false security of his apartment,

Jord leaned against the wall behind the security guard's station and lifted his set of digital Tri-oculars to his eyes. The Hartigers claimed the glasses could provide stats on any building in the city, thus aiding Jord's Earthly education. Jord could hardly look out his windows, let alone stand there long enough to let the oculars explain the specs and history of various skyscrapers. He hadn't used them much. He didn't like to carry technology; he didn't like the way smartwatches and augmented reality units beamed his location to satellites and Hartigers.

The six months he'd spent filming that VR-TV special, with drone cameras hovering around him for most of the day, had been a study in patience.

The oculars might be able to find Frankie in the crowd, though, in case he'd missed her on her way out.

Frankie hadn't wanted to hold a memorial for her parents, but she'd show up. She had to.

He hadn't expected her to quit attending her language lessons. The gaping hole in his weeks had filled up easily at first, as he'd reviewed the contents of the protocol box with relevant personnel and scrambled to staunch the flow of disastrous press coverage. As the weeks dragged, the media moved on to other matters while Pathbound hobbled along, mired in lawsuits, the protocol preventing them from making any major changes for six months.

When Jord found himself dawdling around his kitchen island on lesson days, listening for Frankie's knock, he'd booked double martial arts in the gym and reminded himself with every punch that he only had to hold out a little while longer.

The Hartigers operated in opaque layers, even after death. He'd never understand it.

But as of this morning—and as per the now-hated *Telescope Protocol*—Jord was officially in charge. When Frankie showed up for her parents' memorial, he'd hand her the protocol box and propose they reinvent Pathbound, together. Frankie should have been named to lead Pathbound, though Jord knew why she wasn't; Jord was a successor without rights. One who could be easily squashed, should the need arise.

Michael and Cindy hadn't expected him to hand so much power, so much wealth, back to their own daughter. Once he did, Frankie would be free to send all the search parties she wanted. And why not? If the Hartigers were alive, they'd have made contact by now.

Maybe Jord would go along.

The point was, he had a choice now. The worlds finally showed a little promise.

Between ocular glances, Jord watched over the guard's shoulder at the endless burn of the screen that monitored activity throughout the tower. It was a good thing Earthens had invented eye drops to go with their ubiquitous screens. Otherwise, Jord's eyes would have shriveled into raisins after mere days.

Beside them, the doorman stretched. "The security booth on the seventeenth can see a lot more," he said.

Jord suspected his presence might be interrupting a habit of sitcom viewing, which was just as well. He had never comprehended what was so funny about a drone delivering pizza to the wrong address.

The elevator dinged into the lobby, and Jord straightened. As he'd done several dozen times over the past hour, whenever the elevator dumped more people onto the floor. Ernie and Walter whipped their heads around, too, as if they wanted to know who he was waiting for, but were too afraid to ask.

When Liz came through the doors, Jord let himself fall against the wall, doing his best to hide his disappointment. She had on a rumpled black dress, her jacket slung over one arm. "What are you doing in here?" she asked.

Completing the final exam in doorman training.

Counting the number of times the elevator arrives in the space of fifty-three minutes.

(It was nineteen, stars help him.)

Watching Ernie's hair grow.

"I'm waiting for Francesca," he said.

Liz gave a little half laugh. "Seriously."

Jord didn't know if it would ever be possible to reverse Frankie's feelings after everything he'd done to block her from her parents and Pathbound. He'd stoked the animosity between them, adding kindling every time he rooted out one of her schemes. Explaining why he'd done it could easily make her hate him more. What had started as self-preservation when they first met—she did have a tendency to project a certain Hartiger-brand callousness—had morphed into something much more selfish.

Some days, he was able to convince himself that he did it to protect her from the truth about her parents, the depth of their cruelty. Most of the time, he could admit the real reason: that it was all in service of a desperate attempt to postpone the day when Frankie's expression would harden into Cindy's, and never soften again.

Jord straightened away from the wall. "Ernie," he said, "if you and Walter want to take a coffee break, I can keep an eye on things for a few minutes."

When they doormen had disappeared, Jord turned to Liz. "Have you seen her?"

Liz sighed. "I'm supposed to meet her here any minute. I actually thought she'd beat me up here."

Jord's heart dropped out of his chest, dragging his hope along with it. He knew Frankie had been reassembling the old transport at all hours of the night. She'd accessed the floor through the service elevator by reactivating a former employee's ID—exactly the kind of blip he'd learned to investigate.

He hadn't had the heart to stop her. Frankie didn't grieve any more openly than she'd sought her parents' affections while they were alive. The girl had dealt with their emotional rejection by going after a position in their company, by dreaming up brilliant projects and assembling working prototypes that would have inspired anyone else to hand her a job on the spot. Of course she'd deal with grief by building things. She took action. She buried herself in formulas.

Jord hadn't been able to bring himself to take that away. As long as she'd kept beating at the proper channels, demanding search parties and trying to cancel funerals, he'd been confident she was only constructing a backup plan.

He had a feeling he was about to pay for that mistake. "Up here? From where?"

Liz leaned over the desk, reaching for the tablet. "The control room. She begged me to come to the memorial."

Jord pulled the tablet out of her reach and selected the control room on Walter's screen. The guard was faster with these things, retrieving answers in a few seconds. Jord always fumbled.

"She didn't swipe out," Jord said, already moving toward the stairs. No time to wait on the elevator.

Liz hesitated behind him, biting her lip. "You don't think..."

He didn't think. He knew.

Frankie was on her way to another world.

TEN

FRANKIE

By the age of thirteen, Frankie had known enough to initiate the interworld launch sequence on her own. She'd never had to hack anything to learn the access codes; decrypting was more effectively accomplished through observation, and surreptitious videos of typing transport operators.

She'd watched. She'd learned the password rotations. She'd paid attention.

Now, she selected the launch sequence for Suhainn. Once she pressed enter, she'd have five minutes to secure her seat.

Once she pressed enter, the transport would go to Suhainn, with or without her.

Frankie gripped her bag as system checks whirled across the screen. As she waited, she mentally inventoried the items in her pack: granola bars, dried fruit, and water; all-purpose charger plate; backup all-purpose charger plate; first-aid kit; blanket; stunner; notebook and pen, in case she had to go analog; a mini box of champagne chocolates for Audrey; and finally, Jord's bottle of ibuprofen.

She'd considered tossing the pills, forgotten after so many

months, but the pragmatist in her had won out. Anti-inflammatory medication might come in handy anywhere.

She pulled her helmet on, coughing at the smell of new plastic as she snapped the chinstrap. It seemed silly to wear one at all, given the speed at which the interworld bypass squeezed the transport through space, but her parents were geniuses. Or at least, Mom was. They wore helmets, so Frankie would, too.

The system checks flipped to solid green. Good to go.

On the dock, the transport gleamed.

Frankie bit her lip. Her parents were in Suhainn. Audrey was in Suhainn. No one had evaporated in space, and neither would Frankie.

She had to do this. No one else would.

Her fingers barely trembled as she keyed in the code and pressed enter.

The screen glared red: *Initiating launch sequence. Destination: SUHAINN.*

Frankie hopped off Liz's platform and ran for the dock. She bounded through the doors, flung the pack into the transport, and threw herself in after it. It took a few seconds to untangle the mess of seat belts, but once she clicked them into place, the doors began to ease shut.

She checked the countdown clock on her watch. A little over sixty seconds had passed. She could have strolled here. She tucked the pack behind her and adjusted the helmet. It squeezed her ears, but there was no help for that. She wouldn't have to wear it for long.

The right-side door jerked open, and Jord landed in the seat beside her. "You can't go to Suhainn by yourself."

He said it like it hadn't been a month since their last encounter, like he was picking up in the middle of an ongoing fight. But he couldn't stop her this time. The transport was leaving Earth, and so was Frankie.

She reached over as far as she could and shoved his shoulder. So what if he landed beneath the transport? He could roll, couldn't he? "Someone needs to rescue Audrey and my parents," she said. "Get out."

Unfortunately, the belts prevented her from getting a good grip, and the door clicked shut. Jord said something in Suhainnan he hadn't mentioned in their lessons, then tightened the straps around his body.

"You haven't got a helmet," Frankie said.

"I imagine I'll survive."

Her stomach turned, uneasy, and she suddenly wished she'd paid attention to this particular aspect of interworld travel. What would happen to him without a helmet? OK, yes, he was annoying. That didn't mean she wanted him to die. "Your brain will get scrambled."

"As you just tried to seal my fate as the first person to be run over by an interworld transport, forgive me if your concern feels disingenuous."

Frankie ripped the plastic shell from her head and jammed it onto Jord's, batting his protesting hands out of the way as she wrenched the visor into place. She was not about to be responsible for his death. Her parents would kill her. "I hope it squeezes your ears," she said.

He fumbled at the strap as though to shove it back toward her, but the engines escalated into a roar, and it was too late.

Experiencing a departure with her feet planted on Earth was intense. This... this was the center of a cyclone, a living roar that wormed its way between her ribs, under her nails. This wasn't easier to take than a commercial space launch. It was much, much worse. Her eardrums were going to burst. Her teeth were going to drop out of her skull, right before the pressure squeezed her brain into toothpaste.

One more apology she owed Audrey.

For the first time, panic gave way to a loud, flailing part of her brain that shouted at her to stop this plan *right now, right now, right now*.

Too late. Frankie clutched the seat as the transport catapulted them into the interworld bypass. With smoke in her nostrils and copper on her tongue, she forced herself to watch. Somewhere in her dreams, she'd imagined there would be something to see. Beyond the bubbles of blue fire that skimmed along the windows, there was only darkness.

Jord leaned on the headrest, eyes closed beneath the visor. Not clenched, not tense, just closed. As if he thought he might be able to nap through this. Well, sure. If you've experienced one interworld launch, you've experienced them all. Except the disastrous one.

That one had probably felt a little different.

Frankie had certainly never imagined a normal trip through the bypass to feel so... unpleasant. There was pressure in her ears, and the blackness through the porthole made her feel like she was in a cave. Or a tunnel.

Frankie hated caves, and tunnels. She never knew why the bypass couldn't simply open straight from one dock to another, like crossing a threshold. If they could get there in thirty-four seconds, couldn't they get there in one? Apparently not.

The transport lurched to a stop, and Frankie's body strained so hard against the straps that she half expected them to snap. The engines powered down. In their absence, loud silence poured in. Frankie couldn't see a thing through the windshield.

"Are we stuck in the pathway?" she asked.

Jord unfastened his seat belt and pulled off the helmet. "Electricity is limited here. They don't keep the lights on all the time."

"They've got solar panels."

"Still not worth it. Have you got a flashlight?"

"Didn't bring your own?"

"You didn't give me time to pack."

Frankie activated the flashlight on her watch and eased the door open. How had he known to find her on the dock? "Because I don't need you."

"This once, Francesca, I think you do."

She spoke Suhainnan. She'd studied the maps. She didn't need anyone, least of all Jord. Frankie hopped out of the transport and shouldered her pack. She flashed the light around. With floors and walls made of stone, the Suhainnan transport dock was more like a garage. A small one.

Or a submarine. Instead of sliding doors, the exit consisted of a ladder and a hatch.

Jord stood frozen beside the transport, staring at the ladder.

"What?" Frankie said. "Not looking forward to explaining how you abandoned your world for indoor plumbing?"

"It's not quite as I remembered," he said.

"You haven't been here in years. Maybe they moved things around."

The paltry light cast his face in shadow so that it was impossible to see his expression, let alone read it. "It's not too late to go back."

Frankie started up the ladder. The rungs were rough with rust. "Actually, it kind of is."

"How so?"

"I don't know the codes for the return launch."

The ladder shuddered as Jord clambered up behind her. "I don't think I heard you correctly."

Frankie reached to fumble with the door. There had to be a handle somewhere, or a latch. It was impossible to fish for it while twisting her wrist to shine the light, and also holding the top rung. Frankie chose groping in the dark over falling to the concrete floor. "Once I find my parents, they can bring us home. Now that I've brought them a transport."

Finally, she'd done something that they would have to acknowledge. A daring rescue, accomplished through scientific know-how and Hartiger-level boldness, would win everyone over. A worthwhile endeavor by Mom and Dad's standards, and by Audrey's. Win-win-win.

"And if you can't find them?"

"Then I'll contact Liz, and she'll help us."

"And if the coms are still down?"

"Will you be an optimistic person for thirty seconds?"

"Because you're known as Gloria Sunshine?"

Frankie's fingers closed around the latch. "This wasn't supposed to be your problem. You want to help? Help. Otherwise, go visit your old girlfriends and stay out of my way."

She pushed. The hatch opened with a wrenching squeal, and a column of sunlight poured down the ladder.

Sunglasses. Weeks of meticulous list-making, and she hadn't remembered to bring sunglasses. Squinting painfully, Frankie made herself finish the climb. Not the most dignified way to enter another world for the first time, crawling in the sand. She stumbled to her feet and looked around. Everything was bathed in white light. Her eyes stung.

Wherever they'd landed, it was eerily quiet. True, she was used to the roar of New York. But there ought to be water gurgling. Trees rustling. Vendors calling wares.

Frankie inhaled, expecting to smell saltwater and sea marshes. Instead, she almost choked on the dust in the air.

They'd emerged by a wall made of tree trunks. It looked hastily constructed, like a model she might have thrown together with popsicle sticks as a kid. It stretched as far as her watering eyes could make out, in either direction.

"Where are the canals?" she asked, taking a step toward the

wall. "Why is the air so dry? I thought Suhainn was all water and boats."

Jord climbed the rest of the way out of the hatch. He propped the door open and came to stand beside her. "I've got a simple explanation for that."

Frankie waited. When he didn't continue, she said, "And the fee for this information is...?"

Jord shaded his eyes, peering up at the wall. "I'll give you this one, free of charge," he said. "We're not in Suhainn."

ELEVEN

JORD

Stale wind stung Jord's cheeks with bites of hot sand, while a bell cried long, metallic tones that buzzed between his eyes. Frankie turned a full circle, assessing the situation, their surroundings, as if it were a mathematics problem.

Suhainn had boats zipping down azure canals. Air infused with salty humidity. Suhainn had the people he'd almost allowed himself to hope he might see. Neighbors, tutors, friends. A brother.

Here, a rickety wall stood before them. At their backs, alcoves were carved into a cliff, the top ledge of which disappeared into waves of sunlight.

Frankie faced him, the wind already teasing her curls free of their tie. "Did you know about this place?"

Seeing as he had no idea where they were, he found it difficult to answer that question. Michael and Cindy kept secrets. That was never a surprise.

He hadn't thought they might be hiding inhabited worlds. Or at least, this one appeared to be inhabited, what with the buildings and all. He certainly hadn't thought their daughter would head off to one, and without an escape route.

"I didn't," he admitted. "Is there a signal? Can you call Liz?"

Frankie gave herself a shake and lifted her wrist. She pressed some buttons on the side of her watch, waited, then shook her head. "Nothing."

Jord cursed the Hartigers. Michael and Cindy knew about this place. They had to.

But there wasn't time to contemplate what secrets they'd buried here. His ears half-registered approaching footsteps, and then there were people streaming out of the cliffs, surrounding Frankie and Jord in a matter of seconds. Soldiers, wearing helmets with strips of metal guarding their noses and chins, swords gripped in gloved hands.

They stopped, several of them exchanging confused glances. A woman in front rolled her eyes. Odd.

Feet shifted. Leather creaked. And then, all but one of the soldiers dropped their weapons, swords and spears clattering to the ground as if hit by a spell.

The one who still held his sword—the commander, Jord decided—stood unmoving in the center of the semi-circle. He had a burly figure, light brown skin, and a close-cut beard. A golf ball-sized dent marred the left shoulder plate on his armor.

After a pause, he lowered his weapon, too. His eyes were locked on Jord. "Very funny," he said. "Feeling better, then?"

And Jord understood him. The words, anyway, if not their context. No sign of water in this world, no sign of the sky he remembered so well in his dreams, yet this stranger spoke to him in Suhainnan. And seemed to know him. How?

Jord felt Frankie's eyes on him. No doubt she thought he was lying about where they'd landed. He couldn't entirely blame her, but he'd never seen this man before in his life.

The commander sheathed his sword, the blade sliding into its leather case with a whisper, then removed his helmet. He looked weary, the corners of his eyes pinched with pain. "Tell me the rules of this game, so I might know how to play along."

"We came here by accident," Jord said.

"Fine." The commander motioned to his soldiers. "Escort these *strangers* to the nearest bottle of *afan dreoch.*"

"What's that?" Frankie asked. "*Afan*—what?"

"Drink. A strong one," Jord said.

"I don't get it."

Neither did he. The soldiers folded around them in a loose escort, marching them a scant few feet before stopping abruptly in front of a narrow passageway. A tunnel, burrowing deep into the cliffside.

When Jord hesitated, the commander affected a shallow bow. "After you."

"Where does this lead?" Jord asked.

The commander shrugged. "This is your game."

Jord shook his head, as if he could rattle the man's words into something he understood. None of it made any sense.

Frankie, however, pressed her lips together and shot him a look he couldn't read—defiance?—before plunging straight into the darkness. She never let fear sink its claws in. If she ever felt it at all.

Jord couldn't even open his apartment shades.

He fell in beside her. The passage veered immediately to the right, snuffing the daylight into a darkness so thick it felt like something he could chew. Light in New York was never truly absent. Smoke detectors blinked, drone modules remained illuminated, hallway sensors reminded you of their constant vigilance. Jord would have found the tunnel almost comforting, if he'd had any idea where they were headed. He had to assume he'd been mistaken for a friend, or he and

Frankie would have been skewered by now. But the reception was so odd, the shared language so disorienting, that he had no idea what to think. Or what might happen when the misunderstanding came to light.

He skimmed his fingertips along the wall, the rock cool beneath his touch. Grounding.

Another turn, and two spots of fire pricked the shroud ahead like tiny lighthouses.

Jord sensed the expansion of the space before his eyes drank enough of the meager light to see anything of the room where they'd emerged. He stayed close to Frankie, while the commander lingered on his other side.

The room—a cavern, in truth—was empty. Or so Jord thought, until the candles flinched. It was barely a flicker, an interruption he might not have noticed if the movement had not stopped the commander in his tracks.

And because the soldier stood so close, Jord heard the man's breath catch in surprise as a new voice floated out of the darkness. "Yesterday, it was fireballs in the sky. The day before, our dwindling supplies. My answer is the same today, Reyche. Go away."

Reyche swallowed. He turned to stare at Jord, open-mouthed shock scrawled across his features. He assessed Jord for a long moment before turning to face the voice. "The Earthen carriage. It—it brought—"

"Did it bring ducks, Reyche? Did it bring that orange jelly the Earthens used as garnish when we were children?"

Jord felt more confused than ever, but Frankie said, "Are you asking him for sweet and sour sauce?"

The shadow snapped his fingers. "Indeed. It was both. Did the carriage bring that?"

"No, your highness. It brought Earthens."

"Pity."

Reyche cleared his throat. "Prince Kol. I think you will want to see these Earthens."

"I cannot imagine so."

Reyche withdrew a torch from his belt. He stepped forward to touch the torch to the candle, where it blazed to life.

The prince lounged in a wooden chair, a shadow clothed in black. As Jord's eyes adjusted, he saw there was but one candle, the flame doubled by the surface of a large mirror. These items sat upon a table beside a bottle and a mug.

The man in the chair raised his hands to block the light that bloomed through the cave as the rest of the soldiers ignited their torches, locks of long hair falling around his face. "You murder my skull, Reyche," he said, his voice muffled. "In times like these, we all deserve the dignity to die as we please, without skull-murdering light inflicted upon us."

"Prince Kol, please. Look," Reyche said.

Slowly, the Prince lowered his hands.

His hair curled long, almost to his shoulders. But aside from this difference, and the black clothing, the resemblance could not have been plainer.

He was Jord's identical twin.

Frankie actually gasped. Jord felt the absurd impulse to laugh.

Give this prince a haircut, a suit, and—especially—a bath, and he could stand in for Jord's next television appearance. No one would ask a single question.

Michael and Cindy had to have known that he had a twin living in some world they'd never bothered to mention. Royalty, no less.

Jord cursed the Hartigers. All of them.

Other-world Jord retrieved his mug from the table and swallowed a long draught. "Reyche," he said, "this batch of *afan* is giving me hallucinations."

"Have you considered not drinking it, Your Highness?" the captain returned, regaining his composure.

Frankie, of course, was already talking. "I was right," she said. "This is an alternate world. This place is what... a desert version of Suhainn? At war? We could be looking at multiple universes with multiple apocalyptic scenarios. It could make complete—"

"I can hardly understand her," the prince said.

"—sense," Frankie finished.

Jord half expected her to drop to her knees and start scratching diagrams on the floor. He was curious to know whether she found this situation at all worrisome. She was looking back and forth from Jord to his twin, as if the Hartiger in her had identified specimens for study. "I'd need more data," she said.

It was both disconcerting and, despite the situation, somewhat amusing, for Jord to watch his own face passing through the stages of confusion many people experienced when Frankie honored them with one of her speeches.

No one forgot their first meeting with Frankie Hartiger.

Prince Kol refilled his mug with a hand that was unsteady enough to make Jord wonder how long he'd been drinking. Drops streamed down the side of the cup in little waterfalls. *Afan.* Honey on the tip of the tongue, with the promise of a bite behind it. Jord had smelled it often, in the governor's home.

The series of accidents and interruptions that would have had to occur in Suhainn to make Jord a prince... No, it wasn't possible. Jord kept his past from Frankie, not because it was tied to some secret crime or Hartiger conspiracy, but in truth, he was nothing more than a servant. Page-class, yes—educated and already working for the governor when the Hartigers had taken him—but a servant nonetheless.

Frankie thought little enough of him already. She didn't need to know that.

"Earthen girl," Kol said. "Am I understanding correctly that you can see him, too?"

Frankie folded her arms. "Unfortunately, yes."

Of course she wasn't worried. She'd probably already figured out how to drill through the walls and escape.

"Do I get a vote?" Jord said.

Kol held the mug in Jord's direction, and for a moment, Jord thought he was being invited to drink. "Figment of my imagination," the prince said, "should I drink more *afan* this evening?"

"I'd imagine not."

"Precisely what a delusion would say. Reyche?"

"I can see him, Your Highness."

Poor Reyche had clearly endured this sort of performance before. He didn't even sound annoyed.

"Brilliant," Prince Kol said. "You've finally brought me something worth looking at."

"Happy to oblige," Reyche replied. And with only the barest dry note in his tone, too. Under other circumstances, Jord might have asked for lessons.

The prince turned to Frankie. "And you are?"

"Frankie Hartiger."

The prince froze, his energy cooling so suddenly that Jord moved closer to Frankie without thinking.

The Hartiger name was a match, and she'd struck a flame into the dark.

Kol whipped around to face the mirror. The mask of insolent humor had vanished, leaving fury and confusion in its place.

"Your Highness," Reyche said, his voice taking on a placating tone. "Your wise woman has not answered in weeks."

Jord risked a glance at Frankie, who raised her eyebrows. She still didn't look frightened. She looked like she wanted to take notes.

Kol gripped his mug and stared into the mirror as though preparing to do battle with it. "Summon her."

Reyche reached for the prince's shoulder, then seemed to think better of it. He withdrew his hand and stepped up beside Kol instead, his helmet tucked beneath his arm. "In times of distress, she answers."

It sounded like a piece of a story, or a snippet of psalm from an Earthen holy text. An odd kind of phone number. The candle cast an eerie glow on the faces of the two men, hollowing their eyes into pools of black, while Kol repeated the words under his breath.

Where in the universes had Frankie landed them?

As Jord was beginning to think Kol and his captain were both crazy, the mirror... melted. It was the only word Jord could summon for it as the prince's reflection disappeared, replaced by a whirlpool of mercury. Kol gripped the mug so hard his arms shook, and Jord thought it might break between his hands.

The storm settled into a solid wall of silver. Jord held his breath. Beside him, Frankie leaned on the balls of her feet like she might leap into the shimmering pond to see where it led.

The prince had the same eager look in his eyes. Perhaps the universes should have paired these two, instead of sending Jord to her.

Then again, perhaps the universes had done just that.

In a blink, the silver swirled away. The reflections returned, solid, as though they'd been there all along.

Frankie let out a breath Jord recognized well enough. Disappointment.

Jord felt only relief.

Tension quivered through Kol's arm as he held onto the mug, staring into the mirror like a child betrayed.

When he launched the *afan* at the glass, even Frankie jumped. The mug burst, leaving a spiderweb of cracks in the mirror and raining amber *afan* across the floor as Kol dropped to his knees, bowing his head. Whether in despair or in prayer, Jord couldn't have said. The two had a tendency to coincide.

Suhainn had no gods. This place might.

Reyche motioned to the soldiers, and they resumed their formation around Jord and Frankie, leading them out into the arid world and immediately into a cave with bars installed in the rock. Reyche dragged a hand across the door. The lock clicked open, and before Jord had time to consider how the mechanism worked, the soldiers guided Frankie and Jord inside.

Jord had a feeling that this cell would not be furnished as comfortably as his Earthen one.

Frankie moved to the back of the cave, but Jord stayed to face Reyche. "Tell me something," he said. "Why do you hate Earthens so much? Why does the name Hartiger invoke rage?"

"That's two things." Reyche glanced toward the prince's cave. He was younger than Jord had first assumed, maybe twenty; the lines of concern at his eyes made him seem much older. "Prince Kol is right to be careful of Earthens."

Jord wrapped his fingers around the bars. "I'm not Earthen."

"Suhainnan?"

Jord nodded, a bubble of hope rising in his chest. Reyche had heard of Suhainn. "Can you get us there? Operate the transport?"

The captain regarded him carefully. "You truly did not mean to come to Rogur."

Rogur. Was that what they called their world?

It sounded like a curse. "Truly," Jord said.

"Only they can get to Suhainn." Reyche nodded at Frankie. "The same way you came here."

"And something about that offends you?" Frankie asked, her tone biting. "Why do you even care?"

Reyche motioned to the soldiers, and they scattered. His thick eyebrows were drawn together in worry. "You're the reason our magic is dying. You're killing our world."

TWELVE

KOL

Kol stayed on his knees for a long time, caught between sinking and rising.

If the point of rising was to pour more drink, and the drink would send him to the ground eventually, then he might as well stay down. He was well acquainted with the feeling of this rock floor against his cheek.

Perhaps some benevolent entity had sent his twin to Rogur, to take on the troubles of a prince until this world should grind to a stop. Perhaps that was why his wise woman refused to answer. Kol asked for help, the wise woman sent Earthens. If so, her sense of humor was crueler than he'd have guessed, saving his life just to provide such an exit now.

She claimed to know his purpose. It was the only evidence that he'd ever had one at all.

Steps sounded down the passageway, and Kol pushed to his feet, covering the too-quick movement by turning to the table for his *afan*. He did not need Reyche hovering over him in concern. After the massacre that had forced them out of the capital, his captain's list of worries was long enough.

Only when glass crunched under his boots did Kol remember he'd smashed his mug. No matter. The bottle would do.

When the soldier cleared the doorway, Kol could tell that it was not Reyche, even in the darkness. Based on her petite stature, and the whisper of her boots on the cave floor, Kol guessed Lara.

He swallowed a wad of disappointment. "Sent you to check on me, did he? What did he say?"

Lara shifted her feet.

"He's your captain. I'm your prince. What did he say?"

"'Make sure Prince Kol finds his way to his feet, by any means necessary.' Sir."

Kol almost allowed himself smile at that. Almost. No doubt this soldier could drag him up by one ear, if she wanted to. "How fares your leg?"

"Twinges, your highness. But it's fine."

She was lucky. No infection. Of all the impossible attackers that had accosted them in Caisrach City, the one that'd inflicted Lara's injury had been among the worst.

What had awakened the army of gods to descend upon his people, Kol still couldn't say. One night, legends had simply walked out of the palace tapestries—or so it had seemed—and begun to kill. Bren the Voiceless, slitting throats as he'd ascended the stairs. Saraya the Wolf Mother, combing the streets with her pack of ferals, one of which had been responsible for the wound to Lara's leg. On and on they'd come, impervious to swords, answering no prayers and taking no quarter.

According to the reports that Reyche insisted on continuing to gather, clemency had later been granted to those who'd prostrated themselves on the bloodied cobblestones, bending knee to the now-living gods. Kol didn't blame the citizens who'd stayed to bow. If their prince was ill-favored by the gods, why should his people suffer for it?

And ill-favored, he most certainly was. Dozens of gods had returned to Rogur, and Kol claimed only a single ally among them. Elandria. She hadn't even been present when the city was taken—who knew where the fickle serpentess lurked?—yet she'd called to Kol from her mirror and delivered safe passage out of Caisrach City. Reyche's mistrust of her was well reasoned, but none of their party would have made it out alive without her aid.

And perhaps they shouldn't have. A prince ought to go down with his palace, fighting until his final heartbeat. What was the point of scraping a few more miserable weeks out of life? Kol couldn't save his loyal few, or escape those who would see him murdered.

Trapped. They were all trapped.

"Well, soldier, you see me on my feet," Kol said. "How often are you to check on me?"

"Every half hour."

Already featured on Reyche's list of worries, then. Kol strangled the neck of the bottle. "Very good. Don't let your captain down."

Lara recognized the dismissal. Kol watched her go, then wandered to the cavern wall, still cradling the bottle. He had not cared much for the palace, either, with its mosaic of balconies, but he did wish for windows. He wished for fresh air.

Kol dropped into the chair, and lifted the bottle to his lips.

THIRTEEN

FRANKIE

Sand crusted Frankie's eyelids, burrowed under her nails, caked her throat in a layer of grime that couldn't be swallowed away. Not without the water in her pack, which the soldiers had unfortunately realized they should confiscate.

Leave it to Frankie to botch a rescue attempt by landing herself in the wrong world. This detour might be a fascinating one, what with the cranky doppelgängers and angsty soldiers, but Audrey and her parents were still stuck in Suhainn without a transport. Frankie needed to get there.

Instead, she was trapped in a cell. With Jord. He sat on a slab of stone in the corner with his elbows on his knees. He might have been waiting for a bus.

"So," she said, "you're royalty here."

Jord shifted to sit up straight, then tossed his rock in the air and caught it. He shouldn't be able to stay so calm when Frankie's nerves were on fire. "If you happen upon Earthen twins, Francesca, do you speak to them as one organism, with shared mind and purpose?"

Frankie tested the bars, moving down the line to give each one a shake. Solid. "You know what I mean."

"Yes." Jord gave the pebble another toss. Up. Down. "You've cemented your alternate-worlds idea as truth, and this gentleman as an alternate version of me, when there could be a dozen other explanations."

"I've been working on this theory for years," Frankie said. "Let's hear yours. Oh, right. You don't have theories. You have a rock."

He took a long time to answer, so long that it became painful to hold his gaze. He thought too much about what he said. It was hard to trust that.

When he finally spoke, his voice was soft. "Truce."

Frankie opened her mouth, ready to fire off a retort, then closed it. "What?"

"I call a truce. Amnesty. Cessation of hostilities. Like in our lessons. We need to work together if we're going to get back to Earth."

Like in their lessons? As if his kitchen counter had been some kind of a neutral zone? Frankie couldn't separate the Jord who'd conjugated verbs with her in his gloomy apartment from the one who undermined every attempt she made to advance at Pathbound, and prove herself to her parents.

Maybe there was a version of Earth where Frankie didn't leave every session with a weight in her stomach, wondering why they couldn't be friends instead of sworn enemies.

A moth dipped between the bars and skimmed along the ceiling of their cave, wings whispering against the rock. It looked like a normal, Earthen moth. Nothing otherworldly about it.

Jord was the last person she wanted on her side. But he wasn't wrong, either. They needed to get out of here. As much as she hated to admit it, his talent for diplomacy might have its uses.

Before she could say as much, her pack landed at her feet.

Frankie twisted to see Jord's twin—god, there really were *two* of them—looking down at her from the other side of the bars. Whiskey-like fumes wafted around him, so strong that she wondered how he could have breathed near the candle without igniting his furniture. In place of the broken mug, he carried the full bottle, hanging onto the neck as though it were the only thing holding him to this life.

As she got to her feet, he passed a second object through the bars. "Reyche thought this tube might contain a weapon. Alas, it's a sheet of parchment. How boring."

The plastic cylinder was all too familiar. A protocol box. Frankie took it. "Where did you get this?"

"That would be a question for your extraordinarily good looking companion," the prince said, tipping the bottle to his lips. The drink streamed out of the sides of his mouth and down his chin.

Jord came to stand beside her, close enough that their shoulders touched. In brighter light, she might have been able to search out some scar, or a tell, to distinguish him from the prince. As evening faded to night, she wasn't sure she'd be able to tell the difference.

Frankie held the box up to the torchlight. Printed in block letters was the word TELESCOPE. So this was it. The mysterious, search-party-prohibiting protocol. She'd assumed Jord would be privy to some of its contents. Not all of them. "Why do you have this?"

Jord stood so still, he might have been a statue.

"There used to be a forest here," the prince said, as though in answer to her question. "Trees, tall as you can imagine. Squirrels and badgers, all kinds of forest creatures."

"Badgers like open spaces," Frankie said absently, flipping the tube to read the small print on the bottom. She'd never even held one before. How pathetic. "They'd prefer it now."

If Dad were here, he'd probably fire up her wildlife tracking system. Analyze the badgers, or whatever, since he was so in love with that idea.

Telescope protocol: in the event that communications are lost, the box read.

Prince Kol flung his arms open, splashing liquid out of the bottle. Surprising that there was any left at all. "In that case, welcome all you badgers. Come, build your homes. Someone ought to benefit."

His voice was so much like Jord's that the words cut through her distraction, though it was too nonsensical for her to think of a response.

Jord reached for the protocol box, but Frankie pulled it away. She unscrewed the top and slid the paper out. The more she tried to steady her hands, the more they betrayed her. *Once six months have passed, Pathbound Enterprises is to continue normal operations under the guidance of Jord Mathison.*

No. No way. This could not be happening. They'd left Jord in charge of Pathbound? *Forever?* "You faked this," she said.

But she already knew he hadn't. The parents who failed to rush home when their daughter had shattered her leg in an elevator shaft, who she'd disappointed so badly that they didn't even want her at their dinner table? They wouldn't hesitate to grant her legacy to their golden replacement child. Jord could do no wrong. "You're too young," she said.

"Not in Suhainn."

"Suhainn," the prince said, spitting in the dirt. "Did you know that every time your carriage cracks through to other worlds, it drags earthquakes and plague across Rogur? We're the egg. You're the needle. You drain our juice with every journey."

Everything he said was complete nonsense. Then again, it was impressive that Kol could form a sentence at all.

Two of them. Frankie couldn't even deal with one. She kept her focus on Jord. "You're not from Earth. Is this legal?"

"That would be the entire point, I imagine. Easy to pass along, easy to take back." Jord wrapped his fingers around the bars, holding them with the same fervor his twin exerted on that bottle. "Ask me how I knew you were leaving."

Frankie glared at him. "What does that have to do with anything?"

"I was waiting for you outside the memorial service. I'd hoped we could work together. As partners."

She shook her head. The rest of his story might be true, but Jord had been edging her out of Pathbound since he'd first set foot in the tower. Sure, he wanted a truce now, when her skills could get them out of this dump of a world, but there was no way in hell he'd offer to share that kind of power. "I don't believe you."

"And I don't blame you for it. But everything is different now."

Nothing was different. Nothing had changed. Her parents had chosen Jord over her, again. And this time, the decision might have been permanent.

Kol banged his bottle against the bars, and Frankie jumped. She'd nearly forgotten he was there. "Aya preserve us all," he said. "What are you fighting about?"

"Nothing," Frankie said. She threw the protocol box on top of her bag. Jord was lucky she hadn't thrown it at his face.

Kol scoffed. "The gods awaken, the magic dies, but all these two Earthens care about are their petty love affairs."

Jord made a strangled sound and whipped away from the bars, pacing to the back of the cell.

He didn't need to sound quite so disgusted.

"Aya," Frankie said, forcing herself to unclench her fists. "Is that the woman in the mirror?"

Kol shoved a finger through the bars and pressed it to her mouth. "Shhhh. No one else knows her name."

Frankie batted him away. "Why? What does this... Aya care, if people know her name?"

Kol frowned, confused. "Did I say that? No, that's not right. Aya... She put a pin in the stars. Elandria lives in the mirror. Not that there's much of a difference. If you've met one awakened god, you've met them all."

His ravings descended deeper into nonsense by the sentence. Behind them, Jord continued to pace. She hoped those shoes were pinching his feet.

"Didn't you say you have magic?" she asked. "Can't you use it to get out of here? Can you get us to Suhainn?"

Prince Kol scoffed. He reached for his pocket, missed, and tried again. He withdrew a black ball and held it in his palm, its surface shining in the firelight. "We *had* magic. You keep stealing it."

"Not on purpose," Frankie said.

"Not on purpose," he mimicked. Was he a prince, or a kindergartener? "This stone once contained the power to summon anyone I wished, be they halfway across the room, or the realm. Now, it's no more than a rock."

He opened his fingers, allowing the ball to slip to the ground, where it landed in the dirt with a dull thud.

"Sorry," Frankie said. "That isn't my fault."

Kol grabbed the bars and pulled himself close, his face an inch from Frankie's. The liquor on his breath would ignite in a snap, the fumes nearly overpowering. She held her ground as her pulse pounded in her throat. The prince was unpredictable. Well, so was she.

She felt Jord return to her side, though whether to protect her or help Kol get rid of her, she couldn't say.

Either way, she preferred Kol.

"You arrived in time to watch our world burn," the prince said. He pushed away and launched his bottle at the wall, banishing its shards into the darkness. "So watch. From this cell. Burn with it."

Frankie waited for him to stagger away—in search of another drink, no doubt—before dropping to reach through the bars. Her fingertips grazed the stone. It was too far.

Jord crouched beside her. "Are you all right?"

Frankie ignored him and rummaged through her backpack, hoping he wouldn't see the way her hands shook. She didn't need him to know she was afraid. She didn't need his concern.

"Did he hurt you?" Jord asked.

Frankie's fingers closed around the length of rope she'd stashed in the inside pocket. She slid it out and tied a knot in the end, like a noose. When she fumbled, she sucked oxygen into her lungs, trying to calm her body as she picked it up. "He barely touched me. Don't be dramatic."

"What are you doing?"

Frankie considered looping the rope around his legs and giving it a good tug. Instead, she tossed it between the bars. It took her a few tries to lasso the stone, but finally she was able to draw it close.

The size of a tennis ball and black as obsidian, the stone weighed heavy in Frankie's hand. She turned it over, though she wasn't sure exactly what she was looking for. A fiery vision, perhaps.

"He might come looking for that," Jord said.

And then what? He'd lock them up? Frankie was pretty

sure she could take Prince Kol down with a well-placed nudge. She rolled the glassy stone across her palm, examining. No gods appeared, no crystal-ball mists, but after three rounds, her skimming fingers caught on a flaw. A minute depression in the surface. A button.

She pressed it. Nothing happened.

Excited, Frankie dove into her pack and ripped out one of the charger plates. She touched it to the stone.

The crystal ball ignited in a flurry of images, an irrefutably *digital* flood of faces, villages, lakes, and fields.

"Not magic," she said, turning her back to the bars. "It's a screen. A glorified phone."

"Manufactured magic. Sounds Hartiger-like to me." She couldn't make out Jord's exact expression, though she could easily imagine him rolling his eyes.

"If you mean brilliant, then yes," she said. "This world isn't dying. The charge is just draining out of their tech."

"What about the dead forest and the earthquakes? The plague?"

Well. Maybe it was dying a little. If Kol was right, then Frankie's entire understanding of the interworld bypass was based on a foundation of misinformation. What could the transport be doing to the physical landscape of an entire world? Rogur, he'd called it.

The transport wasn't supposed to pass through other worlds. It wasn't supposed to hurt anyone.

Frankie ran her thumb alone the smooth surface of the ball-screen. "We can fix it. My parents will help us."

"Oh, excellent plan. Any other ghosts you'd like to petition for assistance?"

Frankie hardly heard him, her mind busy cataloguing the other magic they'd encountered. "Kol's mirror has to be a screen, too. Which means this Elana... Elnia?"

"Elandria."

Frankie thought of the silver whirlpool in the Prince's mirror. It certainly had a slice of dramatic flair. Flashy magic-trick flair.

Michael Hartiger flair.

She drummed her fingers on the bag, thinking. "Right. This Elandria person. She's got tech that works. She knows enough to keep her solar panels working, and instruct Kol to do the same." She looked up. "Jord. Elandria must be my parents. They're not in Suhainn. They're here."

FOURTEEN
FRANKIE

Who else but Frankie's parents would know how to restore tech like this? Frankie was sure that if they asked Kol how long he'd been talking to this Elandria person, the answer would be equal to about six Earthen months.

Jord fixed his attention on the stone, like he expected it to spout a full manifesto. He looked ridiculous in his suit vest and tie, plaid button-down underneath. This dustbowl of a world had caked his shoes within the first hour.

Surely he was arranging his arguments against her, evidence that her parents were dead, methods for pulling his newly acquired rank on her. As if it mattered here.

Frankie wasn't going to give him the chance to try. She scrambled to her feet. "What other magic did we see?"

Jord joined her. "The locks."

Frankie was already feeling for them with her fingers. The bars were still warm from cooking all day in this frying pan of a world, and they were rough with rust—as was the lock plate on the other side. Frankie ran her hand along the square, feeling for anomalies, while Jord watched anxiously over her shoulder.

She could practically feel his energy, his breath shallow in his throat. She gritted her teeth to keep herself from shoving him away.

The plate had to conceal some kind of an ID reader. After a moment, Frankie located a trio of sharp pins at the corner. "All Reyche did was drag a hand across the doors, and they opened."

"I don't understand what you—"

Frankie grabbed Jord's hand and shoved it through the bars, pressing his finger against the spot where Reyche had gained entry. Jord gasped in surprise, wrenching his hand out of her grasp.

Before he could speak, the door swung open.

Jord stared at her. "How...?"

"DNA. It recognizes you as the prince."

Alternate-world doppelgängers were like twins in more than appearance. Good to know.

Jord looked at his finger, where a bead of blood was popping up. Pathbound scanners detected DNA by touch. Apparently, this one used a needle. Older tech. Also good to know. "Warn me next time you do that?" he said.

Frankie shouldered her pack. "Let's go."

She slipped out the door and moved sideways along the cliffside. The night air felt like a cool relief after the heat of the day, the stuffiness of that cave-slash-cell. A breeze whipped between the wall and the rocks, stirring the dust into little swirls like eddies in a stream.

Reyche had implied his numbers were thin, so they shouldn't have a problem finding an unguarded section of wall. It didn't look hard to climb.

More than anything, this place reminded her of an old fort from a VR history module of the Old West. Quick to build, quick to dismantle, with rickety rope bridges and watch towers stacked up like blocks. Spots of fire flickered along the top of the wall at intervals, like fireflies blinking in the night.

What would she find beyond the wall? At the top of the cliff?

What would Jord do to her if she paused for a second to snap a photo on her watch?

When they reached the entrance to Kol's cave, Frankie hesitated. They ought to scurry by it. Move as fast as possible. But the mirror was no more than a few feet away, just on the other side of the rock. A link to her parents. To Audrey.

Jord moved in beside her. "We have no idea when a guard might note our disappearance. We have to go."

Frankie scanned the darkened walls, the torches casting odd phantoms onto the battlements above. A shadow might appear any moment, a soldier on patrol. "What if my parents are on the other end of that mirror?"

"I'll grant it's a reasonable theory. But we need to get to the transport."

There was the person she knew and hated. "You'll grant it. Thank you. But if you recall, I can't launch the transport."

"You'll figure it out. I have faith in you entirely."

Lies. "Well, you shouldn't. We brought the transport, and when we find my parents, they can operate it. That's the plan. So we should call them and get directions."

In order to rescue them from a dying world. Frankie knew she ought to be scared right now, but the adrenaline of the tech-slash-magic discovery had her more excited than anything.

Her parents were safe, which meant Audrey was safe. They'd have made sure of it. And Frankie was going to save them all.

"What's wrong with attempting to reach them with the seeing stone?"

Frankie dipped a hand into her bag and showed him how

the pictures had darkened. "It needs more charge. And before you ask, my watch can't find a signal at all. The mirror's our only shot."

Jord sighed. "Put me on the record as opposed."

As usual. Frankie glanced around, then slipped into the tunnel. She had to fight herself to keep from holding her breath, instead forcing slow breaths of moldy air into her lungs.

The cavern was darker than it had been earlier, the candle burned to a stump. What a gloomy place to sulk, with stalactites melting from the ceiling and constant dampness seeping into every crack. No wonder the prince was so miserable.

Kol's chair sat empty.

Frankie dove for the mirror. "Call Elandria."

The mirror-screen didn't even flicker.

"In times of distress, she answers," Jord said.

With a silver burst of light, the mirror whirled to life.

Frankie looked at Jord, and he shrugged. "I have a good memory. Though I'd really rather use this to call Liz."

Not possible without an interworld signal, and not without finding her parents and Audrey first. It was too late, anyway; the silver bubbled its delirious approximation of liquid, the screen so crystal clear that her brain wanted to dip a canteen into it and drink. Now that she knew what it was, she almost couldn't believe she'd been fooled. This had her father's signature all over it. Flashy sleight of hand. He used the environment to distract.

Even Jord touched a finger to the screen.

One moment she was marveling at the ingenuity of it, and the next there were arms around her throat, choking her from behind. Frankie blinked, struggling hard enough to make her captor stumble.

"What have you done with the prince?" the soldier asked, dragging her back toward the center of the cavern. She was shorter than Frankie, by quite a bit, but that did not seem to be affecting her ability to cut off Frankie's air. Frankie gasped, fear and surprise mixing with lack of oxygen as she clawed at the elbow that squeezed her trachea.

Jord's hands were open in surrender as he stepped toward them, tentative, as though he might negotiate a deal. Great. Because this was the time for his slow, cautious thinking. "We haven't seen him."

"I was with him not thirty minutes ago," the guard said. "He does not leave the cave at this hour. Where is he?"

Do something, Frankie thought, willing Jord to some kind of useful action as she struggled to breathe. *Fight.*

Jord took a step. One step, when Frankie's throat was burning. Her heart pulsed in her ears, her hearing dimmed by the rush of blood. Another ten seconds and she'd pass out. She couldn't reach her pack, where the stunner should still be tucked among her things—assuming no one had recognized it as a weapon.

And clearly Jord planned to hesitate until Frankie stopped breathing. She combed her memories for hints from the cursory self-defense seminars she and Audrey had taken as a part of physical education.

It was hard to think with little black spots growing in front of her eyes.

"Where is he?" the soldier repeated, giving Frankie a shake.

If she didn't get out of this, they'd be back in the cell. There'd be guards this time, and no one to rescue Audrey.

Frankie lifted her heel as hard as she could, landing a blow to the soldier's knee. The woman crumpled, crying out in pain, and Frankie untangled herself to stagger to her feet before the mirror. She whirled around, expecting another attack, but the soldier only crawled toward them. How hard had Frankie kicked her?

Jord grabbed Frankie's arm. "We have to go."

"Obviously," she choked. "Thanks for the help there."

"You had it in hand, clearly."

Right. Well, it wasn't like she should have expected him to put himself in harm's way for her. Why had he followed her here again?

As Jord pulled her across the cave, the mirror—the screen—solidified into an oval, with a hooded figure standing motionless at the center. Frankie squinted, trying to make out a face, a detail in the background. Anything that might confirm her suspicions and lead her to her parents.

The silhouette lingered for a moment, and then the screen went black.

Jord held fast to her wrist, and they dove blindly for the mouth of the tunnel.

When Prince Kol stepped in front of them, Jord skidded to a stop.

Frankie wouldn't have thought it possible, but the prince's condition had plummeted during his brief absence. He'd crossed the alcohol-is-poison boundary he'd been careening toward earlier, leaving him draped across the rock, obviously incapable of standing on his own. The smell was worse, too. He'd been sick.

"I'm afraid you're too entertaining to release," he said. Slurred, really. "Now, what have you done with my favorite soldier?"

Before Frankie could answer, Jord punched him in the nose.

Kol toppled backwards, slamming his head on the wall, and Jord pulled her out the door. "Let's go."

All Frankie could think, as they navigated the shadows and out into the bleak world, was that she didn't know Jord Mathison at all.

FIFTEEN

FRANKIE

The prince had been right about the forest. A few steps out of his makeshift fortress, and trunks rose around Frankie and Jord like specters, bare but for a few murderous branches. Even a city girl knew forests should have nighttime activity. Crickets. Owls. Prowling cats. Or Rogur's version of those things. But the trees kept a watchful silence, which was good when it came to the prowling cats, but a bad sign for the forest's health. Musty odors billowed up from the forest floor, smelling like the pages of an old book about to crumble. Almost good, in a weird way, until you realized you were breathing death.

The cliffs remained their steady companion, gray and endless.

Jord, of course, walked with quiet assurance as they made their way through the midnight woods. Even hampered by his ridiculous tweed vest, his arms never brushed the skeletal branches that snagged Frankie's shirt every few steps. She'd pulled her sampling kit out of her pack, pausing here and there to collect soil and pebbles and bits of leaves, imagining what tests the labs might run to determine the forest's cause of death.

She only regretted that she hadn't brought the tools to obtain a core sample. Surely no one could fault her for that oversight.

If there was a transport dock on Rogur, maybe there was a lab, too. In which case she could locate it and snag more equipment.

As the sun made a feeble attempt to heave itself over the horizon, Jord deigned to throw a few words in her direction. "If you keep stopping every five steps, that handsome but dreadfully misguided prince will have us back in our cell by noon."

"Handsome?"

"I certainly thought so."

Modest. Not that Jord was bad looking, but nice eyes could only get him so far without a personality to match.

"It's funny," she said, "I would have thought if you had a twin, you'd be the evil one."

He stepped lightly to avoid a branch. "Is this an Earthen concept? I knew twins in Suhainn. They were both perfectly decent citizens."

Knew. He always talked about Suhainn as though it were a thing that was dead and gone. Didn't he plan to go back? "Not an Earthen concept, a soap opera concept," Frankie said. "You know, the hero wins and everything seems like it's headed for happily-ever-after, but they have a series to continue and fans to please so they invent an evil twin to cause more trouble."

Maybe he truly didn't know. It was hard to picture Jord watching television, or snapping VR goggles over his eyes for a full-sensory story experience. It wasn't exactly Frankie's chosen pastime, either, though Liz had introduced her to a full complement of entertainment over their years of operations-floor vigils.

"There's time yet," he said. "This Prince Kol of ours could very well turn out to be the hero. No doubt he feels we're here causing trouble for him."

"This world isn't headed for happily ever after, though."

Jord glanced at the sky. "No, it isn't."

Maybe after this, people would finally agree that guided tours were a waste of Pathbound's significant resources. There was too much to study.

Frankie could get them started. Gather data. Figure out the source of the trouble in this world. Surely her parents would be impressed with an accomplishment of that caliber.

"We need to find Mom and Dad," she said. "I know Kol was talking to them in that mirror. If they're alive, so is Audrey."

"Francesca, right now we need to locate water and, if possible, food. Your canteens won't last us much longer. But so far, I've seen no animal tracks, no insects, and no sign of birds."

"Which means no hunting?"

"It means no water. Or at least, that I can't find my way to it."

The only water she'd ever seen him locate was the swimming pool in Pathbound Tower. "OK, who were you, in Suhainn? How do you know all this stuff about birds and insects and whatever? I realize it's late to be asking you about yourself in a serious way, but in my defense, you never exactly invited personal discussions over ping pong. Who are you?"

"Ping pong?"

"Are you a prince?"

"Not remotely."

Frankie waited. But Jord didn't say anything more. He kept walking, scanning the ground and the surroundings by turns. A second ago, he'd been almost amiable. One mention of her parents, and he seemed to remember his true nature.

"Fine," she said. "Don't tell me."

Jord stopped and unbuttoned his cuffs, then rolled his sleeves to the elbows. "Excellent," he said. "I won't."

"You're impossible."

He made a show of finishing his sleeves and loosening his shirt at the collar. Finally, he met her eyes for the first time since they'd been locked up together. "It may be difficult for you to understand, but I do not owe you my life story."

He turned away and resumed his hike. Frankie could only hurry after him, abandoning all attempts to quiet her steps. "I tried to be your friend, you know. When you first came to Earth."

"Yes," he said. "And I declined."

Despite her mother's instructions to stay away from Jord after the meteorite-protocol incident, Frankie had knocked on his apartment door two days later with a presentation aimed at welcoming him to Earth. She'd thought it through, carefully designing holograms to demonstrate fashion and culture. She'd included a food tasting kit and had tried to make everything as visual as possible, because she wasn't sure if he understood English yet.

She'd wanted to be helpful. She'd wanted to learn from him.

And Jord? He'd turned her in to her mother without so much as a word to Frankie.

He certainly had declined her friendship. Given a good night's sleep, Frankie could muster a comeback for the ages. As much as it hurt to let him win, nothing that sprang to mind would be worth his disdain, so she trudged behind him in silence.

Let him find water, and squish caterpillars for dinner, or whatever. Once they'd found sustenance, he could do what he wanted while she located the lost tour group. If she felt benevolent, she'd find him when it was time to go home.

As Frankie continued to fume, Jord stopped.

"What?" Frankie said. "Did you see a deer? You're going to strangle it with your bare hands?"

"Listen."

At first, she heard nothing. Her city ears too readily filled the silence with a ringing tone, loud enough to vibrate her sinuses whenever she stood still. After a moment, though, a low hum found its way through.

She was thinking it might be the transport, rattling back at the fortress, when Jord pointed up.

A fireball hovered low above the treetops, looking for all the world like something that ought to be heaved out of a catapult. Only instead of obeying the laws of physics—which appeared to govern Rogur as strongly as they did Earth and Suhainn—by pausing in midair. Fire licked the space around it, a lacework of sparks.

"A drone," she said.

If she got close enough, she'd dismantle it as easily as she could a car back home. And she'd find Pathbound logos on the parts, too. She was sure of it.

Jord raised his eyebrows. As if to say, *So what?*

Frankie started to shrug out of her pack, fully intending to scale a tree so she could get within grabbing distance. But the drone flew off. Slowly this time, as though beckoning her to follow, and skimming close enough to the branches that she worried it might ignite a forest fire. But it zipped by without incident, buzzing alongside the cliff. Frankie practically had to run to keep up with it.

"I'm not sure this is wise," Jord said.

"You're free to go."

Finally, the drone paused. When Frankie stopped, too, it shot up the rock wall.

If its operators expected that to stop her, they were wrong.

Even city kids could scale a cliff. She dropped her pack and started to climb. If she stopped to think about how stupid this was, she might give up.

She forged on.

Her nails splintered as she stuffed her hands into the cracks in the rocks, Jord pacing below like a wolf waiting out its prey. He hadn't left her, not yet. She couldn't help feeling a sliver of relief.

She was maybe fifteen feet up when she reached a narrow step among the cracks and crevices of the cliff. The drone hovered above, circling a wider shelf that looked like it could be the mouth of a tunnel. It was hard to tell from here.

Frankie couldn't work out a path that would get her safely from her shelf to the waiting drone. This section of the wall might as well have been made of glass.

It was a measly few feet. And she wasn't aiming for the shelf or the tunnel; she was aiming for the drone. She gripped the rock with her left hand and checked the placement of her feet. When she was sure of her balance, she rose to her toes and released her right hand.

Up close, the flames looked like sparking pinwheels. What kind of fuel would be sustaining them? It had to be a sophisticated hologram of some kind.

She stretched for it.

"If you die here, I may very well end up in prison," Jord called.

Frankie ignored him, pouring her full concentration into the reach. The drone hovered, just beyond her fingertips, as though trying to get close enough to ID her.

Or lead her through that tunnel. The longer she hesitated here, the more certain she became that the drone meant to lead them. A guide, or a trap?

Frankie hopped. With her free hand, she grabbed the drone.

Her flesh sizzled, pain lancing through her palm. Frankie let go and fumbled her landing, boots glancing off the narrow shelf as though it were frosted with ice.

And then, she fell.

For a moment, Jord actually held his breath. As if by ceasing to pull air into his lungs, he might will Frankie not to fall.

She caught the shelf with her fingers, her body slamming back into the cliff and rebounding with so much force he felt sure she was about to lose her grip. She held on, legs flailing.

All he could do was watch helplessly from the ground while she scrambled for purchase, her feet glancing off the cliffside as if the rocks were slicked with oil.

Could he catch her from here, if she slipped? He would have to try.

But Frankie gained a foothold. She clung to the rocks, chest heaving. Even from here, he could see the sheen of sweat on her brow. "Are you all right?" he called.

She tipped her head back, and he knew what she was going to say before she opened her mouth. "I think the drone was leading us to a tunnel. Up there."

"You cannot be serious."

But she was. Of course she was. She was already heading for it, attempting a new approach from the side.

By the time she heaved her body out of sight, Jord thought he might collapse out of sheer concern. He stared at the face of the cliff, trying to decide whether he could possibly ascend behind her. If she could barely make the climb with no vertigo to hinder her, how would he fare when the world tipped on its side? On the other hand, she might disappear into the tunnel without him.

The girl was a force of nature. He couldn't hope to keep up.

"What's the view like?" he asked.

"Blurry," she said, legs dangling over the side of the cliff that had almost murdered her. "Fields beyond the forest, and maybe a road. I can't make out much more."

Jord checked his pocket for his tri-oculars before remembering Reyche's search-and-seizure. "I had oculars on me. Look in the pack."

A pause. "I can't believe you thought to bring these and I didn't. Why do you have oculars? I thought you shunned all things digital."

She'd never accept them as evidence that he'd been waiting for her back at Pathbound, hoping to make her a friend. Resurrecting that conversation would only lead to trouble. He shaded his eyes, trying to get a better view of her. "Good thing I tagged along."

A chime cut through the silence, and Jord startled. "Could you try not announcing our location to the entire world?"

"It's the oculars. They know where we are," Frankie said, ignoring his concern. "They're programmed to recognize Rogur. There's a village... a lake... This is impossible..."

Not impossible at all. Her parents had clearly known this world. Perhaps her grandparents had, too. Who could say what they'd been doing here?

"This is an impact crater," Frankie continued. "These walls... We need to get geologists out here. There's definitely a road... hmm... and some kind of anomaly. A structure the oculars don't recognize."

"A newly constructed welcome center, perhaps."

"No, it's—"

Jord didn't get to hear what she thought it was. A twig cracked through the eerie silence of the forest, and he whipped around just fast enough to see that he was surrounded.

But not fast enough to stop strong arms from slamming him into the cliff. His head hit the rock, skewing his vision. *Stay aloft*, he thought, beaming the words to Frankie like a prayer.

"It's him," his attacker said in Suhainnan. Roguran. "He's in disguise."

Oh, excellent. Jord struggled, but the man held him firmly against the cliff, rock cutting into the small of his back. "If you think I'm Prince Kol—"

"No talking," his captor said. A milk-white scar slashed diagonally across his face, puckering the corner of his eye. It cut mercilessly through his dark beard to twist his lip into a permanent uplift. Whatever had done the damage had taken a slice of his nose as well.

Could this be the work of Kol's mysterious gods? The man held him firmly, but there was no malice in his expression. Just fear. He was no doppelgänger, and yet somehow—something in the lines around his eyes, the iron of those biceps—the man reminded Jord of his language tutor in Suhainn. A tree of a man, with a sharp sense of humor who allowed just enough leniency in his classroom to make loyal followers of all his students.

The memory stung. Jord didn't make a habit of thinking about Suhainn, of the people he'd left behind. He shook the thought away, surprised by its weight.

"I'm not who you think I am," he said.

"You cannot conceal your identity behind a haircut and an Earthen wardrobe. We know who you are."

Jord and the prince were mirror images. He couldn't explain that to himself, let alone Kol's own subjects.

Another member of the party sidled forward to peer over the first's shoulder, a woman with a braid coiled into a bun at her neck. She wore trousers and a knitted scarf tied around her neck. "It's him, sure enough," she said, her accent clipped. "You found him, Tomas."

Jord found it difficult to dredge up so much as an ounce of resentment toward her. The Hartigers had been playing in her world, as surely as they played in Suhainn.

The man gave Jord a shake, his forearm nearly cutting off Jord's breath. "Knew the prince had a fortress nearby."

From what he could see over Tomas' shoulder, there were plenty of injuries among the half-dozen citizens that stood clustered behind the woman: arms propped in slings, all manner of scars, and two people leaning heavily on walking sticks.

He saw himself in every single one of them.

Jord cleared his throat, attempting to draw breath. "Was Kol not—I mean, what is your business with the prince?"

"The gods dislike your reign. The broken bloodline," Tomas said. "We're here to demand you give up the throne, officially. To appease them."

If magic was technology in disguise, what could these mysterious gods be? Hartiger manipulations? Flesh-and-blood enemies masquerading as legends? Or something else entirely?

"Broken bloodline," Jord said. "Is Kol a bastard?"

It was Frankie who answered.

"In personality, definitely."

Jord sighed. Of course she wouldn't stay aloft.

Her pack landed on the ground with a thud. She followed, leaping off the cliff to knock Tomas to the ground.

Freed from the Roguran's grasp, Jord pushed off the rock. There should be a way to solve this without a fight, without violence, even with four men already moving to help their friend.

These were no soldiers; they hesitated, as Jord had when Kol's guard held Frankie in the cavern. He'd held back because he'd wanted to approach the situation with reason. He'd feared for Frankie's life, and for the soldier's.

These people? They held back because they lacked organization.

Jord battered his way through the group, dodging clumsy elbows and doing his best to avoid landing any actual punches.

He had no desire to hurt anyone. And despite the current misunderstanding, these people looked like they needed tea and fruit—and a good night's rest.

Frankie untangled herself from Tomas and tried to scramble away, but he grabbed her foot and dragged her toward him. "The pack," she shouted in English. "Get the pack!"

Trying not to wonder what she might have in there, Jord dove for the bag. The woman seemed to have understood Frankie's meaning; she reached it just as he did. He wrenched it from her arms, nearly pulling her off her feet. She tripped. He backed away quickly, unzipping the main pocket.

"What am I looking for?" he asked.

"Stunner."

Of course. She'd brought multiple charger plates, after all. Why not a stunner?

Someone jumped him from behind, and he whirled to shake them off. The man landed on two feet and launched himself back at Jord, teeth bared. "You left us, anyway," he said, breathing hard. Jord dodged, and his attacker overshot to stumble into the cliff.

These people were exhausted, and probably hungry. Desperate.

"Please," the man said. "The days stretch out of season, withering the crops. The south floods, while the north is parched. Please. The gods may not even punish you, if you return."

The implication being that they might.

Frankie was still trying to ward off Tomas, hitting wildly in the man's direction. "Jord. The stunner."

But Jord's attacker swung a heavy fist toward Jord's face. He ducked, barely. "Bit occupied."

Frankie landed a kick to Tomas' face with a crack that sounded much like the breaking stick that had alerted Jord to the man's presence. He fell back, and Jord flinched as the man clutched his scarred nose, blood gushing into his mouth and dripping off his chin.

Frankie didn't spare him a glance. She grabbed for the pack, retrieved the stunner, and exposed the crackling wires.

There, she might have stopped. The people froze at the sight of the tech, a tableau of round eyes and slack jaws. To them, it would be a magic wand. Capable of anything. The lone woman of the group, the one with the scarf, raised her hands to her waist. Jord caught a flicker of silver as she slipped a dagger out of her sleeve.

But despite the weapon in her hand, the woman didn't take a step. She didn't move.

Frankie did. She lunged, avoiding the blade to jam the stunner under the woman's arm. The dagger fell, and the woman dropped to the ground with a scream that reverberated through the forest, her agony amplified by the acoustics of the trees.

Horrified, Jord watched as Frankie picked up her pack, still holding the stunner over her head. Embracing that sorceress aesthetic her parents had worked so hard to weave into this poor world, perhaps. Her hands were skinned raw from the climb, with bruises already blooming along the knuckles.

Frankie didn't give any sign of pain, or doubt. She started backing away as the people attended to their friend. The woman was breathing, blinking. Alive.

"She'll be all right," Jord said, trying to believe it himself as his eyes locked on the fallen woman. "Let her rest. She'll recover."

None of the people looked up.

If any of them had still believed in their prince, that faith was utterly squashed now. Yes, the woman had held a dagger. But she hadn't taken a step. She hadn't moved.

They might still have found common ground.

Perhaps he was naive to think they should be able to move through this world without fighting its inhabitants, and foolish to compare them to Suhainnans. Perhaps Frankie had been in the right. She certainly didn't seem to question it.

In fact, for a moment there... For a brief instant, when her eyes had narrowed on her target, her mouth smoothing into that determined line? For a moment, she'd looked exactly like her mother.

He couldn't let her call her parents. If Michael and Cindy were alive, they'd laud her accomplishment in making it here. They'd take her into the fold.

So he waited. He waited through their now-silent journey through the forest, until darkness impeded any further progress toward whatever destination Frankie had in mind—something she'd made out from the oculars, though she didn't explain, and he didn't ask. He waited until they took shelter at the base of an especially thick tree, until they'd choked down granola bars and spread a blanket over their legs.

He waited until her lashes dusted her cheeks and her

breathing evened out, and then, for good measure, he waited a little longer. His eyelids dragged, and his hands shook with exhaustion, but he held out as long as he could, focusing on the sweep of stars above, before unbuckling the pack. Slowly. Carefully.

He dug in, closed his fingers around the seeing stone, and pulled it out of the bag. Shadowy trees gaped within the glass, the stars winking beyond.

With all the force he could muster, Jord launched the stone into the forest. He stared after it for a long moment, willing it to be gone forever, and the Hartigers too. Wishing there were some way to find Audrey without Cindy and Michael and all the despair they brought with them.

Wondering if it was too late, anyway.

He closed the pack, taking care to fasten the buckles as silently as possible. He replaced it at his side and leaned his head back on the tree, the image of the disappearing stone still zipping through his mind when Frankie said, "I'm going to need to know why you did that."

SEVENTEEN
KOL

Kol dreamed of monsters. Ten feet tall, invincible, storming his city and sweeping his people out of the way, crushing bones in their fists and chewing rocks for strength.

They weren't gods. They were demons with a talent for storytelling.

Kol opened his eyes and wished for death. He was familiar with this brand of headache, a pickaxe working its way relentlessly through his skull. For some reason, his nose also hurt.

"You're awake. Good. I was about to bring the bucket."

Kol squinted in the direction of the offensively loud voice. His mouth tasted sour. "Reyche. Excellent. Why am I crumpled in a doorway, and why is it difficult to breathe through my nose?"

"You let the prisoners escape. You've been passed out here ever since."

Kol sat up and put a hand to his forehead. "Prisoners. Ah, yes. I thought I'd dreamt them."

"Three bottles of *afan dreoch* will do that."

"Only three? Scorched earth, I'm losing my touch."

Reyche extended a hand to help him stand, but Kol used the wall to pull himself up instead. He still had a few shreds of dignity to uphold. Besides, if he took his captain's hand now, he might be tempted not to let go.

They'd stood on that precipice before. The only thing Kol had to offer was worry and despair.

Kol stalked into the room as steadily as possible—if there was one negative to *afan dreoch*, it was that it left a man with weak knees—and over to the table. He poured water from a pitcher that had miraculously appeared there, before collapsing into his chair.

Reyche stood at attention, hands tucked in the small of his back. So ridiculous, this formality between them. "Before you get too comfortable, you're needed at the gates."

"I believe you mean *you're* needed at the gates, Reyche."

"Some of your citizens have found us."

"Oh? And why is that?"

Reyche swallowed. "One side demands your abdication. They want you to give yourself up to the gods in Caisrach."

"Natural enough, but not appealing."

"Another party joined them, however. They came from Lariasc." Reyche continued his report as though Kol hadn't spoken. "Now the two groups are fighting amongst themselves. The ones from Lariasc still believe in you. They want to defend you."

Kol sometimes wondered what he'd have to say to crack Reyche's soldierly demeanor. Not so long ago, he'd been capable of coaxing a flush out of his captain with a single whispered comment. Whatever his reasons for staying, Reyche was doing his utmost to master the art of stoicism.

Lamentable, but probably for the best.

"They claim to have come across you in the forest, and that your Earthen associate tried to murder them," Reyche said.

"I don't doubt it."

The crease between Reyche's eyebrows deepened. If he wasn't careful, it would become a ravine of a wrinkle. Though likely he would not live long enough for that. "Does it not concern you that the Suhainnan masquerades as you?" his captain asked.

In the face of a world dissolving at his fingertips, what was a single twin to cause him trouble? "In fact, I commend him for it. But indignation suits you."

"I'm serious, your highness."

But wasn't he always? "So am I. If the Suhainnan wants to impersonate me, he's a fool. You said it yourself; my people want to murder me."

"Only some of them."

"And what do the others want?"

"They would have you rise to the occasion." He paused. Tapped his fingertips along his belt. "They would have you save them, my prince."

It was, incidentally, what Reyche wanted, too. He dragged Kol into war councils at least once a week to harangue him on the topic.

Kol couldn't save anyone. He'd failed them once; additional attempts would only increase their plight. Better that the gods should enact their rule, and that the people should accept their fate.

"How misguided of them," Kol said.

Reyche dropped to a crouch beside Kol's chair, finally dropping that tedious formality. Better. "The village of Lariasc is loyal. We might garner support there, rebuild our army."

And promptly die at the hands of the gods. No, Kol would not lead his few remaining soldiers to their graves. He would not watch Reyche die with them. "Request denied."

Reyche stood eerily still, the ever-deepening eyebrow

wrinkle the only sign of his distress. "The only reason you are still a prince is that a handful of people have chosen not to stop thinking of you as one."

"That is your failing, Reyche, not mine."

"Sometimes battles are lost. That does not mean limping off to wait on death. You can win this war."

Kol reached beneath his chair and withdrew the bottle he'd hidden there. He splashed an inch into the mug. Of all people in the world, Reyche ought to know that waiting on death was infinitely better than seeking it out directly.

"Some wars are futile," Kol said, lifting the glass in the gesture of a toast. "At least Grandfather left these caves well supplied. By all means, invite the people in. Share our stores. I've made my choice."

Reyche gripped the arm of the chair, muscles trembling. "The nightmares haunt me, too, my prince. I cannot escape them. But neither can I allow you to give in."

Reyche's nightmares could be nothing in comparison to Kol's. Reyche wasn't responsible for protecting the people whose blood now painted the palace walls, whose bones had shattered as monsters tossed their screaming bodies from towers and balconies.

Reyche was not their prince.

"The only reason you are captain is that everyone else is dead." The words brought a cascade of images leaking through his headache, blood and bodies and broken bones. His people had tried to defend him. They'd lost their lives, and for nothing. "Go, if you wish. Leave me to die on my own terms."

EIGHTEEN

FRANKIE

As soon as dawn nudged at the sky, Frankie was on her feet and searching through the undergrowth, the oculars pinned to her eyes as she tried to find Kol's seeing stone. Jord shadowed her steps, refusing to offer any explanations as to why he'd thrown it away.

Her hands hurt like hell after yesterday's climb, her knuckles blackened with bruises. The skin on her fingertips was sheared away so that every touch meant a burning sting.

She endured it. She deserved it. All night, she'd dreamed of electric prongs sinking into flesh. In one dream, Frankie had withdrawn her knife from the pack instead of the stunner, and watched as the Roguran woman died with the blade between her ribs. In another, Frankie had missed her mark, and the woman killed Jord.

"I know you're in distress," Jord said finally, "but we ought to consider putting more distance between us and the fort. The stone is gone, Francesca."

Frankie brushed her palms on her pants in angry motions. "I know why you threw it. Your whole friendship proposal doesn't work if my parents are alive, does it? Why? Will they tell me what crimes you committed in Suhainn?"

He dipped his hand into his pocket, no doubt grounding himself on that ridiculous pebble of his. "Forgive me, but I'm not the one who took a Taser to an innocent citizen."

Before she even knew her intention, Frankie was flying at him, knocking him into a tree and pummeling him with her battered fists. He held up his hands to shield himself from the blows. "If you would kindly put the stunner away before accosting me."

Frankie hadn't realized she'd withdrawn it. She stopped.

"Incidentally," he said, "why do you have a stunner?"

At least she hadn't uncapped it this time.

Frankie backed off, throwing the weapon to the ground, followed by her pack. "That woman had a knife."

"She didn't take a single step. She was scared."

"She would have killed you. She'll live."

He just shook his head. "Why are you doing all this for your parents? They don't deserve it."

"They don't deserve their lives?"

He held up a finger. "If you're right and they've truly survived all this time, they'll make it long enough to get home on their own."

"I'm going to save them," she said. "And I'm going to save this world. That man back there said the days are lengthening. It's a clue. And if I can find one of my parents' labs, I might get enough information to figure out what's going on."

He blinked at her. "And how do you intend to find one of their labs?"

She'd expected him to object. But if he was so opposed to the idea of finding Mom and Dad, maybe the detour sounded appealing.

Well, it wasn't a detour. There was a good chance that

finding a lab would mean finding Mom and Dad, too. In any case, making their way toward an Earthen structure was the best course of action.

"I saw a cell tower from the cliff," she said. "You know, before I saved your life."

At least he had the decency to flinch at that. "There's a cell tower near their lab in Suhainn. You think the setup might be the same."

Exactly. She picked up her pack, shoving the stunner inside. Her parents would be impressed. And Audrey forgive her. Frankie would prove she deserved her best friend, as well as a spot at Pathbound. "I'm going. You can cower near the transport, for all I care."

She could do this. She just had to make it to this lake. From the cliff, it had been nothing more than a shining spot on the horizon, but the oculars promised it was close.

Maybe Jord would fall in. His presence was more excruciating than all of Frankie's injuries, combined. She couldn't stand anything about him. The way he walked, and breathed, and refused to apologize.

Worse, without even the slightest conversation to distract her, Frankie's mind kept returning to yesterday's fight, and the feeling of the woman's body shuddering under her hand. She was angry at Jord because he was right. Since she could never admit it to him, she was stuck alone in her head, with only her guilt for company.

The woman would be fine. Wouldn't she?

Whenever the images returned, Frankie firmly directed her thoughts to the new goal. She could help save this world. She just needed to pay attention, keep her eyes open, continue taking samples. The transport might be causing the distress, but how? Her mind shuffled through ideas, from altered magnetic fields to introduction of foreign bacteria. She needed more data.

The dead forest offered no answers. The trees surrounded them in endless monotony. Without guidance from the oculars, she'd have been convinced they were traveling in circles.

They walked in silence for hours, until the trees ended abruptly before a field. She and Jord couldn't talk to each other, let alone make a decision together, yet they stopped simultaneously beside the last of the trunks to stare at the sunburned vista. The road snaked through patches of bare farmland, useless and abandoned. Another blemish to fix. Another wrong to set right.

And, on the horizon, something odd. It almost looked like a giant head and shoulders were peeking out from behind the farthest hill.

Jord had spotted it, too. He stared ahead, brow furrowed, as Frankie lifted the oculars.

It was a statue. A colossus, really, its slender arm raised as though to pick up the road and use it to lasso the lake. The other hand held a shield that glinted like a sunset. At its back, the walls of the lakeside village were nothing but a smudge.

The oculars blinked. "It's the anomaly I saw from the cliff," she said, her voice rough from hours of not speaking.

She offered the glasses to Jord, who took them warily. As if he feared she might shove him to the ground as soon as he was distracted. Not a bad idea. "Fascinating," he said. "I'd come to the conclusion the anomaly must be a newly constructed Pathbound Enterprises steakhouse."

"Not ready for your brand of humor yet," Frankie said, snatching the oculars out of his hands.

"I apologize. I'll attempt to be more abhorrent."

"Mission already accomplished. Let's go."

"Wait. We need to hide my face." He held up a hand. "Don't say it. Let me guess. I'll do this world a favor by hiding it, and you as well. Or perhaps we'll lose our power to frighten the enemy if I hide it. Whatever witty insult you have in mind, thank you. Can we skip it this time?"

Frankie flushed. Maybe she was capable of wounding him, after all. She got out her blanket and rooted through the backpack until she found the cord that would connect a backup solar panel to the charger plates. The reverse sides of the charger plates were solar panels, self-recharging, but even backups needed backups. She ripped a few holes in the blanket and threaded the cord through, creating the ugliest drawstring she'd ever seen.

"Who knew your talents included fashion design?" Jord said as he shrugged it over his shoulders. The cloak looked lumpy and strange, but it covered his vest. And the hood cast a shadow over his face.

It wouldn't fool anyone who looked closely, but it was better than what Frankie had. As their run-in with the Rogurans in the woods had demonstrated, her outfit was guaranteed to stand out. Not much she could do about that.

Frankie started forward, but Jord hooked a finger around the hem of her sleeve. "Stow the oculars."

"Like I take orders from you."

"You needn't take orders, Francesca. Common sense will do."

She waved a hand toward the countryside. "There's no one on the road. And if we see someone, I'll make up a story about magic glasses."

"In a world where magic is dying."

She pressed her lips together.

"You are not your father," he said.

Meaning, she supposed, that Frankie didn't have the brilliant mind—or the charm—to carry out this sort of a mission. "Thanks."

"It's a compliment, I assure you."

Frankie shoved the oculars into the bag, and they started toward the village.

As they drew closer to the statue, the road joined with another fork, dumping them in with a ragged scattering of travelers. Most of them were barefoot, small sacks of belongings slung over their shoulders. Although strangely enough, Frankie was not so far from blending in. She'd sort of assumed she'd find people wearing long skirts and Shakespearean tunics. But though Jord's suit was grossly out of place, Frankie's clothing wasn't. Most of the women wore trousers.

Her pants were too well fitted, of course, too sturdy in comparison. Even the blanket around Jord's shoulders looked too perfect, too manufactured, next to the rough wool and linen these people wore.

It didn't matter. As they drew close to the village, all eyes were drawn to the colossus. It was the likeness of a woman. At least three stories tall, she carried a shield the size of a car hood. Braids wound around her head, with coins studded throughout like gems in a crown. She was indeed reaching out—not for the road as Frankie had thought from afar, but for the quiver of arrows on her back.

The enormity of the thing was overwhelming. If Frankie didn't know better, she'd have thought she'd stepped into a Virtual Reality module of ancient Rome.

The oddest part—and all the parts were odd—was the fact that the statue was not made of wood, stone, or metal. She looked like flesh and bone.

Frankie itched to touch her, to determine if her tan skin was formed out of clay, or perhaps fabric. But while the rest of the travelers paused to gape along with Frankie and Jord, none of them approached the statue.

One woman had dared to get close. She'd spread a beige sheet of cloth on the grass near the road, maybe five yards from the trench that surrounded the statue's feet. She sat cross-legged in the middle of the cloth, dipping a brush into a palette filled with paint.

There was no doubt in Frankie's mind about the subject of the woman's painting. The statue was formidable. Unforgettable. Could this be one of Kol and Reyche's gods?

"She looks so real," Frankie said, forgetting for a moment that she wasn't supposed to be speaking to Jord. Giant huntresses crowded out the silent treatment. For now.

Jord stared like everyone else, but with eyes narrowed in worry. They'd actually found something interesting to see, and he was worried. She should smack him again. It was so satisfying.

"You must have left Caisrach early, if you didn't hear the story," the artist said, leaning in close to dab her brush against the cloth. She had a blanket slung over her shoulders, though the day was warm. The corner dragged into one of the bowls of paint, but the woman didn't seem to notice.

"We did," Jord said. "What happened?"

"The gods came down," she said simply. "Took over the whole damn place, along with every village in Rogur, save for this one. Lariasc prevailed."

Frankie looked at the goddess, suddenly uneasy.

"The people here beat Aya," the woman added. "They hold the village in the prince's name."

As they talked, a child passed on the road and launched a wad of spit at the goddess' feet. The woman picked up a brush and flicked paint in his direction. "Don't you dare."

The kid kicked at the dirt on the road as he made his way toward the soldiers who guarded the village gate.

"This statue is a monument to that victory?" Jord asked.

The woman dabbed her brush on the canvas, adding points of yellow to the painted goddess's hair. "This is Aya herself."

Not a statue. A body? "She's... well preserved," Frankie said.

The woman coughed, a ragged heave from deep within her chest. "Goddesses don't rot."

The spitting boy was making his way inside the village. As Frankie watched, though, the guard turned several adults away. They sat on the opposite side of the road, looking lost. Refugees. From the other villages, or from the capital. Why wouldn't the guards allow them inside?

"Aya," Jord said softly. "She pinned the stars."

When Frankie turned to the statue, Jord was approaching it. Which... was very un-Jord of him. Even Frankie knew better than to mess with otherworldly god-corpses. "What are you doing?" she whispered, running up beside him. "A goddess might... wake up."

Jord stepped over the trench. It was like a miniature moat, really, a muddy gash in the grass. He stretched a hand to brush the goddess' fingertips, tentative. As though he expected her to melt. "Not a goddess. It feels like flesh, but... it can't be."

Frankie glanced at the people, who watched Jord with tense expressions. They shared her fears, clearly.

"Since when are you an expert on Roguran goddesses?" Frankie said. "I thought Suhainn had no gods."

Jord ignored her and crouched beside the woman, who'd paused her painting. "How did Lariasc defeat Aya?" he asked.

In answer, the woman stood and hobbled away from her painting, shoulders hunched beneath her blanket.

At first, Frankie thought she was simply done speaking to the crazy people who messed with dead goddesses. But Jord studied the painting. In it, the villagers set a trap for the goddess with fishing nets, tripping her so she'd fall into the lake.

Jord met Frankie's gaze, raising his eyebrows as if to say, *Get it now?*

All magic in this world was Earthen technology. Which meant the gods were, too.

"Took three teams of horses to drag her out," the woman said, before descending into another round of wrenching coughs that made Frankie's throat hurt just to listen.

Frankie circled the statue again, wishing she could use the oculars to get a closer look. She felt certain she'd be able to locate some minuscule scar or blemish that, if peeled away, would reveal a control box stuffed with beautiful circuits. "Android," she whispered.

Jord cleared his throat. "Roguran, if you please."

"I don't know how to translate... this."

"Then perhaps you shouldn't try."

Again, with the logic. She glared at him. "What are they doing in this world? Magic mirrors? Giants?"

"Does it alter your plans?"

He was looking at the android, but she detected the slightest bit of hope in his tone. As if the discovery of a robot made finding her parents less urgent, somehow?

"It solidifies my plans," Frankie said. "They're here. Androids don't wake up by themselves."

Jord glanced around. "Gods. And they might, Francesca."

Frankie couldn't win this argument, not without proof, so she chose not to answer. With a last glance at the statue, she stepped onto the road and headed for the gates. Jord could follow, or not. Whatever.

He did.

The guard they approached looked bored. On Earth, she'd have been playing solitaire on her smartwatch. While wearing headphones, and probably doing her nails. "Next plague evaluation's at sunset," she said. "Anyone under twelve can go in now, but you'll have to wait."

Anyone under twelve? Why? "Plague evaluation?" Frankie asked.

If this world had magazines, the woman would have flipped a page in annoyance. She tapped her fingers on the wooden gate. The place looked marginally more solid than the prince's 'fortress,' though not as much as Frankie would have expected. Maybe they'd had to reconstruct the walls after Aya's attack.

"Lariasc hasn't had many cases," the guard said. "Want to keep it that way. Wait for your evaluation, and if you're clean, we'll let you in."

And if not? She thought of all those people sitting outside, waiting. Hoping. "We're kind of in a hurry."

"And I'm kind of wishing there wasn't a plague," the guard said. "We all have our burdens."

Frankie wanted to argue, but it would be reckless to draw more attention to themselves.

And then Jord stepped in front of her. Before Frankie could stop him, he lowered his hood.

Jord had never seen anyone stand up so fast in his life. Not even in the presence of Cindy Hartiger.

This place claimed to be loyal to the crown, and despite with Kol's affinity for *afan*, Jord had little sense of whether that was a good thing or a bad one. Kol might starve his people, abuse them; he might deserve his current punishment, and more.

It was hard to picture him as anything more than an indifferent ruler. Appearances, however, could not often be trusted.

Either way, the village's loyalty to his twin was an opportunity. Frankie's disapproval was potent, her muscles so tense she practically vibrated, but this was the fastest way to get them out of here. Unless she wanted to swim to this cell tower of hers.

She might have preferred it over his company. She'd never understand why he'd thrown the stone away, and even Jord knew that if Cindy and Michael really were alive, getting rid of it only postponed the inevitable.

The guard started to speak. Jord held a finger to his lips and pulled the hood forward again. "We need an escort to the port. Soldier...?"

The woman brought her hand halfway to her chest before pausing. She glanced at the people waiting on the grass and lowered her arm, reconsidering the salute. "Kira, your highn—sir. You're leaving us?"

"Exactly the opposite. I'm going to call in reinforcements."

Somewhere along the road a tone had begun to whine in his head, and the pitch was now increasing so much that it took a concerted effort not to dig his finger into his ear to stop it. He wasn't sure when it'd started, only that it became more irritating with every step. Maybe their attackers back in the woods had banged Jord's head harder than he'd thought. At this point, the ringing approached painful, threatening to upset his balance.

Excellent timing.

"Please," Jord said. "Can you help us?"

Kira's hesitation evaporated. She gave a brisk nod, and Jord felt Frankie relax. He considered holding onto her arm for balance, then decided his chances of staying upright were probably better without her. "These two have clearance," Kira said.

The other guard, whose eyebrows were far more plentiful than his hair, shrugged and returned to his conversation. Jord saw he was speaking with the artist who'd told him about the statue. Though she held them close to her body, her paint-smudged hands trembled.

"You can wait for your evaluation, but it'll be the same as yesterday," the guard said. "You should go to Caisrach."

"Caisrach, right," the artist said. "Where the guards who didn't die or flee will skewer anyone who refuses to pledge allegiance to the gods. I grew up working for the royal family. I'm loyal to the prince."

The guard hesitated, and Jord half expected him to show

mercy. Instead, he shook his head. "I'm sorry. We can't risk contamination."

The woman bit her lip, and despite her tough exterior, Jord thought she might be trying not to cry. On the other side of these gates, he imagined, there would be beds and food, perhaps a friendly face or two. There was safety, however temporary, from marauding gods, even for those with nowhere to go.

In the background, at the edge of his senses, the muffled rush of waves burrowed into his consciousness, and Jord again found himself thinking of Suhainn: of neighbors assembling on roofs to cast fishing lines at sunset and pass news about the day; of the time his friend Denan had tried to leap over the canal outside the hot tea stand. The operative word being *tried*.

Jord looked back to the Rogurans, to the artist who was turning away from the gates. This world was drowning, its prince hiding. There was but one safe haven, and it denied access to sick citizens.

In this moment, he could do something about that. He could help.

If his brother were sick, he'd want someone to do the same.

Keeping his eyes trained on the woman, he said, "Let her in."

Frankie grabbed his arm, but he'd already drawn the guard's attention. "Oh?" the guard said. "And what reason am I to give my commander for disobeying direct orders?"

Jord reached for the hood, and Frankie tried to pull his hand away. "What are you doing?" she whispered.

"Something good," he said.

For once. Maybe Frankie had saved his life back there in the woods; maybe she'd needed to use the stunner to get away from the group. And maybe Jord had no right to fear her, considering his own position at Pathbound and the power he'd accepted without question.

Here, his choice to remain hidden—to do nothing about Rogur's woes, for the sake of survival—here, that argument rang thin, even in his own mind.

He pulled the cloak away from his face. "Tell him you went over his head."

That... seemed like what Kol might say? Unless they didn't use that idiom here. Unless he hadn't quite nailed Kol's accent, or his bearing.

It was like diving into a pond without knowing whether the water was three feet deep, or thirty.

The guard stared at him in disbelief, and the artist looked equally startled. If anyone might recognize the truth, it was someone who'd worked in the palace her whole life. After a beat, she bowed her head. "Your highness. Forgive me, I didn't recognize you."

Jord let out a breath, relieved. "That was the idea."

Between the tone in his ears and the headache that had grown steadily worse since the woods, he wasn't sure how much longer he could maintain this pretense. He felt light-headed. He needed to eat. He needed to get home.

"Your highness," the guard said, affecting a bow. "We—I'm relieved to see you are well."

Jord tipped his chin up. He gave orders at Pathbound, didn't he? Here, he had even more authority. "You need an infirmary to treat the sick."

The guard nodded, like a bobblehead doll. "Of course, your highness. But... we don't know how the illness spreads. What if the town becomes infected?"

"A wall won't prevent that."

"But—"

"The world is on fire," Jord said. "The least we can do is care for those who still believe in us."

Without waiting for an answer, he turned and walked away. A prince assumed his orders would be carried out. Head up, shoulders straight. Toward the water was a safe bet. Kira fell in on his left, while Frankie kept pace on his right. He didn't have to look at her to know she was beaming indignation at him with all her considerable strength. No doubt he'd be hearing her opinions on his speech very shortly.

He shared the face of a prince. Whether by accident, or because they'd landed in an alternate reality, he didn't know. But he couldn't let people suffer when—for once in his life—he had the power to prevent it.

His head throbbed.

"Those people," Kira said, keeping her voice low, "the plague... We cannot defeat it, Prince Kol. Inside or out, they will die."

"You defeated a god," Jord said. "Nothing is hopeless."

She was quiet for a few steps. "We can take Caisrach back. For you."

Jord thought of his dismal twin, drowning in *afan* at the fortress, and he wondered. Did Kol know he had loyal citizens here, waiting to fight his war?

The village of Lariasc was quaint, almost to the point of absurdity. Too perfect, at least on the surface, with its motley collection of half-timbered buildings crammed into a jagged line, charmingly rough cobblestones underfoot. Blacksmith, cooper, tannery. Even an inn with balconies that wrapped around the first and second floors and, if he wasn't mistaken, a garden on the roof.

Yet there were signs of recent distress. The streets were quiet, the few people who dared to step outside moving quickly from one door to another. The buildings showed signs of trauma, too. Cracked beams here, a patch of new shingles there, shop windows sealed with burlap instead of glass.

Aya. An android of a god, sent by the Hartigers for purposes unknown. He'd seen it before, and the knowledge had cost him his world.

The King of Suhainn was known a kindly man, beloved of his people. He was also a complete fabrication, which was how Jord had known to look for androids, and how to root out impossible falsehoods.

Jord had stumbled across the truth in Suhainn, and the Hartigers had swept him away to Earth. If Frankie hadn't been hiding on the transport dock—if she hadn't burst in without permission the way she had—Jord would have died then. He was certain of it.

He should have tried harder to get back to Suhainn, to learn what the Hartigers were doing in there, and what had happened to the real king. What would Frankie do, if she knew the truth? Would she try to help—or would she stun the people into submission?

And what was happening in Suhainn now, with no true king and no Hartigers in control? Jord couldn't begin to guess.

He shook himself into the present and tried to focus on the town around him. Streets. Dust. People. Propped against several of the doors were small green wreaths, each dotted with white wildflowers. The buildings behind them were empty, the windows gagged with boards.

He swallowed hard, willing his stomach to retain its contents as he contemplated the meaning of the wreaths. He paused, stooping for a closer look. The wreath smelled of mint and rosemary. He ran a finger along the circle, scattering bits of the herbs on the threshold.

It was unwise to linger, but he couldn't contain his curiosity. "I thought you said there was no plague here."

"Only a few cases," Kira said. "It did not spread far."

Jord straightened, and the world swayed. He needed to get out of here, soon.

Frankie was still strangely quiet, watching him with a look that for once, he couldn't read. He tried to pretend he didn't notice, but he kept finding himself glancing at her, trying to ascertain her thoughts. What she might do next.

They continued toward the water, and the streets fairly emptied of people—anxious of strangers, perhaps—except for the few vendors, who eyed them hopefully as they passed. Jord slowed before a cart filled with fruit. Though it was as pale and shriveled as he would have expected from seeing all that wasted farmland, the apple-like wares made him want to use his royal resemblance one more time.

He hesitated, and Frankie finally exploded. "Are you crazy? What was that? Your version of discretion, revealing your face to a dozen people?"

Kira shot Frankie a look of alarm. No stopping for fruit, then. How did Prince Kol react to such insubordination? Suhainn had as many ways of dealing with rudeness as the governor had sons—and he had seven of those. Plus a daughter.

Jord didn't have energy for a fight. He'd barely spent half an hour in the presence of the prince, and if he spared a moment of his concentration, he might miss a step. Frankie was still looking at him, though, as if awaiting a complete explanation. "Later," he said.

"Oh, later, great," Frankie said. "I'll look forward to a full report."

Kira's eyes widened, but she led them on without a word.

The street ended, dumping them onto a wide avenue. No merchants here, unfortunately, just three long piers hosting the sorriest collection of boats Jord had ever seen. Coast skimmers, and fishing vessels. Little better than canoes.

The lake, it seemed, would require a more seaworthy craft. Had the oculars not stated clearly that this was a lake, he would have thought he stood at the edge of the ocean. Waves pummeled the pier, rocking the boats like toys.

"We'll need access to a boat the two of us can sail," Jord told Kira.

"Because you can sail now?" Frankie muttered.

Jord ignored her. Every Suhainnan could handle a variety of watercraft, a fact Frankie ought to remember from their lessons. He'd have no trouble sailing any one of these boats on his own, if his vision would stop going double.

Now that they'd reached the docks, though, Kira's pace slowed. "If I may ask, your highness, where are you going to find reinforcements? The South is decimated by flooding, and to enter the North would be death."

"We'll go to the island," Jord said.

As soon as the words were out of his mouth, he regretted them. Too specific. That island might be full of bears, for all he knew. It might be a prison, or the equivalent of the local landfill. He wasn't thinking clearly. He had to get out of here. His neck felt strangely hot, his tongue heavy in his mouth.

Kira stopped walking so abruptly that Jord had to pause and look back a few steps to where she stood, unbelieving, in the street. He said, "Soldier?"

"You can't do that. Your highness."

With thunder in his ears and tadpoles swimming in his vision, he'd hardly be able to navigate these circumstances in Suhainn, or on Earth. In Rogur, with no knowledge of politics, customs, or geography, his sudden lightheadedness could kill him.

The world tilted, and righted itself.

"That island is to be our salvation, soldier," he said. "And I trust you'll help me to get there."

Kira glanced at Frankie, then took a deep breath. "No help can come from that place. It's cursed. You will only die there, and leave us to fight these gods alone. I cannot let you do it."

Oh, good. Frankie's boldness was catching.

He couldn't even face one of her. Two? Impossible.

Perhaps that was how she had felt when she'd seen Prince Kol.

Words. He needed to say words now. He shook his head, his throat dry.

Something sharp connected with his ribs, an elbow—Frankie's? Or had someone else brushed by him? No, not enough people here for that—and Kira's eyes were narrowing, as if she couldn't quite peg what was out of place.

"The crown is on the verge of collapse," Frankie said. "We'll all die anyway. You think those monsters will stop attacking Lariasc? You can't trick all of them into the lake."

Kira came forward now. Her expression was, unfortunately, lost to Jord behind a wall of fireworks. "Your clothing is odd, and you speak with a strange accent. I've never seen you before."

Frankie scoffed. "Have you seen everyone in this world? Are you an expert?"

"My prince," Kira said. "Are you sure you're not traveling with one of them? A goddess, disguised?"

Oh, Frankie was going to love that. Being compared to a goddess might not impress her, but an android? That had to be the height of flattery.

When Frankie caught his arm, Jord realized he'd stumbled. "The nearest vessel," she said. "Now."

Jord was vaguely aware of footsteps, boots on gravel—why was everything so loud here?—and for a moment he remembered the fortress, how Kol's troops had run as one unit. The tadpoles swamped his vision and exploded in a private show of splatters that blocked his view of the street.

Lightning crackled, so loudly that he wanted to cover his ears—unless the sound was coming from within his ears, which seemed possible—but he found himself unable to move his arms. Frankie pressed something hard against his temple—he knew it was Frankie, her muffled voice, her smell of citrus still distinct after days without baths or fruit—and then there was wood beneath his feet. He wanted to say there was no need to take him by force, that he'd go willingly wherever she wished, but the words would not form.

The ground rocked, gently at first, then more forcefully. A familiar feeling, the roll of waves. So familiar, in fact, that for a moment, Jord thought Frankie had brought him home.

TWENTY
KOL

"Apparently, I've been kidnapped," Kol said. Twice in as many days, too, after Reyche had dragged him to Lariasc against his will. "What an adventure."

What intrigue he would have missed, had his captain cared little enough to leave him behind. Gods thundered through cities, mirrors came to life, and yet Kol's entrance into Lariasc numbered one of the strangest moments in recent memory.

While he'd known of the slain goddess that towered before the walls, warning Lariasc's enemies away like the gods' equivalent of a head upon a pike, her proximity made his insides squirm. She was larger than the monsters he'd fought in Caisrach, her quiver still armed with cruel arrows.

The goddess had not been the strange part of this day. It seemed, to his surprise, that the prince had already made one appearance in the village today. Quite a benevolent one, at that. By the time the real Kol had arrived, the soldiers had been in the midst of preparing a hospital for sick refugees.

Reyche didn't see the humor in it. A pity. The captain

paced the inn's common room, his wide stride carrying him from one end to the other in five steps.

"The Earthen is impersonating you," Reyche said. "He could be anywhere."

The papers stuck to the table as Kol shuffled the guard's report. Delightful. If Reyche didn't hand the liquor over soon, perhaps Kol could lick some from the furniture.

"For what purpose?" Reyche continued. His feet sounded steady against the floorboards, but his hands quivered frenetically before him, betraying his nerves. "Where are they going?"

"I've a guess."

For the first time since he'd pocketed it in the woods, Kol withdrew the seeing stone and placed it on the table. The glass was cracked beyond repair, though he could not guess what might have happened to it.

A mystery.

Best of all, for the first time in at least a year, the sphere glowed green. "The Earthens restored the magic in the seeing stone."

"Please tell me you haven't been foolish enough to contact Elandria."

"Indeed I was that foolish. It happens to be my specialty. But alas, it didn't work."

Finally, Reyche stopped his pacing and faced Kol, eyes burning. "You do not mean to seek her out, surely. The wise woman is a fraud at best."

Kol set his palm atop the stone and rolled it over the table, enjoying the rumble of the wood beneath. He did mean to seek her out. Reyche had wanted him to find allies, after all. "And at worst?"

"At worst, she is one of them. A goddess who guided you to your ruin as the unrest in your country tipped to chaos. And you have gone along with her, without question."

Well. Honesty was honesty. "That's enough."

"Your instincts are clouded by the river of *afan* that runs through your veins."

Though not at the moment, tragically. Kol continued to roll the stone, the cracks scratching his palm like glass thorns. "That presumes my instincts were good to begin with."

"Will you spend what's left of your sanity on her, in addition to your money and your power?"

Kol granted Reyche a certain amount of leniency. But there was only so much a man could tolerate. "That's quite enough, Reyche. Have you gone deaf, or simply insubordinate?"

Reyche crossed the room and leaned over Kol's table. "If you are still determined to die, there may well come a day when I will no longer be able to prevent it."

Heat poured into Kol's face, a mix of shame and betrayal. Not once had Reyche held that history against him, or thrown it in Kol's face. Now, the captain wrapped his fingers around Kol's wrist, tightly enough that he could no doubt feel Kol's pulse racing. "If you must seek death, my prince, I beg you. Do not ask your soldiers to die with you."

Kol forced himself to stare into Reyche's eyes. "And would you, Reyche?"

"You know the answer to that."

He could practically see their history passing through Reyche's eyes, a cacophony of moments stolen on deserted stairwells and midnight balconies. The salt of skin, mixing with honey-sweet wine. The captain had never been able to gain control of his expressions. Kol had always been far too adept at it.

Kol wrenched Reyche's fingers off his wrist. "Then get the horses ready."

Reyche straightened, pain and anger at war on his face. He affected a shallow bow, then spun and headed for the door.

"And Reyche?"

Reyche stopped, but did not turn. Kol took his time rising from the booth, doing his best to make his footfalls sound commanding as he stepped after his captain. He could do any number of things to make this right. A gentle hand to Reyche's arm. A firmer one, curled around the back of his neck.

Instead, he said, "My soldiers swore binding oaths to me. Should I order them to blow holes in the ship beneath their feet, I shall expect them to obey."

When Reyche didn't respond, Kol clamped a hand over his shoulder. "Is that clear? Soldier?"

Reyche swallowed, the muscles in his jaw quivering with tension. "Perfectly."

It wasn't that Frankie was worried about Jord, exactly, just that she was seriously considering whether to stop rowing long enough to retrieve the bucket from the bottom of the rowboat and use it to wake him up. A splash of lake water should bring him around. Or, if that failed, a good wallop on the side of the head.

From Lariasc, the clouds gathered above the lake had seemed heavy and motionless, a permanent fixture. They'd burned off once she got away from the shore, leaving her to curse her forgotten sunglasses.

About once a minute, she glanced down to make sure Jord's chest still rose and fell. It was probably a bad idea to douse a passed-out person with lake water, anyway. It was definitely a bad idea to hit him on the head.

He'd done something *nice* back there. It was so... un-Jord-like of him.

Frankie took a moment to remove her hat from the pack and prop it over his face so he wouldn't burn.

For an hour, Frankie rowed, and Jord breathed. Her aching

arms worked mechanically while blisters bubbled across her palms, threatening to rupture with every shift of the oars.

Finally, as the sun made overtures toward the horizon, Jord stirred. He pulled the hat off his face, sat up, and said, "So? How was my impersonation of the prince?"

OK, *now* was the time to smack him. "The fainting would have been more believable with a flask in your hand."

"Good note. I'll keep it in mind for next time."

He was too pale. He was never far from ghostly, true, but his eyes had this glassy look to them now. He didn't look healthy. "Are you OK?" she asked.

He fished into the pack for the canteen and drank deeply. "Fine."

But his hands shook as he screwed the cap on. Frankie paused her rowing and reached into her pocket for the fruit she'd nicked for him in the port. When she tossed it to him, he stared at it like he'd never seen a piece of fruit before.

"Don't overthink it, just eat it," Frankie said, picking the oars up. Her arms protested. She ignored their shaking and pushed forward.

"You stole this."

"You think I don't know better than to pick a fight with you when you're pretending to be royalty? Yes, I caused a distraction and I stole it."

"For me."

Trust Jord to get all weird about fruit. What did he want, a blender to go with it? "Look, we have a deal. I supply you with fruit. Especially when you look like you're about to keel over and die. Will you eat it already?"

He took a bite.

"Does it taste like an apple?" Frankie asked.

"More like a crunchy fig. With, I don't know..." He bit into it again. "Ginger?"

"Weird."

"Want some?"

Fresh fruit would be nice right about now, but he needed it more than she did. Frankie wrinkled her nose. "Not even a little bit."

"How long have we been on the water?"

"About two hours, I think. Time is weird here."

After this, she should have no trouble getting a team of astronomers here to study the planet's orbit. Plus biologists to test the plants—was there actually ginger in the apple thing?—agriculturists for the problems with the crops, and what, meteorologists? To figure out why the climate was changing so drastically. Geologists, too. For kicks, and for the crater.

She had to remember to collect a water sample before leaving the lake.

"I should row for a while," Jord said.

Frankie's arms begged her to agree, but she shook her head. "What happened back there?"

"I could ask you the same thing."

He obviously wanted to know if she'd dealt with the Lariasc problem the same way she'd attacked the people in the woods. She flushed. "I merely implied that I'd stun you with my magic wand, if they didn't let us go."

"Just checking."

As if he hadn't landed his own punches in the forest. "Are you sick?"

"No. A few days of poor eating and sleeping, combined with excessive physical exertion. I'm fine."

Yeah, right. "Maybe if you'd leave Pathbound Tower every now and then, take a walk, get some fresh air. You'd be in better shape."

She expected him to make a comment about the number of hours he'd logged in Pathbound's gym—it was a lot—and how he swam laps on a daily basis. Instead, he said, "I can't leave the Tower."

"You've been in New York for years. How scary can it be?"

Jord bit into his apple-fig, finishing his bite before responding. "It's not that I *won't* leave the Tower. I *can't* leave it. Although, fixing that little detail was to be my second order of business after they named me manager. Once I'd spoken to you."

Frankie stared at him. He took another bite of his fruit, then bent his head low and pointed to a pink scar on the back of his neck. It was no more than half an inch long, but even from here, she could see it was raised and raw. "If I go more than a few steps outside the Tower, this implant triggers temporary paralysis. The chip clamps onto my spine, or administers a drug. I don't know."

Frankie knew.

She knew the implant was a mechanical neural jammer, and that it worked by interrupting the signals between the brain and the spinal cord based on dictated parameters from a central database.

Frankie knew exactly how it worked. Because Frankie was responsible for its design.

She forced her arms to keep working, to keep rowing, to do anything other than show how deep her horror ran. That angry wound on the back of his neck, the mechanism sewn inside his skin. Did he know it was her doing? The way he was looking at her, his brown eyes calm and wide, she didn't think so.

Her mouth was salt and cotton, her lips chapped. "You've tried leaving the tower, and it stopped you."

"I didn't need to. The first thing that happened upon injection was a demonstration."

She pictured him sprawled at her parents' feet, the line of blood running around his neck, and she wanted to be sick. She had never intended for the implant to be used on humans. Never. Certainly, she'd looked at human spinal cords while building the initial prototype—they were large, and there was so much data to work with—but she hadn't meant... She hadn't pictured this. Not once.

But, a voice whispered in the back of her mind, shouldn't she have pictured it? Wasn't it the duty of a scientist to consider the moral implications of any creation? She'd never been much for biology; it was Mom's field of study, and Frankie had—as ever—been looking to make an impression. In eighth grade, she'd applied what she knew about computers and engineering to the human body, inventing a system for controlling the movements of otherworldly wildlife. It was supposed to be a solution for keeping the otherworldly animals they wished to study contained within a limited radius.

It was the one invention her parents ever praised, the one invention her father had ever hinted was genius enough to bother trying to repeat.

No, she'd never considered they might use it on a person. It was supposed to be for birds and hedgehogs. Badgers.

But then, she'd never mentioned its existence to Audrey, either.

Frankie realized she'd stopped rowing. She swallowed a lump of nausea and started again. She might be imagining it, but she thought she could make out a strip of land shimmering in the ocean ahead. "Did you... did you know it wouldn't activate if you followed me here? In the transport?"

Jord scrubbed a hand through his hair.

Frankie decided to take that as a no. She wouldn't have placed bets on his chances, either.

The trip here might have killed him. And it would have been her fault.

"In case you're wondering whether I deserved to be carted

to Earth and injected with a personalized restraining bolt," Jord said, "I may as well confess. I was nothing more than a page in Suhainn. A servant."

Frankie hadn't been wondering whether he deserved it, but that did sound like something she'd say. Was she really so mean, so completely unfeeling, that he'd think her capable of responding that way?

She knew the answer. She didn't like it.

"That's not a confession," she said, the words sticking in her mouth like stale gum. "A confession is 'I stole Frankie's necklace' or 'I slipped rat poison into the Pathbound grant manager's soup.'"

Or, *I'm responsible for your captivity.*

"You frighten me."

She should frighten him. She thought of Audrey's disgust when Frankie had tripped him at the party all those months ago, of the look on his face after she'd stunned the woman in the woods. She might not have been thinking of him when she'd designed that implant, but she ought to have wondered why it had delighted her parents so much that its creation had bought her a ticket to their dinner table that evening. Were there lines she wouldn't cross?

All this time, she'd thought that Jord's story was... what, exactly? Had she really believe him to be some kind of a criminal? Her parents had never intervened in Suhainn's workings before. Why would they have begun with Jord? Jord wasn't a second child to them, or an employee, or even their crony. He was their prisoner. But why?

No wonder he'd wanted to get rid of the seeing stone. No wonder he hated her.

He should hate her so much more.

She cleared her throat, uncomfortable. "Wouldn't my

parents... I mean, wouldn't they have wanted to make sure you could get back home to Suhainn?"

Jord finished his fruit and tossed the pit into the ocean, then wiped his hands on his pants. "No, Francesca, they most definitely would not. Now, I think it's my turn to row."

He invoked her name like a barrier to further questioning. She wasn't going to get any more answers from him now. He must still be lightheaded, to have told her this at all.

Frankie handed him a second apple-ginger-fig, then retrieved the oars before he could protest. "I see land. I want to be able to say I rowed the whole way."

When Jord glanced over his shoulder to check out the view, the scar was so obvious that Frankie wondered why she'd never noticed it. She knew the answer, though. She'd simply never looked.

She didn't know why her parents would have brought a Suhainnan servant to work for them on Earth, but her whole perception was turned on its head. He must have been living on Earth in fear. This whole time.

Jord didn't argue about the rowing. By now, he should know when it was fruitless to try. He dug into the pack for the roll of bandages and held them out to her. "For your hands," he said, when she gave him a questioning eyebrow.

Right. That would have been a good idea from the start. But Frankie couldn't bring herself to move toward him. All the abuse she'd leveled at him over the years, and she'd never stopped to consider that the gulf between them might be less about Frankie and more about Hartiger.

Had their places been reversed, she wouldn't simply have tossed the seeing stone into the woods. She would have shattered it into a million pieces.

If he knew her hand in this, he'd abandon her as soon as their feet hit the sand.

Jord shook the roll in her direction. "Take the bandages, Francesca. You didn't implant this thing in me, did you? Besides, it's not all bad. The scar twinges when it's about to rain."

He smiled, like he knew what she was going to say. How could rain matter to a person who would never feel it? The thing could warn him of an incoming missile, and he'd be stuck watching it fall, incapable of escape.

TWENTY-TWO

JORD

Jord had been fortunate enough to suffer no illusions, no hopes, of ever returning to Suhainn. What he'd seen, and what he knew about his home world's king, would keep him on Earth for the rest of his life. There'd never been any point in denying it.

He hadn't meant to tell Frankie about the implant. Eventually, maybe, but not now. The story had simply bled out of his brain. Gushed. He wanted to blame it on the still-blurry world, the mild throb in his head, the very present fear that his senses would fail him again.

In any case, there was no taking it back. And now that it was out, he didn't want to.

At length, they reached the island.

They wrestled the boat across a strip of beach and over a patch of waist-high grasses that separated the sand from a forest so dense it was practically a jungle. Birds called, animals rustled in the undergrowth. Smells of seaweed and damp earth tangled with a sweeter floral scent.

As soon as the boat was secure, Frankie set off along the edge of the forest as if on a mission.

Frankie Hartiger was always on a mission.

Jord trailed several steps behind her. He didn't like how obvious their footprints were here, but there wasn't much to be done about it. "Are you looking for a welcome sign?" he asked.

"No, genius, a path into the woods."

Jord bit back a smile. She'd been so tentative with him on the boat after he'd shown her the implant. Guilty, as though she were somehow to blame. It wasn't as though he'd have told her about it, if she'd noticed the scar sooner and asked.

"And if the inhabitants of this island didn't want their path to be found? Assuming they exist?"

"Someone was here at one point," she said, "long enough to build a cell tower. And I think I'm smart enough to find a path."

"Your intelligence was never in question."

It said more about his luck than his skill when he looked down to see a ribbon of soil scattered across the sand at his feet, leading to a delicate parting among the grasses to their right. A trail, leading from the woods to the beach. Jord pushed a branch aside to peer into the undergrowth.

The path was narrow, hardly discernible, but it was there. And Frankie had walked right by it.

Sometimes, the universe was good to him.

"Francesca."

"What? What is it now?"

He cleared his throat. She sighed in exasperation and turned. When she saw him holding the branch, her eyes widened for a second. "See? That's terrible camouflage. One branch?"

Well. She was nothing if not predictable, in one sense anyway. "Is there even a point in—"

Frankie ducked under his arm and headed down the path. "Nope."

Though twilight still clung to the beach, he'd barely passed the first few trunks before the green-tinged light faded to near blackness. Frankie had already activated the flashlight on her watch.

One moment he was catching up—his body still felt heavy, slow to awaken after his illness—and the next Frankie had stopped so suddenly that Jord walked right into her.

She raised her wrist to shoulder level, using her watch to illuminate the barrier that now stood before them.

So far, the walls they'd seen in Rogur had been made of wood. Logs at the fortress, boards at Lariasc. Basic and functional. This fence made him feel as if they'd stumbled to Earth a few steps from a military base. It was made of closely knit chain link, with spirals of barbed wire wrapped around the top.

"A lab," Frankie said. "I was right."

He hadn't doubted she would be. He only wondered what —or who—they might discover inside.

She was already moving, throwing herself toward the question with her typical gusto. She had to be exhausted, but she aimed her light at the bottom of the fence with impressive focus. When she dropped to her knees, he understood why; she wriggled through a hole in the fence, and—mercifully—paused to wait for him, fingers drumming impatiently on her hips.

He supposed he should be grateful she'd checked for holes first, before trying to lead them over the barbed wire. He crawled, mud seeping through the knees of his pants, the fence catching on the back of his shirt.

As soon as he was on his feet, Frankie took off. Jord rushed to keep pace with her, his body gasping for equilibrium. "Maybe we should wait until daybreak," he said.

"We have a light," she said.

Nothing would keep her from a Pathbound laboratory. She wanted to save Rogur, which was an admirable goal on its surface. But how much could he ever trust her, while she continued to pursue her parents' admiration in this way? No matter how kindly she'd responded to his story, she had not paused in her goal, and he would do well to remember why she was here.

When she found her parents, everything would change. She'd turn against him, too.

Despite the footprints on the beach, this place didn't look like it had seen any Hartigers in a very long time. The lab—if that's what it was—was a functional box of a building that the forest seemed set on vanquishing. Vines crawled up the walls as if to swallow them whole, giving the place a furred appearance. A trio of rodents skittered out of their path as Frankie and Jord ran for the doors, where the vegetation hung more loosely around the frame.

Now that they were here, perhaps Jord would have the opportunity to convince her to call Liz and get them back to Earth.

Or perhaps that was a fool's wish.

Frankie reached for the rust-spotted handle and yanked. The door opened.

"Too easy," Jord said. "We should—"

Frankie hooked her arm around his and pulled him inside.

"See?" she said, giving the flashlight a cursory flick across the space. "There's nothing here."

Nothing but darkness and rot.

And a breath of wind, gusting toward them.

The light glinted against a moving object, and Jord yanked Frankie to the ground an instant before an enormous ball whistled over their heads. There was a sharp spike adhered to the bottom, looking murderous and hungry as it pierced through the spot where they'd been standing.

"A trap," he said, breath catching as Frankie used her light to track the ball's retreating swing. "So much for the lab idea."

The ball dove back toward them with a swoosh, cresting a few feet short of its last peak. He half expected Frankie to throw his arm off, the way she'd tried to do on the day of the Pathbound disaster. But she remained still beside him. "If they set traps, then there must be something to see," she said. "We'll just have to be careful."

Right. Why would he have expected deadly traps to sway her from her task? "Because that's a quality you're familiar with?"

"Not really, but I happen to know it's printed on *your* business cards."

Perhaps she saw more than he thought. The ball returned, though it was beginning to settle nearer the center. A strange kind of trap, especially for the Hartigers. They tended to show a bit more finesse. Maybe they'd been in a hurry.

Or maybe it wasn't their design.

Frankie got to her feet and headed for the edge of the room. "We'll work together. That was what you wanted, wasn't it?"

Universes help him. "Yes."

She offered him her hand. "I'll trust you if you trust me."

What would she say, if he were to tell her he'd trusted her all along? That it was her inability to rise to Hartiger-level standards that made it so? Her outstretched hand might have been a beacon of hope. It might have been his salvation, for the warmth it brought to his chest.

In all the endless worlds, no one had ever been quite as stupid as he was. He took her hand. His head still felt fuzzy, but at least he wasn't dizzy anymore.

A quick tour with the light illuminated circular walls, with numbers and calculations scrawled upon them in neat columns. He'd have expected Frankie to dive for them, to pore over the numbers and obsess over deciphering their meaning. But though she lingered briefly on the marks, she quickly moved on.

More to see, apparently.

The walls encircled a giant pit of sand, over which the ball now swung. It was adhered to the ceiling somehow, though Jord could not make out the fixture. A strange sort of sculpture for a strange sort of entry hall. That, at least, had the signature of Hartiger flare.

The passage around the perimeter appeared to be clear. They proceeded with caution, hand in hand, watching for hidden trip lines and lasers.

A second door waited at the end of the room. This time, Frankie opened it with caution.

No deadly wrecking balls made to take off their heads. "A lab," Frankie said, as though the entry hall had caused her to doubt it. She squeezed his hand. "It really is, Jord, look."

It might have been one of the research facilities back at Pathbound Tower. Well, aside from the rust and overturned stools, and the vines dangling from grates in the ceiling. Cabinets ran along the walls, with stainless steel tables arranged in the center.

At the end of the room, past another set of open doors, he thought he could make out the corner of a glass aquarium. He shuddered, wondering what species of wildlife the Hartigers might have trapped in this place.

Frankie shone the light around the room, pausing when it caught the gleam of a tripwire strung between two lab tables. It was attached to a cage of spikes. Crude, but effective.

"I can deactivate that," Jord said. Now that they knew what to watch for, navigating the lab should be doable.

Frankie stepped forward.

The floor flipped out from under her feet. One second it was a solid metal panel; the next, her weight was dragging Jord to his knees, his hand her only tether. If not for the friction of the bandages, she would have slid away.

Even so, it was a near thing.

"I can't hold on," she said, the words half muffled. "I can't. I'm slipping."

Jord didn't want to imagine how long the fall might be, or what horrors lurked there. He lowered himself so the edge of the drop was beneath his shoulders, trying to retain his calm. He stretched for her other hand as her feet scrabbled fruitlessly for the wall. Unlike the crater cliffs, this drop was sheer metal.

He couldn't see the bottom.

"Reach for me," he said. "I'll pull you up."

She swung for him with her other hand and missed, swaying so much he almost lost his grip. "Again," he said.

"My hands," she said through gritted teeth. "They hurt too much."

He never should have let her do all that rowing, after yesterday's climb. No matter what she said. "You have to hold on," he said, edging further over the pit. Vertigo tugged at his brain, but he tucked it away, ignoring the drops of sweat that tickled along his hairline.

He stretched his arm as far as he could, praying for balance, and caught hold of her fingers.

She let out a breath like a sob.

Grasping her bandaged hands as hard as he could, Jord heaved her up over the edge, pulling her to him as they collapsed back against the wall. She was shaking so hard he thought she might come apart in his arms, and for a moment, neither one of them could move. He wasn't sure he'd ever be able to let go.

He'd almost lost her.

"See why I don't like heights?" he said into her hair.

She laughed, half sobbing into his neck. "Why are you even helping me?"

He thought of his panic when he'd realized she was trying to take the bypass by herself, the absolute emptiness of a world—any world—without her in it. And even though he knew she might turn against him the minute she reunited with her parent, there was a deep, unmovable part of him that hoped—that had always hoped—she'd choose him.

He could move an inch, even less, and drop his lips to her hair. To the skin beneath her ear, the softness of her throat. Every part of her was pressed against his body, and he wanted... he wanted to catch her lips between his. He wanted to stay here for a good long while.

He swallowed. "Why wouldn't I help?"

"The trip might have killed you. My parents kidnapped you. I'm only ever awful to you, just..."

Not only. Not always. "To be fair," he said, working hard to regain his senses, "I thought I'd be able to stop you before the transport left."

"This world sucks so much."

"No arguments there."

She pulled away. He wanted to hold her forever, but made himself relax his arms, shifting to the side. "I did *not* expect the Indiana Jones treatment," she said. "At least, not from the lab. What the hell was Pathbound doing in here?"

"Far be it to me to say anything positive about your family, but this doesn't look like their work."

Frankie sat back against the wall and pulled the canteen from the pack. They passed it back and forth while she surveyed the room. Probably planning all her experiments. But they couldn't use this lab. Not with traps set to kill them with every step.

Jord tried to breathe, tried to keep the world in focus. Something still felt off. He needed to eat more, or drink several canteens of water. A few hours of sleep, and he'd be well. He just needed rest.

Suddenly, Frankie whipped her head to the side. "Foucault's Pendulum!"

"I'm sorry?"

She leapt to her feet. Jord followed more slowly, his body still shaking from adrenaline and the aftermath of her touch, his head protesting the barest movement. "The ball," she said. "It's a Foucault's Pendulum, of course it is! They were measuring the rotation... If the transport... yes..."

She was already hurrying back the way they'd come, beaming her paltry light through the space. She dropped to crawl beneath the still-swinging ball, wiping her hands back and forth in the sand. "Foucault's Pendulum measures the rate of a planet's rotation," she said. "The people in the woods said the days are lengthening. What if it's because the transport rapidly slows Rogur's rotation? The shifting seasons, the dying crops, the earthquakes... Those symptoms would fit."

"Didn't Superman reverse the Earth's rotation without ill effects?"

"That's why comic book science is dumb." She stopped crawling to point a finger at him. "And don't think we're not going to discuss how you know that."

He wasn't about to admit he'd gotten it from the old film, not the comic. He'd never live it down. "We can't stay in here," he said.

Frankie finished her sand smoothing and hopped out of the ball's path. "Of course we can't stay. We'll be safer out there, and we should try to call..." She trailed off, apparently remembering that finding her parents meant finding the people who'd imprisoned Jord. "Well, anyway. We should see what else we can see. We'll come back here tomorrow and check the results."

At this, she pointed to the circle, where the spike on the bottom of the ball was dragging a line across the sand. He wasn't sure exactly what it meant, but Frankie did. That was enough.

"Don't you need to check the results against pre-transport numbers?"

Frankie blinked at him. He thought she looked... impressed? No. That couldn't be. "Jord. You know how to science." She flashed the light along the markings on the walls. "Luckily, someone left us a record. If Rogur is slowing down, we'll form a plan. If not, then it's back to the physics drawing board."

Jord supposed it was as good a plan as any. She certainly seemed to know what she wanted. They stepped out of the lab together.

And a net landed on top of them.

The ropes were thick and rough, clearly hand tied. Where had it come from? Frankie was already struggling, trying to lift it, but Jord could see the bottom was cinched tight.

"Aren't you two in a bind?"

Frankie startled at the sound of the voice. She flicked the light around the empty courtyard, searching for the source.

"Up here."

Frankie shifted the light toward the roof, where a young woman sat on the corner, swinging her legs. "Who are you?" the girl asked.

English, Jord realized. The girl was speaking English. "You're Earthen," he said.

The girl dropped off the roof, caught the limb of a nearby tree on the way down, and landed on bent knees, straightening like an experienced gymnast. With the moonlight shining on her face, Jord could see she seemed to be of East Asian heritage, and not far from their age. She had her hair cropped close to her head in choppy layers.

"Didn't ask who I am," she said. She raised her arm, and dim light or not, there was no doubt about the fact that she was holding a gun.

"Now," she said. "Who are you?"

Another girl slipped through the gate, merging into the shadows as though she were made of grace. "Bex," she said. "Wait. I know them."

Beside him, Frankie's entire body went still. The girl moved into the light, and Jord's breath caught in his throat.

The second girl was Audrey LaRoche.

TWENTY-THREE
FRANKIE

Audrey stepped into the moonlight, dangling a pair of sickle-shaped blades from two fingers as casually as Frankie had seen her carry heels and a handbag. She had her black curls tied up in a headband of floral-print cloth, revealing a healing cut across her forehead. She wore cargo pants and a cropped T-shirt, and her arms were covered in scratches.

Audrey. She was OK. She was *alive.*

Audrey didn't move to release Frankie and Jord from the trap. She stepped up beside the other girl, her expression so stony that for a moment, Frankie wondered if she might be looking at another doppelgänger.

But then Audrey said, "That's Francesca Hartiger."

Francesca? What, like she recognized Frankie from a picture in a zine or something? Jord wrapped his fingers around Frankie's wrist in warning, and Frankie clamped her mouth shut. Because the other girl—Bex, Audrey had called her— wasn't lowering her gun.

The barrel was freckled with pocks of rust, but Bex's stance was wide. Confident. She knew how to use that thing, and the glitter in her eyes promised she would not hesitate. Her clothes were big for her, the shirt knotted at her waist above a utility belt made from a strip of cloth. Frankie caught the grin of a cartoon cat on the left hip pocket, its head folded ruthlessly in half.

"The daughter?" she said.

Audrey nodded. "We're friends."

She said it like they hadn't spent hours lying side by side on Frankie's bed, or Audrey's, talking about their froufrou school and making plans for the future. This was *Audrey*. Who never tried to give Frankie a makeover, who always had her back.

Who finally got sick of checking Frankie's thoughtlessness, right before getting trapped in a dying world full of killer androids. What would she say, if she knew about Jord's implant, and Frankie's hand in it?

No wonder this wasn't the reunion Frankie had hoped for. She made herself address the other girl. "You know my parents?"

Bex's lips twisted in disgust. She'd have spat in the dirt, Frankie thought, had she not been busy holding them at gunpoint. "Oh, sure, we go way back. I remember them fondly as the people who marooned me here seven years ago."

Frankie hadn't had a proper meal, or a good night's sleep, in nearly three days. Her hands felt like they'd been oiled and slapped on a griddle, which hurt only marginally more than the suspicious look on her best friend's face.

At this point, there was no hope for competent cognitive function. "They marooned you on an island? Like a pirate?"

Surely a girl like this would have the wherewithal to lash some tree trunks together and paddle her way to the mainland.

"No, Baby Hartiger. They marooned me in this *world*."

Jord sighed. "Of course they did."

Bex nodded at Jord. "And you are?"

"Her valet," he said.

Frankie stared at Bex. "Why would they maroon a... what, ten-year-old?"

"I was nine, actually. Tagged along with my dad and a bunch of scientists they sent here. What, Mommy and Daddy Hartiger don't discuss their crimes over family teatime?"

Implants. Marooned scientists. Quite an excellent day for the Hartiger family name. What else were they hiding?

Audrey touched Bex gently on the wrist. "Let's take them home. We can talk there."

Home. On Earth, Audrey's home was the opposite of Frankie's, brimming with voices and music, fresh flowers and cooking smells. Frankie was always angling to visit, even though Pathbound Tower was closer to school.

Audrey's home on the island was probably a hut. Or a treehouse.

Bex held Audrey's gaze for a long moment before lowering the gun. She didn't put it away, but it still felt like a victory. "OK. Cut them loose."

Audrey had to stand on tiptoes to slice through the top of the net. When she was finished, she turned straight back to Bex without meeting Frankie's eyes. "We'd better get moving."

Frankie brushed the net off her shoulders, trying to rid herself of the phantom weight it left behind. Like she'd missed a thread—or dislodged a heavy insect. She ran her hands through her hair, checking for stowaways. "And how far is 'home' from the lovely death-trapped laboratory?"

"You liked my welcome basket?" Bex said. "A little prize for the Hartigers, in case they come back."

"You caught the wrong Hartiger," Jord said.

Bex shrugged. "You made it out."

"It's a bit of a walk," Audrey cut in, answering Frankie's original question with uncharacteristic curtness.

Too bad. Standing here was more of a challenge than Frankie liked to admit. Her arms trembled fiercely after all that rowing and ducking and falling into pits. Her hands felt raw, the bandages damp with blood.

And she wasn't the one who'd passed out today. Jord pretended to be holding up well, but Frankie was beginning to suspect that 'pretending' might be his default setting. Back in the lab, the way he'd held her... But if he knew about the implant, he'd hate her more than ever, no matter what friendship he might have pictured before they'd landed here.

Audrey tucked the knives into sheaths at her waist and waited for Frankie and Jord to untangle their feet. Frankie freed herself first and offered an arm to Jord for support. "How are you feeling?" she asked him, in Suhainnan.

"You're the one who fell into a pit. I suggest you watch your step moving forward. I don't know about you, but I prefer my arms to remain inside their sockets."

Frankie actually smiled at that. When had his voice stopped grating on her ears?

Before she could respond, Audrey laughed. "Wow," she said, in English, as they followed Bex into the moonlit jungle. "Things have changed between you two."

Jord ducked around a branch. "You speak Suhainnan."

Audrey shot a frown back over her shoulder. "I understand a lot of *Roguran*."

"She learned it so she could spy on the Hartigers," Bex said, a hint of pride sneaking into her voice. "She wrote it in code. Pretended to be writing songs, while secretly recording conversations. So she could figure out what they were up to."

Audrey grinned. The first smile Frankie had seen from her, and Bex was the one to tease it out. "I did do that."

Frankie blinked. "In six months?"

Her friend lifted a shoulder. "I've got the ear. It's not like I understand every word. The structure's pretty simple, though. But Roguran and Suhainnan are...?"

"Same language," Frankie confirmed.

"What happened?" Jord asked. "On the transport?"

Translation: why was spying necessary at all?

Audrey didn't answer right away. For a few seconds, there was only the sound of their footsteps squelching into the damp leaves. "The transport landed in this deserted fort thing," she said finally. "Obviously not Suhainn. Your parents were upset, but somehow not surprised. They brought us to a village, then spent a month acting shady. Cindy disappeared for long periods of time. The rest of us had no idea what was happening."

"There weren't soldiers when you arrived?" Jord asked.

"Nope. Just dust and cliffs, and an abandoned wall."

Kol had still been in his palace. Interesting.

"Audrey figured out that the Hartigers were looking for a group of scientists they'd abandoned here. My group," Bex said. "She escaped, and she came to find us. To warn us. She figured maybe a couple of villains who left their own employees behind in another world might want to hurt us."

Frankie shook her head. Why would her parents get stranded here and then suddenly decide to seek out Bex and her group? It didn't make sense. "You lost me."

"Basically," Bex said, "your parents are assholes."

"That much we know," Jord said.

A few days ago, Frankie might have argued. They might not be top-notch parents, but she'd always assumed that sacrifice was a trade-off. That she'd one day join the ranks of the Pathbound greats and understand why they couldn't make it home when she needed them.

She'd thought she'd be happy to gain that knowledge. Impressed. Proud. Not horrified and sick.

Frankie said, "You're saying that instead of trying to figure out how to get home, my parents spent months searching for Bex and the marooned scientists. Why?"

"Why do evil villains do anything?" Bex said. "Clearly they decided to tie up some loose ends when they found themselves stuck here."

"I think there's more to it than that," Audrey said. "Bex disagrees."

"Where are the other scientists?" Frankie asked.

Bex spit into the woods. Frankie took a grim pleasure in having predicted that. "It's just been Dad and me, for years now. He was the medic. Your parents showed up here a couple months ago and kidnapped him. They'd have taken me, too, except that Audrey figured out their plan and got here first, and she made me hide in a tree."

Frankie could picture that. Audrey rowing out here on her own, finding Bex, urging her to silence. Although it was a little hard to imagine Bex shutting up for any length of time.

People like Audrey left security behind without a second thought, to save strangers. To save lives.

People like Frankie? Well.

"But why did they leave you in the first place?" Frankie asked.

"Nope," Bex said. "That's it for this information station until you reciprocate. How did you find us?"

Frankie didn't know if she should start with the drunken prince, his deranged citizens, or the giant android hulking over the other side of the lake. "It's a long story," she said.

"Full of twists and turns," Jord added.

Bex snorted. "You two are first-rate storytellers."

Might as well keep it simple. "We thought if we could find a Pathbound lab, we might be able to figure out why Rogur is dying. We tracked our way here using digital tri-oculars."

Bex threw a glance at Audrey. They seemed to be capable of full glance-only conversations. "I know exactly why this world is dying, Baby Hart. And so do your parents."

And Frankie thought she hated being called Francesca.

Bex stomped in a puddle, sending globs of mud flying up around her feet. "Your parents sent scientists here, right? Astrophysicists, geologists, botanists, and Dr. Dad. And yet somehow, they didn't think we'd catch onto the fact that the interworld bypass is bad news for this world. Well, we did. Only it turned out your parents were already aware of that detail. They brushed it off, and we threatened to blow the story open on Earth."

Frankie wasn't sure how many more Hartiger truths she could face today. "So they left you behind."

And abandoned Rogur.

Bex snapped her fingers. "There it is."

"We can find them, and your dad," Frankie said. "The people in this world think Earthen tech is magic, and that it's dying too."

"No shit," Bex said. "Another fun Hartiger manipulation."

Frankie reached for a sour response, and found she didn't have one. "Well, there's one person whose magic still works. Have you heard of Elandria?"

Bex stopped walking. She turned slowly, raising the gun again. "Elandria?"

And just like that, the conversation was booby trapped again. Like anything Frankie said might end with her hanging upside down from a tree. She glanced at Jord, who shook his head. "That's the name," he said.

Bex turned to Audrey. "She's lying. Maybe she was your friend before, but she isn't now. She's working with them."

Frankie reached out for Audrey. Bex raised the gun higher. "I don't know what she means," Frankie said. "Elandria's some legend they have here, about a wise woman who lives in a mirror. According to the prince, her name is Elandria."

"Well, that would be something," Bex said.

This time, Audrey didn't step in. She folded her arms and waited.

Audrey knew how desperately Frankie had wanted to travel between worlds, how much she'd wanted her parents to notice her. Audrey had said it herself; Frankie didn't hesitate to knock people out of her path to get what she wanted. So of course Audrey would believe Frankie capable of becoming a monster. Frankie couldn't even fault her for it.

No achievement would ever unlock Audrey's forgiveness, or her friendship, because Frankie always had an ulterior motive.

Audrey didn't consider her own gain when she'd set off to save Bex and her dad. Like Jord in Lariasc, helping those people in the prince's name. Frankie had been obsessing over how to save Rogur, true, but had she thought even once about what that would mean for the people?

She hadn't. She'd looked them in the eyes, seen their injuries, and still she thought only of herself. What *she* wanted. She'd even injured them in pursuit of it. It was no different from designing an implant to control wildlife without considering what the wider implications might be—without asking how her parents planned to use it.

If she couldn't change that, she *would* turn out like her parents.

Maybe Audrey knew that. Maybe Bex did, too.

And Jord? What did he think?

When Frankie didn't say anything, Bex shook her head. Like Frankie's silence was confirmation of guilt. "I know all about the crazy mirror lady, Baby Hart. But she hasn't got a name. And Elandria is *me*."

Frankie focused on keeping her jaw united with the rest of her face, her sluggish brain struggling to make sense of the declaration. For the first time since dropping out of the tree, Bex smiled. More of a sneer, really, and far too satisfied.

Frankie wondered what kind of prison Bex had built for traitors and Hartigers. Bex was probably picturing Frankie locked inside.

Jord spoke first. "You've been chatting with Prince Kol through a screen he thinks is a magic mirror?"

Bex stared at him. "No," she said, drawing the word into a long syllable of disdain, "I haven't spoken to Prince Kol in years, since we fled the capital right after we got marooned here."

Bex knew Kol. That was interesting.

"Elandria was my princess name when I was a little kid," Bex explained. "Before your lovely parents stranded me here, I used to dress up in floofy outfits and tell everyone I was a fairy princess, or a warrior princess, or whatever I felt like that day. But the princess's name was always Elandria."

A hundred questions. A million.

Frankie was still working on the whole Bex-as-princess image, but Jord said, "And the Hartigers knew about this game?"

Bex gestured toward Frankie. "I didn't think so, but clearly she does. Which means they've got it in a file somewhere, and she's seen it. Dad and Mom were the only ones there. Since Mom died when I was five, she's not exactly gossiping about it."

Frankie bit back a frustrated laugh. "My parents don't let me access the menus for lunch orders. I'd never heard of this world a week ago. I didn't know it existed. How would I know about your princess game?"

"Then how are you here?" Audrey asked softly.

A splinter lodged in Frankie's chest, digging painfully at her lungs. She didn't know how to convince her friend that they were both on the same side. What would Frankie do, if it turned out she couldn't? "The same way *you're* here."

"Not precisely," Jord said. "Francesca did repair the transport for the singular purpose of saving your life."

He shouldn't be defending her. He should be running away.

Audrey didn't even blink. "And since when have you trusted him? Your parents' crony?"

Jord tipped her a bow. "Thank you, Audrey. Wasn't sure you'd noticed."

"Wait. Shut up," Bex said.

A flash of moonlight, and Audrey's knives were in her hands. "Cat or bird?"

"Bird. I heard the rustle."

"I didn't bring the bow and arrows."

Both girls were already moving, melting into the thick forest shadows. If Frankie waited a beat longer, she'd lose track of them in the dark. So she trudged after them into the jungle, annoyed, vines rising up around her feet as if in protest. Jord kept pace at her side, and she found herself thankful—again— for his presence.

"This doesn't seem like a good time for a hunting detour," Frankie muttered.

The moon flickered. And then, impossibly, it went dark. As if someone had flipped a switch. Silver one moment, black the next. Even the stars, which should have twinkled all the brighter in its absence, were suddenly veiled.

Forcing herself not to panic, Frankie switched on her flashlight. Nothing. She turned it off, then on again. Still nothing. Weird.

A rustle of feathers cut through the air above them, followed by the unmistakable beat of wings. Massive ones. The air pulsed, and Jord twined his arm around hers.

Audrey knocked them back into a tree as the wingbeats descended, sending a stroke of air through the jungle before them. Frankie couldn't see her friend—she couldn't see anything—but she knew it was Audrey. And not just because the marooned girl wouldn't care if some bird pecked their eyes out. Frankie knew her friend.

"No lights," Audrey hissed between gritted teeth. "The bird can see it, even if you can't."

How? That was impossible. *Impossible.* It was so dark, Frankie might have been blind. Her eyes struggled to make sense of it.

An enormous shape crashed to the jungle floor in front of them. Audrey whirled away, blades whining through the night.

Frankie couldn't see anything. If not for the tree at her back and Jord's arm locked through hers, she might think she'd stepped through a hole in space.

"Jord," Frankie whispered, "did a bird turn off the lights?"

"So it would appear."

"That isn't possible."

"I'll inform the bird immediately."

For a moment, everything was still. A living forest's version of still, of course; leaves fluttered, creatures scurried. A sweetly rotten scent found its way to her nose, like forgotten fruit decaying in a drawer.

Frankie felt that phantom weight on her neck again. She raised a hand to brush it away.

She didn't even hear the creature move. One moment she was raising her hand, the next she had a face full of feathers. Jord's arm flew away from hers, and there were feathers everywhere, wings flapping frantically over her eyes, her nose. Her hands were trapped at her sides as feathers drowned her, tearing along her neck and into her ears.

She stumbled to the side, and the bird took her down. She tried to scramble back, but her wrist caught in the vines. She couldn't see a damn thing.

Claws ripped into her legs, feathers clogging her screams.

And then the bird let out a screaming howl. Hot liquid sprayed Frankie's face, and the weight fell away, taking the feathers with it.

A beat, and the moonlight flickered back on.

Bex and Audrey stood over her. Well, Audrey stood over her, sickle blades spotted with blood; Bex was surveying the bird, its body splayed in the dirt beside Frankie. It had midnight blue feathers, and long legs that made her think of an ostrich, only they were attached to a falcon-like form—sleek and predatory.

Bex hauled the dead bird over her shoulder. "Thanks for that. If you hadn't moved like an idiot, it might've gotten away."

Frankie stared at her, still locked to the ground. Jord appeared from farther in the jungle looking dazed, his shirt ripped at the shoulder. It must have knocked him down, too.

He stumbled over to crouch beside Frankie. "Are you all right? You're bleeding."

Her legs were scratched from its talons, her pants in tatters. But it hadn't pierced anything crucial. "Mostly bird blood, I think. How can a bird block light like that?"

"Don't know, don't care," Bex said. "It's one of the deadlier predators out here. Luckily, it's also tasty."

Frankie cared. Was it some an imitation creature, like the androids? Those feathers had felt real enough, and Bex planned to eat the thing, so probably not. Maybe it emitted some kind of a pulse to trick the eyes. But how?

Mom was the biologist. She probably knew.

Frankie looked at Audrey. "How did you learn to—when did you—with the knives—"

Audrey offered her a hand. "It's been a long six months."

Frankie and Jord followed her back to the path, where Bex waited with the bird slung over her shoulder, squarely blocking their progress.

"Really?" Frankie said, working hard to calm her breath. There were feathers in her hair, in her clothes. Her face felt sticky, no matter how much she wiped it with her sleeve. She needed a shower. She needed to get out of this world. "You're still not going to help us, after that?"

Bex didn't so much as twitch a muscle. "I'm pretty sure we just helped you not to die."

"We would understand if you don't want to bring us to your home," Jord said.

Frankie was one disaster away from losing her last scrap of determination, and Jord was still playing the diplomat. It was impressive. She was impressed. With *Jord.*

It was still a new feeling. She thought again of the way he'd held her in the lab, the way his arms had closed around her in comfort. She hadn't wanted to scramble away from him. If anything, she'd been tempted to stay there.

"Neither of us has slept in nearly a full day," he continued. "We've impersonated royalty and rowed across a lake, been attacked by killer wrecking balls and... whatever that bird was. We need to rest before we can sort this out."

No kidding. Frankie didn't think she could stay on her feet another minute.

Bex and Audrey exchanged a look. "Your call," Audrey said.

"OK," Frankie said. "This is ridiculous. Audrey. You're my best—"

"Like I said," Audrey interrupted. "It's been a long six months. Bex and I have spent half of that surviving, together. And she's right. You know something you shouldn't, which means you might be working with your parents now. Just like you always wanted."

Frankie had wanted it, before. More than anything. But she was desperate to believe she hadn't realized what a seat at the Hartiger table would actually mean. She'd never anticipated this kind of cruelty, this deception. Yet hadn't she known there was more to Pathbound, with the secret floors and the square so often dotted with protesters?

She couldn't bear to look at Jord, to see Audrey's doubt reflected in his face. She couldn't bear to imagine what he was going to say, when he discovered how complicit she already was.

Audrey's eyes were sad, but Frankie knew that expression. Her friend wasn't going to budge. "I trust Bex's judgement."

Bex stared at Jord, as if she could bore through his skull and read his thoughts. Apparently, this came down to his trustworthiness.

Finally, Bex tucked the gun into her back pocket. Frankie

would have informed her of a number of potential safety issues with that decision, but at this point she wasn't sure she cared.

Bex wouldn't listen, anyway. She was already walking. "Let's go."

A low buzz had taken up residence in Frankie's brain, and she stumbled every few steps. Her legs were smarting almost as much as her hands, now. Lovely. Jord offered an arm for support, and they helped each other along through the jungle.

Bex ducked beneath a swath of branches, and they emerged into a pool of moonlight where the trail ended beside a cliff with scrubby foliage peeking over the top edge.

Frankie was getting tired of cliffs.

"Why are we stopping?" Frankie asked. "Are you going to scream at us again?"

"Not ruling it out for the future, but no. I'm stopping because we're here."

No way Frankie would be scaling that cliff tonight. Or ever. But Bex moved in the opposite direction, crouching to slide her hand beneath a flat rock at the bottom of the pile.

A trap door.

Bex hopped inside and disappeared. Audrey went next.

Frankie approached more cautiously. A light burned at the bottom of the vertical passage, illuminating the other girls as they descended. It was steady enough to be electric, if Frankie dared to hope for that. The tunnel was wider than a manhole in New York. More like one of those huge drain pipes where TV detectives always found bodies. Though it was hard to tell from here, she estimated the depth at about one story. She'd need a watch scan to be certain.

"Are you looking for the serial number?" Jord asked. "No doubt it's Pathbound made."

Frankie wouldn't usually hesitate, even in the face of dank

tunnels and long drops. "We're supposed to go underground with people who hate me, no questions asked?"

Jord brushed a hand over Frankie's shoulder as he stepped around her, his touch so light it might have been a mistake. "Audrey doesn't hate you. And I don't see that we've got a choice."

Without waiting for a response, he started down the ladder.

He wasn't wrong. Frankie followed, making it a few rungs before Bex called, "Don't leave the rock open, Baby Hart."

Her legs were going to kill her, if her hands didn't. Frankie climbed back up to cap the passage with the door-slash-rock, then continued after the others. The metal wall radiated cold. Streams of water trickled down the sides. It all smelled of mold and sharp rust, and the ladder was slippery under her feet.

Everything in this world involved tunnels and heights.

They followed Audrey and Bex into the light.

The room was eerily familiar. Titanium walls, circular workstation of computers, garage door leading to shadowy corners.

It was the transport control center. In miniature, and laced with rust. No transport dock, of course. Just a hallway. Storage or labs, or maybe both. Bouquets of wildflowers were stuffed into tin cans around the room, purple and orange blossoms blended artfully beside strands of green. Audrey's doing, surely; Frankie couldn't picture Bex gathering wildflowers. Though she also couldn't picture Bex playing princess, so who could tell.

Frankie was still processing the strangeness of the environment when Bex spoke again. "I guess there is one other person who knew about Elandria. Not that it helps."

At this point, Frankie's expectations for actual information were practically nonexistent. Regardless, her brain was too tired to process anything more complicated than *food* or *rest*. Still, she managed to ask, "Who?"

Bex dropped the bird in the corner, then unhooked her belt and tossed it on a table, where it landed with a clatter. "My aunt Liz."

TWENTY-FIVE
FRANKIE

Frankie's brain buzzed. "Liz," she repeated. "Like... engineer-genius Liz?"

"Our Liz's last name is Han, if that helps," Jord said.

Frankie could hardly remember her own last name, let alone Liz's. At least Jord was still functioning, somehow.

"That's our last name," Bex said. "Your know her?"

"She works for Pathbound."

"My aunt doesn't know about Pathbound."

"She lives beneath a rock in the middle of the ocean?" Jord asked.

Bex rolled her eyes. "I mean, she didn't know Dad worked for them. She knew he was on a top secret mission and we'd be gone a few years. They fought about it. She tried to get me to stay with her."

Jord looked at Frankie. "How long has Liz worked for Pathbound?"

"She started when I was fourteen. About three years? A little more?"

"What does she do there?" Bex asked.

"She's the transport operator," Frankie said.

For a moment, they all stared at each other. Clearly, no one in this room had any answers.

"Can those computers talk to Earth?" Jord asked quietly.

Bex shrugged. "In theory. Your girlfriend's grandparents established the first control center here, and moved to the mainland later. It took us forever to find this place. Good shelter, you know?" She fidgeted with one of her cloth pockets, worrying the fabric between her fingers. "We never reestablished communications, after."

Frankie could. These computers were dinosaurs, and she'd always preferred gears to circuits, but... She could probably establish communication. Get in touch with Liz.

End this.

Audrey was here. Bex, too. Maybe they could return to Earth without Mom and Dad. Leave them behind to deal with what they'd wrought in Rogur.

Her great-grandparents had saved Earth from flood and ruin. Her grandparents had broken the barrier between universes. Mom and Dad were supposedly dedicating their lives to science and discovery, too. Not implanting kids with paralytics and marooning people in other worlds.

Were there any true heroes among the Hartigers? Or were they all monsters?

A sick feeling drifted across the rest of Frankie's pain. It couldn't be a coincidence that Liz's brother and niece had gotten stuck here, and that she'd then left one of her fancy jobs to endure the Hartigers' abuse.

No need to start blasting theories into the room, though. Especially theories that implicated the gun-toting girl's auntie.

Frankie shrugged off the pack. If her shoulders could have groaned, they would. "I can reestablish communication," she said. "We'll find a way to get in touch with Liz, and she'll tell us what the hell is going on."

"I'm in favor of that plan," Jord said. "But first, maybe we ought to wash off the blood."

FRANKIE WOKE with her face buried in her arms, the corner of the keyboard digging into her cheek.

She sat up, easing her arms gently off the table. Her muscles felt raw, like she'd laid into her flesh with a meat tenderizer, from her wrists to her neck. At least her arms had stopped shaking.

Her hands radiated a whole different kind of pain. Searing, with a side of stabbing. Jord had forced her to change her bandages and wash the blisters before she sat down to work, which was probably a good thing. She had no interest in experiencing otherworldly infections.

She stood and stretched, looking around the mini control room. It was hard to keep track of time down here. Audrey and Bex were nowhere to be seen, nor the impossible bird's carcass. Jord was sleeping in the far corner, his head tilted at an awkward angle. A single blonde curl dipped across his forehead, shockingly out of place. She found herself resisting the sudden, inexplicable urge to brush it out of his face and tuck it among the others.

Asleep, he looked so young. He spent so much energy trying to be the opposite.

He'd kept appearing last night, while she tried to work. First with the bandages. Then with smoked fish and fruit. He'd even made himself a smoothie, somehow. She hadn't been able to muster the strength to tease him about it.

And then... well, then she must have fallen asleep. She

rubbed her eyes. She had to be close to cracking the interworld signal.

The computers were old. In a classroom on Earth, she'd have relished the chance to play with them. Here, urgency and fatigue crowded out any feelings of fun or adventure. The deeper she dove, though, the more the foundation of the code aligned with contemporary Pathbound systems. The ones they used on Earth now had just evolved.

She had no idea how long she'd been working when the buzzing started.

It took her several beats to emerge from her work fully enough to connect the vibrating sensation with the watch on her wrist. On Earth, the thing tickled her with constant notifications. In Rogur, it had only been silent.

And now, someone was calling. Frankie got up and walked swiftly down the hallway, casting a glance at Jord before ducking into the kitchen where he'd apparently made their dinner. The room was dingy, with spiderwebs bunched on the ceiling and spots of mold along the edges of the floor.

But the shelves were packed with food, and it smelled like pineapple. Not totally bad. Jord had indeed found a blender, which he'd rinsed and propped upside down on the edge of the sink, a choice that felt strangely normal. Domestic.

Frankie accepted the call.

When her father's face appeared on the augmented-reality screen above her wrist, she wasn't even surprised.

For months, she'd been staring at the same handful of photos of her parents in the news, their lives and work celebrated through a few carefully selected moments. Ribbon cuttings and state dinners, black dresses and bow ties. Dad's face looked sharper now, as though Rogur had carved his round into points. Even with all she'd learned today—and she had a feeling it was the tip of the Hartiger-conspiracy iceberg—her heart twisted in her chest at the sight of him. And suddenly, she was just the little girl who'd broken her leg and wanted her parents to come see her, with that same ball of salty emotion choking her throat.

He seemed to be giving Frankie the same assessment. "Francesca," he said, finally. "What are you doing in Rogur?"

She wanted to laugh. "I came to rescue you."

"By yourself?"

Of all the responses... But then, her parents weren't the ones who needed rescuing, were they? Something nudged at her mind. A warning.

Frankie shoved the sad little girl deep inside. She sat up straighter. "Yeah," she said. "I'm alone."

Frankie had always been a terrible liar. Great at subterfuge, at avoiding the truth. Terrible at outright lies. She avoided them.

The wrinkle between Dad's eyebrows deepened. As soon as he got back to Earth, he'd be ordering an injection to smooth that out. "We're almost done here. We'll come find you."

It was embarrassing to admit that some part of her had still expected him to be impressed with her accomplishment. He didn't seem to care, in the slightest, that she'd been resourceful enough to launch the transport on her own, to come all this way in search of them.

Mom would care. She'd want a full report on the security breaches that had allowed it to happen.

Frankie could almost see herself, her inventions, through their eyes now. Like she'd shifted angles on her own life, or sharpened the focus. They didn't want big plans like the ones she'd been designing. They wanted little ideas with big impact. Six months ago, she'd have been thrilled to finally understand that she held the key. Would she have opened up a lab of her own? Started inventing awful machines?

She didn't know how to do better. She'd figure it out.

It wasn't too late to become her own person. Even if that meant defying generations of Hartigers.

"How did you know to call me?" she asked. She toed the peeling edge of the linoleum, wondering what color it had been when they'd first carted it over from Earth. It was brown now, with tinges of yellow.

"Our drones spotted you in the woods near the transport dock, a few days ago."

Which meant he had to know she was lying about Jord. Her throat itched, and she clamped it shut, willing herself not to cough. Maybe the drone had only seen her. Maybe it had been too far away to catch both of them on camera.

Maybe she had no idea what kind of game she was supposed to be playing.

"We've been tracking any live tech since then, hoping to make contact," Dad continued. "There was an artifact near the forest at one point, but it wasn't you."

The seeing stone. "It's not there anymore?"

"It's in Lariasc."

Frankie bit her lip. Had Jord found the stone and pocketed it without her noticing? He did have a tendency to do that kind of thing. But why would he pick it up after throwing it away? And why leave it in Lariasc?

"Have you met anyone on the island?" Dad asked.

"No one."

"But you found the bunker."

She licked her lips. She could claim the oculars had led her here. If the bunker wasn't programmed into them, she'd be caught in a lie. And if it was, Dad might guess Jord was with her—though maybe he already had. The only thing she knew for certain was that she needed to protect him.

It was a weird feeling.

What would they do to him, if they found out he'd come? "I also launched the transport," she said. "Give me a little credit, Dad."

But it wasn't the kind of credit he was ready to offer. He looked up, past the screen, as though for confirmation on the acceptability of her answer. Frankie stomped on the linoleum corner to see if it would crack. It didn't. "Mom's with you, isn't she? Can I talk to her?"

Dad's eyes snapped to the camera. "No," he said. "No, no, I'm alone."

He was as bad a liar as she was. Family trait, clearly. "Yeah. OK."

"Stay where you are," he said. "We'll be a few more days. Then we'll go home."

"Dad," she said. "What happened? How did you end up here?"

"Stay put, Francesca."

The screen disappeared. Frankie blinked at the blank space, feeling strangely empty. It was hard to know what direction to face, without a scheme to impress her parents.

What were Dad and Mom doing, for a few more days? Why had they kidnapped Bex's father? The only thing she knew for certain was that she couldn't just stay here and let them find Jord.

She had to talk to Liz.

Frankie returned to the computers, wishing for an actual seeing stone that could tell her what the hell was going on. Or barring that, a computer manual—and several tons of hot coffee.

Liz would help them get home. Frankie would take Jord up on his offer to run Pathbound together.

And her parents? She just needed to find the will to leave them behind.

TWENTY-SIX
FRANKIE

When a signal icon blinked green in the lower left corner some hours later, Frankie thought she had it. She jumped out of her chair, knocking it to the floor.

A second later, the icon faded to orange. OK. Orange was better than red. Probably.

"I take it something good happened?"

Frankie wrenched her eyes from the screen, surprised to find that Jord was not only awake, but bathed as well. His hair was damp, and, so shocking, he had another smoothie in his hand. It was deep purple, like the outside of an eggplant, which Frankie sincerely hoped it was not. An eggplant smoothie would represent a new level of disgusting.

Bex and Audrey had returned, too. They sat against the wall with plates of food in their laps, shoulders touching as they ate. Frankie considered asking whether they'd fried up some killer bird, then decided she'd rather not know.

If she told them about Dad's call, Bex would freak out before Frankie finished talking, and they'd waste hours on convincing her not to shoot the smartwatch.

And Jord? What would he say?

She should tell him about it. And she would. As soon as they found a private moment. As soon as she was sure the information wouldn't make him faint, or turn on her.

Frankie went back to her code. After this, she'd be seeing blinking cursors on the inside of her eyelids for the rest of her life. She really, really preferred gears to computers.

"I thought so," she said, "but not quite. Yet."

Jord came to stand beside her at the desk. He'd definitely showered, and they definitely had some kind of soap here. He smelled all fresh. She wanted to punch him out of pure jealousy. Of course, if he'd interrupted her work to suggest she take a shower, she'd have punched him even harder.

She was starting to understand what he meant when he said he couldn't win with her.

He pointed to an icon on the other monitor. "What's this, though?"

"I haven't been working on that side."

"It looks like a camera."

"Unless it's a signal icon with pretty little bars, I don't care."

Jord bent to touch the screen.

"Stop," she said. "You're going to mess it up."

"I don't think so."

Frankie swiveled her chair to face him, annoyed. But the sharp words dropped out of her mouth when she saw what he'd pulled up.

A quilt of images flickered across the second monitor, instantly recognizable as live scenes from the island. Frankie hadn't noticed any cameras yesterday, though she must have passed them. The screen showed their rowboat, still tied to its tree, and the chain link fence where they'd met Bex. More pictures flipped by, too many to inventory—fields and beaches, trees and inlets—interrupted by an occasional black patch. Understandable, after all this time. Probably pecked out by light-killing birds. She would have expected more outages, honestly.

"OK," she said, turning back to her screen. "That's good. That means I restored another piece of the network. I just have to figure out how to patch to the interworld signal."

"How fast can you do that?"

"You've been waiting all night. Suddenly there's a dead-line?" The thought twisted guilt into her stomach, since she knew Dad would be on the way soon. In a few days, though. They had time.

"To put it mildly."

When Frankie didn't budge, Jord took hold of her chair and rolled her to the security screen. A well-placed kick, she thought. Or permanent smoothie confiscation. "Yes," she said, "there are coconuts here. Probably monkeys, too. What do you—"

He tapped his index finger on the screen. Before the wide-angled view of the beach blinked away, Frankie caught sight of a ship on the water.

Jord had the sense not to say 'I told you so' before flipping the screen back to get a closer look at the ship.

It was as big as a pirate ship in a movie, and it wasn't passing by. Its sails were down, masts jutting into the grainy sky like the trunks in the dead forest.

Worse, she could make out several rowboats on their way to shore. "Which enemy do we think it is?"

"Guessing it's the royal one."

Prince Kol had hardly seemed capable of leading his soldiers to chase after a couple of Earthens. Though his captain seemed grounded enough. Or maybe the citizens from Lariasc had followed after all.

They sure had managed to make a lot of enemies in a short space of time. "This is because of your face," she said.

"A perennial problem."

"What's going on?" Audrey asked.

Frankie rolled the chair to her work station. "We have visitors."

Bex got to her feet so fast her plate clattered to the floor. "We know how to deal with visitors."

Audrey grabbed Bex's hand and pulled her back. "Bex, you had visitor protocol when there were other people to support you. Your father wouldn't want you to try. We should stay here."

Visitor protocol. Frankie was afraid to mention how Path-bound-y that sounded.

"And let them ambush us?"

"We're hidden."

"We didn't exactly cover our tracks," Jord said.

Frankie buried her head in her work and tried to tune them out. She'd strengthened the island's network, which meant it should be able to see the interworld signal. Shouldn't it? The problem was, she'd never located an interworld signal before, not like this. But maybe it was a matter of...

Green light. And beautiful, beautiful green bars.

Frankie pushed the button to call Pathbound. The others fell silent as the system dialed, and Frankie held her breath. For an agonizing moment, she almost sympathized with Prince Kol's Elandria-induced rage.

Then, the screen dissolved into a whirlpool of silver as it had in the fortress, and Liz's face faded onto the screen. Behind her, the Pathbound control center gleamed.

Home.

"What the hell, Frankie?" Liz said.

Bex hurtled her body onto the platform and shoved

Frankie's chair aside. She knelt in front of the desk, bouncing, her chin in line with the table. "Liz!"

Frankie tried to scoot into the picture. Bex didn't budge. "We don't have time for—"

"Bex," Liz said. "You're alive!"

Liz looked like she wanted to leap through the screen and hug her niece. It should have been a private reunion, and usually Frankie would have been thrilled—or, OK, less impatient—to give them the time to laugh or cry, or whatever reunited family members liked to do. She wouldn't even be jealous of the tears in Liz's eyes, or the fact that she didn't seem to care that Frankie was alive, too.

Frankie still would have given them all the time in the worlds, if not for the screens to the left of Bex's head. They showed a dinghy hitting the shallows, and soldiers jumping into the water to drag it over the sand.

Frankie edged Bex to the side. "Unless you want this to be the last time you two see each other, we need to talk."

Liz wiped her eyes. "Where's Russ?"

Bex looked at Frankie. What, Frankie was supposed to tell the story? Tap into some psychic connection with her parents to locate Bex's father?

Thankfully, Jord leaned over Frankie's shoulder, bracing one hand on the back of the chair, the other on the armrest beside her. "Hello, Liz," he said. "Quick question. Have you been talking to a prince here who, funny story, looks exactly like me?"

Liz's smile faded. "Jord."

"Yes, I survived as well. Sorry to disappoint."

"No. I'm glad you're OK. Both of you. That was really stupid, Frankie. What were you thinking?"

"Um, I was thinking I'd take a jaunt to supposedly safe Suhainn and rescue Audrey and my parents, since no one believed me that they were alive. Except you. Of course, you kept that to yourself and let everyone think I'd lost it."

Liz leaned closer to the camera. "I had to send your parents to Rogur, Frankie, and I had to do it with witnesses."

Liz not only knew that Frankie's parents were alive. She knew where they were, because she'd sent them here. Frankie shook her head, incapable of speech. Even her thoughts were stuttering, unable—unwilling—to comprehend the betrayal.

Luckily, Audrey was still capable of speaking. "Because people tend to ask questions when half a dozen high-profile celebrities go missing," she said.

Liz nodded. "Return without them, and you've got a scandal."

Used. All of them. Audrey's expression was carefully still. Processing. Jord covered his mouth with his hand and gave his head a little shake.

Liz took a deep breath. Let it out. "I had to keep my distance the last few months, Frankie. I just... I'm not a great liar. You'd have seen through me."

"Give yourself more credit," Jord said. "I'd say you're quite an excellent liar."

"I worked at Pathbound for three years, waiting on the right moment," Liz said. "They went off on that tour, finally, and I made them a deal. I played a recording in Michael and Cindy's helmets during the launch: find my brother and his team, and I'd bring them home. No harm. No scandal. I reprogrammed the launch system to send the transport to Rogur. I'm sorry, Frankie. I didn't... You weren't supposed to know how to launch the transport."

Indignation and hurt burned in her throat like a poison. "Of course I can launch the freaking transport," Frankie said. "You should know that. You've helped with practically every one of my plans."

"Yeah, but Frankie, your schemes never quite... They don't tend to come together."

Except the evil ones, apparently.

Frankie had never had a single ally at Pathbound. Liz had attended Frankie's school events, and watched every season of *Mars Colony* with her—why? Because Frankie was a nuisance and a spy, and Liz had wanted to keep her close?

It wasn't fair to be angry. Frankie was, anyway.

But Jord said, "You clearly don't know her at all."

His voice was so quiet, Frankie doubted Liz could hear. But his lips were in line with Frankie's ear, close enough for the words to warm her skin.

And then she realized. He hadn't only spoken softly; he'd spoken in Suhainnan. The words weren't meant for Liz. They were for Frankie.

When she looked at him, he held her gaze, his brown eyes bright and clear. He'd anticipated her plan in time to follow her to the transport dock because he'd known, or suspected, that she could launch the transport whenever she wanted. Of everyone at Pathbound, it was Jord who always knew what Frankie was capable of. The realization was practically blinding, a flare against the night sky.

One ally, then. She had one ally. And she was responsible for his chains.

Confusion bubbled into her throat, dissolving the hurt. Still, Jord didn't look away. Maybe he didn't think she'd turn into her parents, after all.

She'd have to prove him right. And get the implant out of his neck, as soon as she possibly could.

"Nice to see you two getting along," Liz said. Like she cared.

Frankie swallowed hard and shifted her focus to the screen. "And your wise woman act with the prince?"

"Your parents went radio silent, so I connected directly to Kol. He's not always reliable, but he's better than nothing."

Funny. Frankie was pretty sure Kol would say the same about Liz-landria.

On the other screen, the prince in question patrolled the tree line beside his captain. He'd made the journey, after all. They'd find the path any minute, and they'd follow the all-too-obvious trail to the bunker.

"You need to get us out of here," Frankie said. "This world is falling apart."

She could stay to fix it. Brainstorm solutions, help these people. But maybe that was better done from the safety of Path-bound Tower. She'd planned to enlist her parents' assistance, but it was hard to picture them caring.

"All right," Liz said. "Where's Russ?"

"The Hartigers took him," Bex said. "A month ago."

Right. Leaving her parents behind now would mean leaving Bex's father, and the rest of the celebrities as well. But couldn't they return with reinforcements?

Liz consulted something on her desk. A map. An oracle, perhaps. "They should have made it to the transport by now."

"Like I said," Frankie said, "world turned upside down. Gods descending. Or androids awaking. Whatever. You didn't do that, did you?"

"No," Liz admitted. "I talked Kol into leaving Caisrach before they could murder him."

How magnanimous of her. "Well in case you haven't noticed, we're traveling with someone who looks exactly like Kol," Frankie said. "It's not the safest."

"I can't explain that part," Liz said. "Believe me, I've tried. But I'm sorry, Frankie. I won't send the transport to Earth until you find my brother and the other scientists."

"The others are dead," Bex said.

Liz let out a breath. Frankie didn't have time to soothe treacherous souls today. "You're going to leave your niece in danger?"

Liz's expression hardened. "Bex can help. She'll stay with you and help save Russ. Confirm you're telling the truth when you all get to the transport. Bex? Can you do that?"

Bex nodded, her face serious. As if this wasn't completely insane.

Frankie's hands smarted as she gripped the armrests. "We're not going to live long enough to get to the transport. If you—"

"No way," Liz said. "Cindy and Michael have had plenty of time to hatch another scheme. I'm sorry, Frankie, but having you in Rogur? It's extra leverage."

Don't be so sure about that, Frankie thought. So much for the idea of avoiding that family reunion.

"I'll do it," Bex said. "I'll find Dad."

Liz smiled. "Good girl. Frankie—"

Frankie ended the call. She didn't want to hear whatever instructions or apologies Liz had to offer. Not when Liz was holding them all hostage.

Before Frankie could say a word, Bex attacked.

TWENTY-SEVEN

FRANKIE

Bex slammed into Frankie so hard that Frankie toppled off her chair, cracking her head against the table on her way to the floor. Bex landed on top of her, fist connecting with Frankie's jaw before Jord and Audrey lifted her off. She fought them, kicking so hard that Frankie raised her arms to protect her smarting face in case one of Bex's feet managed to get close to her nose.

Or Bex's teeth, which were bared and looked perfectly capable of ripping into Frankie's flesh. Nice girl.

"Bring her back," Bex screamed, struggling hard against Jord and Audrey. "Bring her back!"

Frankie sat up and rubbed her jaw. "Yeah, I'll get right on that."

"I didn't say goodbye."

"Oh, well. Sad for you."

"It's been seven years. She's my family."

"Your family betrayed us."

The irony of that statement didn't escape her.

Bex's whole body was quivering, tears streaming down her cheeks. "To save me."

Frankie gave her best scoff, along with the most exaggerated eye roll she could muster. It was hard to maintain one's dignity after getting punched in the face. "If she wanted to save you, she'd help us get home. She used Audrey. Now she's using you, and me."

Bex lunged so hard her feet practically left the ground, but Audrey and Jord still had a firm grip on her. "She did what she had to do. You'd do the same."

Frankie stretched out her arms. "Wrong. My family got lost here, and I came after them without using other people to do it."

Bex tilted her head in Jord's direction, still fighting. "And him? You manipulated him into playing bodyguard. Admit it."

"I came on my own," Jord said.

Frankie got to her feet, and the room tilted. She shoved the pain back, as best she could. Away. "You see Hartiger, and you think you know what that means. You're not the only victim in the room."

"Fuck you," Bex said. "You, a victim? Mommy and Daddy are oh-so-mean to you?"

Frankie hadn't been thinking of herself. Her gaze shifted to Jord, though he was focused on keeping Bex from slipping out of his grasp. Had Liz known about his alteration? Was that why she'd kept Frankie close? What else did she know? A lot, presumably, if she'd found this place.

Frankie wasn't going to defend herself to Bex.

"We're all stuck here now," Jord said. "We need to work together."

Bex twisted to give him a disdainful look. "Like you're so neutral. Liz is right to use your girlfriend as leverage, and I will, too, if I have a chance. When it comes down to it, Hartigers side with Hartigers. They'll choose her. She'll choose them."

Frankie clenched her fists at her sides, blisters be damned. It wasn't true. Whatever her parents did, whatever they offered, she wouldn't side with them. She could save Jord, save Audrey. She could save the world they'd screwed up so badly.

She'd definitely made the right decision, keeping Dad's call to herself.

There wasn't any point in arguing with Bex, or trying to prove herself. She'd only ever see Frankie's last name. Had Jord really managed to look beyond it? Bex had been marooned in Rogur, and he was a prisoner on Earth. He might be softening toward her, but it was hard to imagine he could really side with a Hartiger. No matter what he told Liz.

And yet... he'd had his chance to go. Jord could have had the implant removed the second he'd signed the paperwork to take over Pathbound. He could have ordered a transport launch to bring him home.

Instead, he'd waited to make a deal with Frankie. He acted like he planned to stay.

Audrey whispered into Bex's ear, still gripping her arm. Bex pulled away, her rage beginning to deflate. "I don't need reassuring," she said. "I don't need any of you."

Audrey flinched and let go. When Bex didn't immediately launch herself at Frankie, Jord released her as well. For a second, Frankie still thought she might have to dive under the table. Bex paced away, agitated.

"You promised Liz you'd help find your father," Jord said to her. "How will you do that if the prince captures us?"

For a moment, even Frankie had forgotten about Kol. She whipped her head to look at the screen, so quickly she almost lost her balance. The Prince was no longer on the beach. She watched as the images blinked past. Flick, flick, flick. Beach, jungle, prison. No Kol. No soldiers.

"They won't find the entrance," Bex said, but she didn't sound certain.

A hollow clang shook the bunker, followed by the echo of feet clambering down the ladder. A lot of feet.

"They found the entrance," Audrey said.

Bex was already moving toward the back passage. When it came down to it, Jord was right; they *were* in this together. Frankie, Jord, and Audrey ran to keep up with Bex as footsteps resounded through the halls, boots on metal.

At the end of the corridor, Bex beckoned them into a kind of barracks, with bunks lined up on the far wall. When Frankie entered—managing to hide her surprise when Bex allowed it— she could see it made sense. This room was sealed off from the others by an iron door that locked with the spin of a wheel. Like something from a ship.

The room contained no food or provisions that Frankie could see, and no other exits. Excellent.

Once they were all inside, Bex shut the door and gave the wheel a spin. Safe. Cornered.

"Tell me you have more guns," Jord said.

Bex rolled her eyes. "Like any of you would know how to fire them."

Not wrong.

"Bex," Audrey said.

Bex sighed and showed them the gun's open chamber. No bullets. "Happy?"

"Yesterday I'd have said yes," Jord said. He looked around the room, as if he thought he might be able to assemble a plan from a dozen straw-filled mattresses, a buzzing light bulb, and a sink. Not even Frankie could fool herself that they might be able to rig an escape out of so little. They were trapped.

A knock sounded on the other side of the door. More of a 'we're here for tea' kind of knock than 'police, open up.' Jord pulled Frankie toward the bunks, as if standing on the far side of the room with Audrey and Bex would save them.

"Chasing you is exceedingly boring," Kol said through the door, "and Reyche is stingy when it comes to drinks. Please, come out."

God, even his voice was like Jord's.

"What's he saying?" Bex asked.

"He says he's been chasing them," Audrey said. "It's boring. That's... a strange thing to say?"

"That's Prince Kol," Frankie said.

"This sounds like a lovely interlude," Kol said. "But you needn't argue about my birthday gifts. I've got a list of suggestions, if you'd like to come out and see it."

"Let me guess," Frankie said, in Suhainnan-slash-Roguran. "Drinks, drinks, and more drinks."

Kol tsked. "More credit. I'd also like a new catapult, and for someone to get the Hartigers out of my godsdamned world."

Audrey translated for Bex, who muttered something about Prince Kol having the right idea. "I feel like I'm on the wrong side of the door," she said. "By the way, he understands English. It's like a badge of honor here. Faker."

"Who is that?" Kol said. "You sound interesting."

Another voice joined Kol's, louder and deeper. Reyche. "We can wait you out, however long it takes."

"Reyche," Kol said, "is that any way to invite people to a party? They're going to think we're aggressive and rude."

Apparently they knew about good cop, bad cop in Rogur. Frankie licked her lips, thinking. She crossed to the door, the ghost of an idea swirling through her brain. "And Elandria," she said. "You'd also like to find Elandria, wouldn't you?"

"Darling, you read my mind."

Frankie wrapped her hands around the wheel and started to turn it.

"What's she doing?" Bex said.

Jord ran up beside her and grabbed the wheel, holding it in place. "Let's consider this for a moment."

Frankie looked up at him, too aware of his closeness, too aware that he would actually listen to her. That he'd been her ally all along. "We're not getting out of here," she whispered. "If we survive, we'll be prisoners again. We could end up ten feet from the transport, but there's no way to get out of this world without Bex's father. We have no idea how to find him."

Jord's gaze bored into hers, as if he could see the wheels turning in her mind. "You think Kol might help us if we surrender."

"Surrender?" Bex said, stalking over to the door to hover behind them. She was like an annoying bug, her stinger always primed. "Are you out of your mind?"

Frankie glared at Jord. "You couldn't have said that in Suhainnan?"

"Audrey would have understood, anyway."

She tried to pry his fingers off the wheel. He held on fast. "Let go."

"At least make a deal with him first," he said.

Bex barked a laugh. "Because he's obligated to follow through?"

He wasn't. But Frankie didn't think Kol would renege. He needed them. Besides, everyone still seemed to think Frankie could be used as leverage against her parents. Jord might have a better sense of the truth, but Kol could surely be convinced otherwise.

Jord was still watching her, searching her face for answers. He had to know that there was only one way out of this room.

Still, he said, "Francesca, you and Kol might have a common goal now. But you want very different end results."

Frankie leaned in toward Jord's ear, the way he'd done with her earlier. When he put himself between her and her plans, he won. Every time. She had to make him understand. "I need you to trust me," she said. "We need allies. Please."

Jord let out a breath that might have been a silent laugh, dropping his chin toward his chest. He said something in Suhainnan that made Audrey laugh. A curse, Frankie assumed.

With a shake of his head, Jord let go of the wheel.

TWENTY-EIGHT

KOL

Kol didn't quite understand why the Hartiger girl had insisted on stopping at this dreary, leaf-infested building before leaving the island. She claimed to be running an experiment that might save Rogur, leading him to expect to see something like the glittery spaces he'd glimpsed as a child, when the Hartigers had visited as honored advisors to the crown. He remembered his mother, straight-backed and stern—as she had been, before the plague—looking over Cindy Hartiger's shoulder and listening to the woman's scientific findings.

The Hartigers brought with them bright lights, impossible potions, and tools as sharp as their lies.

This place, on the other hand, featured a rather large silver ball. Swinging back and forth above a pit of sand.

Kol could not imagine what Frankie found illuminating about it. She measured the lines in the sand, darted to the mysterious markings on the walls, and noted something on a sheet of parchment before racing back to the swinging pendulum.

Kol's twin watched every move the girl made, as though she

might shatter into a million pieces if he blinked too hard. But seeing as Kol was doing his best not to watch Reyche in the same manner, he couldn't rationalize so much as an ounce of judgment, even to himself. The captain had begun this little detour by standing a close guard over the girl and enacting his best glare. When she noticed, she set him to work counting the lines in the sand.

Kol had not decided yet if she actually needed the count, or if she was just getting Reyche out of her hair. Either way, he noted the strategy for later use.

The tall, beautiful Earthen girl watched Frankie as well, though less obviously than Kol's twin. Kol couldn't begin to guess what their history might be.

And then there was the other girl, the one with the choppy hair who'd shadowed the tall one until Kol lost track of her whereabouts. That girl watched everyone. Like she was planning a murder, but had not yet determined whose. It was unnerving. Where had she disappeared to?

He turned, thinking to find her skulking in the shadows—or scuttled away to her hole in the ground—and startled when he found her standing not three inches from his shoulder.

"What'd you do to get kicked out of Caisrach?" she said. "Set another dog loose in the kitchen?"

Kol had been forming a remark involving the penalties for sneaking up on princes, to hide how badly she'd surprised him. Her words froze the joke on his tongue. "Bex?"

She grinned. A cat's smile. "Didn't think you remembered."

They'd only been friends for a few months, the memories blurred by the whirling pace of childhood. Still, he'd often wondered what had happened to the girl who helped him nick Earthen sweets from the Hartigers when they came. She'd always aimed for something called chocolate, and while that was well enough, Kol had favored the way taffy adhered to his teeth and puckered his mouth.

And they had indeed set the hounds loose on the kitchens. Though that had been an accident. Mostly.

"I very nearly didn't remember," he admitted. "I assumed you'd found a way home after the Hartigers... Scorched earth, you've been here all this time?"

"You guys weren't too excited about Earthens after the Hartigers left. So we figured we should find a place to hide."

Kol grimaced. "I never would have... That is, I don't think my parents would... I'm sorry."

"Where are they? Your parents?"

Kol tried to keep his gaze level with hers and failed, dropping it to his feet. His boots could certainly use a polish. And several patches. "Plague. About a year ago. Bit more."

"You're the king now?"

"I didn't take the title. 'Prince' feels more fitting, does it not?"

He should have taken the title, and scheduled a coronation. He'd still been in mourning when the gods had descended. It was no wonder some of the people connected their wrath with his sudden rise to power.

Kol wasn't sure he believed in gods anymore. Just Hartigers.

The current Hartiger-in-residence dropped to the sand to pore over the numbers she'd made on the parchment. Jord watched her, and Kol noted a tremor in his twin's hands. How quickly he tried to hide it.

"Do people still call you the foundling prince?" Bex asked.

"I believe they replaced it with 'the prince who was nearly murdered by gods,'" he said, continuing to watch Jord. Because it was convenient, the conversation being so awkward—but also because in addition to the hands, Jord was not looking entirely well. Off balance, somehow, and pale, though certainly they both suffered from excessive ghostliness to begin with.

Bex didn't respond, which likely meant she expected a real answer to her question. Tiresome, really. "They still call me the foundling prince," he said. "They want me to abdicate because of it, in fact. Some of them."

"What do you want?"

Kol's heart stretched across the space toward Reyche. Instead his eyes again landed on Jord. "It seems a prince should have the power to do good."

He just wasn't sure what that meant, exactly. Just because Kol had the luck of the ages—to land in a childless royal family, as he had—did not make him any smarter, or more talented, than anyone else. Reyche was a born leader. And that soldier back in Lariasc, Kira. She seemed the type to attack problems with efficiency and gusto. Why could she not lead the country to victory?

The Hartiger girl screeched and jumped in the air, interrupting the conversation. "Yes!" she said. Screamed, really. "I was right. Rogur's rotation is definitely slowing. We could do something about that. Knock it back into place somehow."

She talked so quickly, Kol could hardly make sense of it. Jord had his arms folded across his chest. He lifted an eyebrow. "It sounds like you're suggesting we aim an asteroid at the planet."

Frankie waved him away. "In theory, that would work. But we should try to do it without killing everyone."

"Ideally."

"Like jet planes or rockets or something."

Jord was suspiciously serious. So serious, in fact, that Kol thought he might be teasing the Hartiger girl when he said, "Sounds like comic book science to me."

Frankie bit her lip. "Maybe Liz will have an idea."

Jord raised an eyebrow. "We're mad at Liz, remember?"

"Right."

Kol turned back to Bex and selected the easiest question. "What is a comic book?"

She lifted a shoulder. "Earthen literature. Kind of."

Kol studied her for a long moment while Frankie chattered in the background. Bex seemed to be staring into space. "I guess we're going to Lariasc now," she said.

"Is that what you want?"

"I want to find my father. I want to get back to Earth."

She said it like a mantra. Like she'd spent a long time convincing herself. And no wonder; Earth seemed an overwhelming place. He always pictured it strewn with Hartiger tools; metal and glaring lights, numbers and sound, chattering people everywhere. It must be frightening for Bex to contemplate leaving seven years of isolation for a now-unfamiliar city.

Maybe Kol couldn't smash his world back into rotating properly, but he might be able to do something to make Bex smile. That was a start, wasn't it? "I'm not sure Earth has rolled pastry," he said. "But I do. On the ship."

And there it was. An actual smile. "Then what are we waiting for?"

She was already stalking toward the doors, as though to hide her smile from the others. Fair enough. But Kol had seen it.

And yet, a prince's work was rarely complete. As the rest of the group followed suit, Kol fell into step beside Frankie. "A moment, if you don't mind," he said.

Jord froze, his face contorting into an unattractive scowl that reflected poorly on them both. Frankie, though, waved him off. "Go on. I'll see you on the ship."

Kol would have placed bets that they'd soon discover his

twin waiting outside the doors. With Reyche, no doubt. But he didn't argue.

Kol waited until Jord had gone before saying, "You truly believe he's another version of me?"

She folded her arms across her chest. "He says you're a version of him."

An adequate dodge. Kol withdrew the cracked seeing stone from his pocket, the surface fluttering with images from around his world. "Perhaps, then, you can tell me something about restored magic."

Frankie's eyes widened. She started to reach for the stone, then reconsidered. "Where did you...?"

"You need to keep better track of the things you steal," he said, placing it into her hand. "This one's yours, providing you'll illuminate me as to how you fixed it. I can replace it easily enough."

He tried to appear amused. As if it were a matter of mere curiosity.

Frankie slipped the stone into her pocket. "When you fulfill your end of the bargain. Help me find my parents."

"I will do my utmost."

She started toward the doors. He said, "Can you really help it? The... rotation?"

She paused, turning halfway back, and he could see the difficult welcome Rogur had offered so far, written in the bruises and bandages, the scratches on her face. She was even limping, ever so slightly. "I'm going to try," she said. "I swear."

TWENTY-NINE

FRANKIE

While Kol's soldiers began their search for the Hartigers, Frankie got to sleep in an actual bed—with a mattress, blankets, and goose-down pillows—inside a half-timbered inn in Lariasc. There were baths, too, and, finally, Roguran-style clothing. Frankie had traded her shredded hiking pants for linen trousers and her shirt for a blue blouse that flowed around her as she moved.

And there was fruit. Which Frankie delivered to Jord in person, first thing in the morning, by dumping the bag at his feet before he'd even left his bed.

"Francesca," he said, "have you heard of knocking?"

She tapped her foot, impatient. "You swim in the pool every day at home. I've seen you without a shirt, Jord."

"And what did you think?"

She smacked his foot, still safe beneath the bedspread. She was not about to answer that.

Jord raised an eyebrow. "All right. But what if I'm not wearing pants?"

She was powerless to stop the spots of color from blooming

across her cheeks. Jord, making her blush instead of infuriating her. Truly a new world. She threw up her hands in surrender, but she couldn't help smiling at him like some kind of an idiot. She was embarrassed to contemplate exactly what that might mean. "Knocking from now on. So. Are you good for the day? Kol said he'd come by to play something called clicker. Clerker?"

"They have *cluichur* here?"

Frankie snapped her fingers. "That's the one. So? You're good?"

A nod. "And what will be occupying your time?"

"We finally know what's wrong with this world. I'm going to try and figure out how to fix it."

"And touring Lariasc will help with that?"

No. Maybe. She had to jog her brain, shake something loose. Walk. Observe. Interview. "I have to try. I'd invite you along, but..."

"Can't have two princes wandering around," he finished. "Take notes for me?"

Frankie held up her pen, grinning. The bandages on her hands were fresh and clean, such a relief after the ordeal of the island. "Obviously."

Leaving him felt strange. Frankie was getting accustomed to his presence. Five days in Rogur, and already she was losing it.

Her mind had roiled all night with theories about magnetic fields and atmospheric drag and planetary cores, and, when she'd finally drifted to sleep, with Superman destroying the world while trying to save it.

She needed to walk, to move. She needed to think. Why not take in otherworldly sights in Lariasc at the same time?

The streets were quiet. Scents of leather and woodsmoke filled the air, accompanied by the rhythmic clang of a blacksmith's hammer. When Frankie turned the corner, she caught sight of Audrey hurrying away from the inn. Alone. She'd swapped her ragged Earthen clothing for soft trousers that whipped around her legs as she rushed toward the gates.

Frankie hadn't spoken with Audrey one-on-one since arriving here. She ran to catch up with her friend's businesslike stride, but Audrey didn't even turn.

They passed a cluster of kids on the next corner, listening quietly—too somber, these children—as a burly musician drew his bow across the strings of a violin-slash-flute. When he blew into the end, the resulting sound was like something out of a haunting. Not completely pleasant to Frankie's ears, but certainly unusual.

Audrey didn't spare the musician so much as a glance.

"Wait," Frankie called. "The music, Audrey."

Audrey kept going. If she was startled by Frankie's presence, she didn't let on. "That's not my life anymore."

She said it as though Frankie should have realized. And yeah, Audrey had been trapped in a messed-up world for six months, but that didn't mean she had to abandon everything she loved. Music was the whole reason Audrey had wanted to visit other worlds in the first place.

"I don't understand," Frankie said.

Still moving, Audrey flicked a dismissive wave over her shoulder. "You said it yourself. I was spoiled on Earth. The idea that I made any kind of difference to anyone by performing music, when there's this kind of trouble in the universe? It's pointless."

Frankie hurried to match her friend's pace. "So you're going—"

"Reyche told me they set up an infirmary on the outskirts, for plague victims. I figure the least I can do is stir a pot of soup. Be useful."

Frankie tried to catch Audrey's arm, but her friend pulled away. "I don't care if I get sick," she said, eyes shining with tears. "Don't try to stop me."

"I wasn't," Frankie said. "I came out here to think about how to save Rogur. You can help me."

Audrey still didn't stop walking, but she slowed her pace. "Why?"

Frankie wanted to pretend the question was an absurd one. Here was Audrey, risking herself to help plague victims because she cared. The same way Jord had stepped out of his self-preservation bubble and used his resemblance to the prince.

Frankie wasn't good with talking to people, with comfort or soup-stirring. She didn't even want to contemplate how horrible she would be at bedside manners.

But she *could* help by fixing their world. It was all numbers and laws of physics. There had to be a solution.

"Are you still trying to impress your parents?" Audrey asked. "Or have you actually learned something?"

It stung. It was also deserved. Frankie had to make an effort not to hunch her shoulders, instead pulling her back up straighter. "I'm not my parents."

Audrey was moving her hands, her whole body practically quivering with anger. And, Frankie thought, with fear. And who could blame her for that? "Aren't you, though?" Audrey said. "I've been there with you, through all your schemes and plans. While you shoved people out of the way, and treated them like tools in your precious kit. I want to trust you, Frankie, but..."

She trailed off. Frankie waited, to be sure Audrey didn't have more to say, before finishing her friend's sentence. "But even when I'm doing the right thing, I'm usually doing it for the wrong reasons?"

Audrey raised her eyebrows, just a touch. As though surprised Frankie could have put that together on her own. Or maybe she was just considering disputing the 'usually' part. "What will you do if you *can't* save this world? Will you help these people? Or will you call it a Pathbound loss and leave them behind?"

The way her parents had. "I can save it."

"According to you, the planet is lurching to a stop," Audrey said. "I'm no expert, but fixing that sounds like a tall order. You can't just install an engine and cross your fingers."

"So far, it's just slowed. I might be able to—"

"But that wasn't the question," Audrey said. She hesitated. "There's something off about the people in this world, Frankie."

"What, like the way Kol is off?"

Audrey didn't smile. She licked her lips, thinking. "It's the older people, mostly. I spent months befriending them. Listening to them reminisce together. It's like... they all have the same childhood memories. There are slight differences, but..."

She bit her lip, as though trying to decide whether to continue. Lariasc was small, and Audrey was walking quickly enough that they'd nearly reached the wall. Frankie could make out the goddess's scalp on the other side, the decorative coins glinting in her auburn wig. Every step they took revealed another inch or two, until Aya's full head was visible.

"But what?" Frankie asked.

Audrey drew in a deep breath and let it out slowly, as if trying to regain her composure. "Like, there was this one festival all the people here remember. Ask anyone over the age of thirty what it was like to grow up here, and no matter where they live, they'll mention it. Learning to dance, sneaking sips of beer, stepping on a pretty girl's toes. Full moon. Streamers hung from the trees. Lying in bed and listening to the adults laughing late into the night."

"Maybe it was a good festival."

Audrey shook her head. "If you ask my mom about her childhood, she'll talk about trying on her mother's shoes as a little kid, and participating in protests as a teenager. My aunt will tell stories about playing sax in band and sneaking into the neighbor's pool. My uncle remembers the protests and the pool, but not the other stuff."

"OK," Frankie said, trying to keep up. She didn't have family members to discuss memories with, and she hadn't thought to interview Rogurans on the subject. Audrey's perspective was important. A piece of the Rogur puzzle that Frankie had been trying to work out.

"I think they're in danger," Audrey said, "and not just because their world is going to hell."

Maybe the memory thing was a side effect of the plague, or the sparsely populated world. Frankie didn't know anything about brain science, and certainly not psychology. "That part doesn't help."

"No. You know there were four earthquakes when we first got here? A dam broke in the south and flooded an entire village. It's under the lake now." Audrey stopped in front of a long building that might have been an old stable, or a ware-house. There was a pile of boards on the scrubby grass before it, like someone had recently—and hastily—reopened it for use.

"Audrey?"

"Don't try to talk me out of helping them, Frankie. I'm going in."

Frankie couldn't dredge up so much as a sliver of resent-ment at that. She might have stopped Audrey, once, if she'd thought it would serve her own ends. "I wasn't," she said. "I mean, I believe you, about the memories. It's just... I was just going to apologize. I'm sorry I called you spoiled. I'm sorry I promised the transport would be safe. I'm so sorry."

Audrey wedged her lip between her teeth. "You believe me?"

"Yeah. I do. And... and I'll try to help them. I swear I will."

A bee buzzed nearby, so enthusiastically that the air seemed to vibrate. Remembering the light-snuffing bird on the island, Frankie looked around, expecting to find a fist-sized monster bumbling near her head. Nothing in sight, though. Not so much as a flower.

Audrey looked at the door. "Even Bex couldn't blame you for what happened on the launch. It wasn't your fault."

"She really hates me, huh?"

Audrey sighed. "Like you would not believe."

Bex had tried to murder her. Frankie had no trouble believing it whatsoever.

Frankie craned her neck to see inside the infirmary window, wondering if the artist they'd met the other day had made it inside, and if she was going to be OK. She couldn't see anything from here. Just light, distorted by thick glass. "Jord made them do this," she said, as much to herself as to Audrey.

Audrey examined her nails. "What's up with you and Jord, anyway? Not exactly the dynamic I remember."

Frankie shrugged, accepting the change in topic. "I guess I don't hate him?"

"Uh huh."

"And you and Bex? You seem close."

Audrey dug a toe into the dirt. "We're together. At least, I hope we still are. She's pretty pissed I wouldn't let her beat the crap out of you."

Talk about opposites. Bex was all sharp teeth, where Audrey was made of kindness. "Thanks for that, by the way."

"Yeah. Look, I think I'll see if I can find some wildflowers to bring to the infirmary. Maybe cheer up the place. Come with me?"

Frankie wanted to bring up the music again—a song from Audrey could cheer up any room, in no time—but she didn't want to shatter the moment.

The buzzing whirred up again, and this time Frankie was sure she could feel it. She looked down, ready to smash an insect into otherworldly goo.

It wasn't a bee. It was the seeing stone Kol had given her, vibrating from the pouch at her hip. Her stomach gave a sickly turn. "I think I'll go check out the colossus. See if I can find any hints there. Meet up later?"

Audrey actually smiled. "OK, yeah. See you later."

Frankie waited until she'd passed the gates to retrieve the stone. She walked in Aya's direction, casual. Another tourist, checking out the dead goddess. She had to admit, if only to herself, that the machine her parents had crafted was darkly beautiful. A golden-skinned Artemis, tall enough to look past the walls of human creation, yet frozen in time.

The smell of woodsmoke died away here, replaced by grass and dust. She checked the road for signs of movement. Everything was clear and still.

It took a second to figure out how to accept the call. Frankie would have designed this thing to give some kind of a musical chime, a mystical sound instead of vibrations. It was a missed opportunity.

Audrey's accusations fluttered through her mind. She *was* like them, more than Audrey knew. Still redesigning their fake artifacts in her head.

She'd fix that, too.

When Dad's face appeared, it was strangely distorted by the round shape of the stone. His nose bulged, his eyes so tiny they were barely visible. "You lied," he said.

Oh, hey Dad, nice to see you alive, too.

She didn't say anything. He went on. "We've been watching you, with Audrey LaRoche, and the doctor's daughter. We've been looking for them, Francesca. What did you think we were doing?"

Igniting wars. Imprisoning doctors. The usual.

"We saw Jord in the woods, too," Dad continued. "I convinced your mother you'd have separated from him by the time we spoke to you. Given your history. But she was right. You're still together."

Her mind churned, urging her to offer some story. Some explanation. Something. "Where are you?" she asked.

"In Caisrach, at the palace. You'll bring the girls to us, and Prince Kol. Ditch the others."

Her throat tightened. "Ditch them?"

Frankie glanced at the gate. Still no one watching. A reedy thread of music floated over the wall as though caught by the wind. "What are you going to do when you get to Earth with a bunch of people who know what you've done?"

Though she couldn't see his hands in the stone, she pictured him waving her away. "They won't remember any of this. Bring the girls. Bring the prince."

They wouldn't *remember* any of this? What the hell was that supposed to mean?

But Frankie knew what it meant. It meant erasing memories, or modifying them. How, she couldn't have said, but certainly Pathbound had the means. She couldn't help thinking about what Audrey had said about the Rogurans' memories. Had her parents done something to them, too? Poisoned their water or something? But why?

With horror lumping in her throat, she swallowed. "What about Jord?"

"Leave him."

The screen went black.

Frankie stared at her reflection, as warped and strange as her father's had been. The stone was an eye. They were probably watching her right now. Taunting.

They were going to erase memories. They were going to leave Jord behind.

Only if Frankie let them do it. She dove toward the goddess and plunged the stone into the muddy trench at Aya's feet. She ripped her watch off next and drowned it behind the stone, wishing she had the oculars and the charger plates. She'd throw them into a watering can as soon as she got to the inn.

For the first time in her life, she wanted to purge every piece of tech in her possession.

Water soaked instantly through the thin material of her pants, but she stayed kneeling in the mud at the goddess's feet. Her parents planned to modify memories. In itself, that was a common enough Earthen technology, though she doubted they planned to collect the proper agreements. Especially for the replacement part. What was their plan for the memory replacement, anyway? Fond thoughts of a resort vacation? Sorry that pesky cosmic radiation erased your photos?

That must be what they'd been doing with the Rogurans. Replacing their memories with vague sketches of some festival. But what had they erased?

If Frankie refused to bring Bex, Audrey, and Kol to them—what did they need from Kol, exactly?—she had a feeling they would not spare her.

She needed to find a way to rescue Bex's father. And there was no way she could ditch her parents here, the way she'd hoped. Rogur wasn't ruined yet, but they'd see the job done.

Maybe she couldn't save its rotation. But she could sure as hell save the place from Mom and Dad, and get them to the transport—under the watch of a military escort. Their lawyers would quickly absolve them of their crimes in Rogur, citing absent jurisdiction. But memory modification was only ever performed after careful psychiatric evaluation. And administered as therapy with a patient's consent.

Even the intention to modify Earthens' memories would carry hefty charges. Jail time. Which would allow Frankie time to comb Pathbound for more secrets.

She couldn't leave them here for Rogur to deal with. They'd tear the place apart. They already had.

Her brain rushed to plan, but her limbs felt too heavy to move. From here, on her knees in the dirt before their monstrous invention, victory seemed impossible. Her parents had no trouble pushing Kol from his throne, manipulating this world like a doll's house. She couldn't beat them.

Jord. She had to tell Jord. She should have done it as soon as her father called her on the island, but she'd gotten so distracted by Liz, and then... and then she'd been too afraid of what he'd say, how he'd look at her. But he'd trusted her on the island, when she'd wanted to make a deal with Kol. It was her turn to reciprocate. She'd tell him about the calls, and the implant. She'd tell him everything.

He'd listen. They'd figure out a plan, together.

Frankie stumbled to her feet and broke into a run.

THIRTY

JORD

Jord hadn't expected Kol to make *cluichur* his first priority of the day. But he'd barely bathed and dressed before the prince appeared, eager to engage in a game. "There's a garden on the roof," he said, when Jord opened the door. "We can go there without fear of observation, if you're willing."

The inn was hardly Pathbound Tower, with only three stories to climb, yet stepping onto the rooftop patio gave Jord's head a dip of vertigo. He was glad when the prince dropped his game board on a table near the center.

"The inn has boards in the library, but I prefer to play on my own," Kol said, collapsing into one of the chairs as if finishing a race.

The roof smelled of roses, with the gurgle of water still audible in the background. That, at least, Jord found comforting. He pulled another chair up to the table. "You brought your *cluichur* board with you when you escaped the palace?"

"It has a sea monster in the center," Kol said, as if that explained everything.

Cluichur was a game of strategy and luck, where players

navigated tokens from the outer rim of a circular board to the center. Choose your path—one of four labyrinthian roads—and place your token. Sure enough, Kol's board revolved around a serpent, fangs bared, body coiled in such a way that the tail became a part of the maze.

In Suhainn, the center represented a reward of some kind. Even cheap cloth boards had sketches of treasure boxes and feasts. "Is it typical in Rogur, to put monsters on a *cluichur* board?" Jord asked.

Kol just smiled.

Sea monsters aside, the *cluichur* board was only marginally interesting on its own. It was the hexagonal dice—and the moves they dictated—that made it a challenge. A player could opt to roll the white die and be assured of moving forward—but never more than four spaces at a time. If he risked the black and gray dice, though, they might advance him as many as sixteen spaces—but could easily throw him back just as far.

Jord withdrew the Suhainnan rock from his pocket and rubbed it between his fingers, willing the smooth stone to ground him in this world. His only constant.

Kol forfeited the first move, watching as Jord placed his token on the most direct route. That was the funny thing about *cluichur,* though. Everyone who played considered their favored path to be the most direct.

Jord spilled the dice. Six gray, two black. A gain of four spaces.

Kol considered the board, rolling his coin around the edge of the circle as though he couldn't decide on a pathway. "Strange, isn't it? Our resemblance?"

Jord certainly couldn't disagree. "Frankie believes we come from different versions of the same world."

"And what do you think?"

"I wouldn't know." There had hardly been time to think on

it, let alone form a theory. Jord wasn't one for scientific theories. He spent most of his energy simply trying to survive.

The prince let his coin fall flat, on the entrance to the same path Jord had chosen. An unorthodox move, though not an illegal one. "There's knowledge, and there's instinct."

Jord's temples throbbed in response, as if attempting to collapse his skull. And here he'd thought he might get through the morning without any pain. He ignored it. "Aside from the language, the *afan*, and this—" He indicated the board. "—there's nothing here to indicate that Rogur is a copy of Suhainn."

The prince gave the dice cup a lazy shake. "And yet, who's to say how much impact a single decision can have? Perhaps there are worlds that started as twins, yet diverged so completely that the only connection is... *cluichur*, perhaps. While in others, I simply skipped a night of drinking, and the world carries on almost precisely the way this one does."

"Did the Hartigers arrive in those worlds?"

"Who's to say?"

The idea that multiple versions of the Hartigers could be traveling between worlds made Jord want to empty the contents of his stomach onto the patio. He tried to hide his nausea behind a roll of the dice, cursing at the three-move penalty. When he reached for the stone, his hand betrayed him with such a violent shake that the token skittered across the board.

It wasn't only the vertigo that made his head spin this morning, nor the mention of multiple universe-skipping Hartigers. He'd slept. He'd eaten. And still, illness clawed at his gut, at the fringes of his skull.

"In one version of events," the prince said, "you skip between worlds. You begin to feel unwell."

For someone who spent a lot of energy pretending to be

cavalier, Kol's eye was remarkably sharp. Or perhaps he'd seen these symptoms often enough to make them all too apparent.

Jord drew in a breath to steady himself. The air felt thin. Insufficient. "And what happens after that?"

Kol retrieved the stone, then sat back in his chair. "Fever's next. The timeline gets murkier here. You're strong. It may take some time."

The smell of the roses on the patio was beginning to cloy. Jord wasn't certain he wanted to know any of this. And yet some part of him had already suspected. "You're not afraid of catching it?"

Kol tilted his head, just a touch. His eyes were hooded. "We can't figure out how the plague is contracted. Young children aren't affected. It might level one entire village, and kill a single person in the next."

The prince moved his piece back a space and handed the cup to Jord. "We haven't got a cure," he said, conversationally. "It's going to be terribly surreal for me to watch you die."

With so much death swirling around the prince, he certainly had the experience to recognize its shadow. For Jord, the subject was too abstract, the prince's attitude too nonchalant, the very setting of the revelation too sunny and pleasant to invoke fear.

Could they make it back to Earth, before...? Could he look at Suhainn's blue sky, hear the water lapping along the canals? Could he speak to his brother one more time? And Frankie...

At this point in the game, Jord would usually play a round or two with the white die for guaranteed progress. Instead, he threw black and gray into the cup, barely swirling it before tossing them out.

Kol whistled. "Advancing eight. That's quite a roll."

"You can't tell her," Jord said.

"Wouldn't dream of it, darling."

Darling? "Did I miss the part where we braided bracelets and bonded with trust exercises?"

The prince blinked at the board. "I don't understand what any of that means. It sounds dismally boring. But allow me to impart some of my hard-earned wisdom."

"I don't need advice from you."

Kol leaned back in his chair, stretching his legs out before him. "You know, I wouldn't have thought so. You're considerably more sober than I am, on a regular basis no less, and you seem to actually care about the world. Worlds. Which is why you ought to tell her."

"I doubt she cares."

Kol dropped the white die into the cup. "Safer to think that way, isn't it? Perhaps some version of you already told her. Perhaps she's already concocted a cure."

Jord couldn't suppress an eye roll. And a thread of sympathy for Reyche. "Back to the versions. I thought we'd abandoned this line of inquiry."

Kol tipped his head to the side, the barest hint of a shrug. "It's endlessly interesting. But then again, you appear to like women. I only like men. That's no choice."

"And there, your theory fails."

"Your lover's theory, not mine."

Whether from boredom or propriety—likely the former—Kol changed the subject, and they played on for several more games. When the prince eventually gave up on *cluichur* and disappeared into his cups, Jord chose to remain on the roof. Closer to the sky than he usually preferred, but the waves provided a comforting soundtrack. A fresh breeze lifted strands of roses from their arbors like colorful streamers, and though hints of thunder murmured in the distance, the day was otherwise tranquil. No sign of ill weather. Not so much as a patch of dark clouds.

If he removed this day from the context of Hartiger conspiracies, doppelgängers, and otherworldly disease, there wasn't much more to wish for. But then Frankie appeared from behind a curtain of flowers, and Jord remembered there was always one more thing.

He hadn't expected to see her again until after dark, or maybe tomorrow. But she paced toward him now, lips set in a determined line, one he knew well. On a mission. She was agitated, her cheeks flushed pink, hair flying in every direction. She had her pack slung over her shoulder, as if she meant to make a break for it.

What would she do? If he told her?

He didn't realize he'd gotten up from his chair until she reached him. He set his book on the table. "Done exploring already?"

Frankie grabbed a strand of her hair and tugged on it. "What? Oh. No. I've had enough exploring for a lifetime."

He placed a hand on her forehead. "Call the medics. You must be unwell."

She was supposed to bat him away, or call him a vampire with his cold hands. Maybe smile at his joke. Relax her shoulders. Tell him what had happened.

She stared at him. Not angry, just... lost? It wasn't an expression he could place, and that was perhaps the most worrisome thing of all. On someone other than Frankie, it might have looked a lot like fear. In the distance, the thunder intensified. Some strange Roguran weather pattern? Or something else?

Frankie opened her mouth to speak, and he heard the breath hitch in her throat. He pulled his hand away, not wanting to cause her more distress. "What happened?"

She caught his hand in hers, and his heart gave a painful stutter. For all the time they'd spent together, in Rogur and on

Earth, she rarely touched him. Now, she held his fingers like she trusted them more than gravity.

For a moment, he feared Kol might have told her about his illness. The prince wouldn't have been his first choice of confidants, but it wasn't as if Jord had shared the information willingly. He hadn't exactly been able to hide it.

Frankie said, "Please. Promise you won't hate me."

He truly didn't know how he ever could. He'd tried, with as much concentration as he'd given every aspect of his job at Pathbound. He wanted to reach for her, pull her close. He wanted to promise her everything, anything to get rid of the look on her face.

He said, "Tell me what's wrong."

Bex exploded onto the roof, scattering blossoms as she ripped through the ring of arbors. "What the hell did you do?"

The color drained out of Frankie's face, as though someone had spun a dial. "How could you possibly know already?"

The thunder resumed, its low tone vibrating the boards beneath his feet. Strangely rhythmic. More like drums than thunder, really.

Bex pointed in the direction of the wall. "Kind of hard to miss."

Frankie looked past Jord, toward the street, and he found he didn't want to turn from her. Could he not stay in the previous moment for a second longer?

The thunder increased its pressure on his feet.

He turned.

The goddess who pinned the stars was trudging toward the inn, the top of her head barely visible above Lariasc's rooftops. Not thunder, then. Footsteps. Huge, giantess footsteps.

"I'm inclined to give you the benefit of the doubt," he said, his fingers still locked around Frankie's, "but I do have to ask. Did you wake up the goddess android?"

She shook her head, tears collecting in her eyes. "No."

Jord let out a breath, annoyed with himself for thinking she would.

But Frankie wasn't finished. "I've been talking to Dad," she said, her words rushing out on top of each other. "But I drowned all my tech. He can't reach me anymore."

Jord's stomach went cold, heart freezing where a moment ago it had burned. She'd been in contact with her parents already, and she'd kept it a secret. He shouldn't be shocked. He shouldn't even be surprised. It was just he'd always feared, wasn't it?

Jord released Frankie's hands, and a piece of him snapped. "Well," he said, working hard to keep his voice steady, "it seems they've called in reinforcements."

THIRTY-ONE

FRANKIE

When Jord let go of her hand, Frankie had to stop herself from snatching his back. They'd spent too long on opposing sides of a battlefield she still didn't completely understand, with Jord too afraid to make a move beyond defense, and Frankie setting off land mines wherever she stepped.

He'd never see her side. He'd never even try. Why had she ever thought he might?

She needed to tell him about the implant, now, before someone else did. The words stuck in her throat. Impossible cowardice.

"How long have you been talking to your father?" he asked.

The little trust they'd gained over the last few days felt like flakes of gold panned from a river. Precious. Hard-won. She'd tossed them all away. She could hear it in his voice, rough and injured. He didn't look well; his hands shook, and she didn't think it was due to her confession alone.

She could only deal with one crisis at a time. As if in response, the village wall cracked in the distance, Aya moving ever closer.

Audrey and Reyche rushed onto the roof, toting buckets of water. What were they planning to do, splash the android to death? It had taken a swim in the lake to pause her circuits in the first place. Reyche had a crossbow slung over his arm, too. Little good that would do.

Frankie kept her attention on Jord, as far as that was possible with a multi-ton giantess headed their way. "Dad called me on the island," she said, her traitorous voice giving way to a tremble. She cleared her throat. "Something felt weird about it, so I lied and told him I was here alone, but Kol... He found the seeing stone in the woods when they were looking for us. He gave it to me."

Jord scrubbed a hand through his hair. "They've been watching us. That's why you drowned your tech."

She nodded. Her word was as good as useless now, both to Jord—she could see it in his eyes, the hurt, as though they'd been close companions for years instead of days—and to her parents.

"It didn't occur to you that I might know enough about their habits to predict this, had you told me about it?" Jord asked.

It honestly hadn't. She'd been kind of busy learning about Liz's role in all of this, and making bargains with drunken princes. At least her regret was quickly giving way to anger. That, she was used to. "You can spare me the self-righteous indignation," she said.

Bex wedged her body between them, as though she expected this argument to come to blows. "I'm not saying I agree with Baby Hart, on anything, but maybe save the lecture for later. We've got a bigger problem."

Under other circumstances, Frankie might have enjoyed the irony of that statement. They did, in fact, have an indisputably enormous problem.

As a statue, Aya had been oddly enchanting. Eerie, and despite her size, somehow fragile.

Now, as she crashed through the village, she looked ready to crush everything in her path. She towered over the highest buildings, footsteps shaking the ground and making the inn shudder beneath Frankie's feet. Even the android's coin-spangled headband shot shards of sunlight bouncing everywhere, sharp as the arrows in her quiver. People scattered as she clipped the corner of a building, raining debris onto the street below.

Luckily, this was no Godzilla encounter, with millions of citizens diving for safety. A handful of people ran to avoid Aya's thundering footfalls, the musician discarding his instrument on the roadside. Whether it was plague or war that had made the village so quiet, Frankie had no idea. At least it would keep the carnage to a minimum.

"You did this," Bex said, flinging her arm out toward the approaching android. "Fix it."

"I could have brought you to them, no questions asked," Frankie said. "We could be on our way home."

"And why not?" Reyche said. "Isn't that what you want?"

Frankie shook her head. "They plan to erase our memories. I kind of thought Audrey and Bex might be opposed to that."

"You don't get points for meeting the standard for basic humanity," Bex said. "That's the Hartiger talking."

She wasn't wrong. But Frankie would have to deal with her genes later.

"Go hide," Frankie said. "I'll handle the goddess."

She started for the corner of the building, where she could draw Aya's attention.

Jord intercepted her. "Please promise me you're not intending to talk your way out of this. They're not susceptible to reason, or ethical arguments. Tell me you know that."

Frankie shoved past him, but he stayed right behind her. "Will you get somewhere safe, please?" she said.

"Safe doesn't exist, Francesca. Don't—"

Frankie made it to the corner, and Jord stopped talking, though he stayed with her as she stepped onto the lower railing, balancing her knees against the upper. She could only hope Lariasc had decent carpenters.

To her surprise, Reyche was only a few steps behind. He joined her, a few yards to the left, crossbow primed. "Where is she vulnerable?"

"That's an excellent question," Frankie said. Where was the goddess's control panel? Maybe Reyche could shoot that. One well-placed arrow might be enough to fry her motherboard.

The fake goddess did not move as gracefully as it had seemed from far away. Pathbound's security bots were cone-shaped for a reason; they maneuvered easily on wheels, and the wide base made it tough to tip them over.

Aya's steps were smooth, but slow. She didn't corner particularly well. It might have been a side effect of her lake encounter—the villagers should have left her to rust at the bottom—or simply a condition of the precarious two-legged design she shared with humans.

"We might be able to trip up her mobility if we fire some arrows at her knees." Frankie pointed at Reyche's crossbow. "But it'd be temporary. I think."

Beneath the shuddering of her steps and the aftermath of the tremors they caused, Aya brought with her the electrical hum of fans, the creaks and groans of intricate machinery.

Frankie threw her arms up and waved.

When Frankie's presence registered, the goddess slowed to a stop. Her shin bumped a vendor's cart, spilling fruit across the street like balls on a billiard table.

"Our conversation wasn't over, Francesca," Aya said, her Roguran accent fast and clipped.

It was the way Mom spoke. So this was a puppet show, then, with Lariasc as a picturesque backdrop. Curtains twitched in the building across the street as huddled forms watched the standoff, like Frankie and Aya were about to draw six-guns.

Frankie wanted to scream at them to get somewhere safe, before the goddess plucked them out of their houses like dolls from a toy house. But she couldn't even get Jord to do that. He lingered a few paces behind her, like he didn't trust her not to hand them all over.

She wouldn't do that. Still, if it was up to Frankie to protect them, they might be screwed.

"Where are they?" Aya-slash-Mom demanded.

"These people haven't done anything wrong," Frankie said. "Stop messing up their town."

"What's your goal here, Francesca? You have only to gain from bringing the girls to Caisrach."

Frankie hoped Bex hadn't heard that. She didn't budge. "I won't do it."

Aya drew an arrow from her quiver. Frankie doubted even the most sophisticated android would be able to shoot one cleanly, and Aya was not the most sophisticated. Frankie would have made her smaller. Wide and powerful, instead of tall and precarious. Her design was pretty, but inherently flawed.

But when your arrows were as big as car axles, you didn't have to shoot them.

Aya punched the arrow into the roof of the inn, a few steps from where Frankie clung. The railing snapped with an ear-rending crack, flinging Reyche over the side. Frankie could see the tips of his fingers, clinging to the edge. Jord threw himself across the gouge in the roof to grab the captain's hand.

Aya straightened, keeping a firm grasp on the arrow. It swung clumsily behind her, and nearly pierced the building across the way. "Since when do you care more about strangers than you do about Pathbound? You're a Hartiger."

And Hartigers cared only for their own agenda, their own greed. Jord had learned to manipulate that greed, early on. Frankie had never even seen it. They were *Hartigers*, for crying out loud. Their reputation was everything. But if she'd paused her own agenda, if she'd paid even an ounce of attention, she'd have seen the truth.

Out of the corner of her eye, she saw Jord help Reyche onto the roof. She didn't turn toward them. They were moving. They were alive.

"Look what we're capable of building," the goddess said, stretching her arms wide. "You're meant to be a part of this, Francesca."

"Since when?" Jord shouted as he and Reyche staggered to their feet. There was blood on his forehead, and running down the side of his face. "Since when have you looked twice at her?"

He was so angry at her. So angry, and still he defended her.

Aya stopped. "He doesn't know, does he?" she said. Had she been human, she might have laughed. "Ask her, Jord. Ask Francesca who's responsible for your leash. Ask her who built your implant."

Jord looked to Frankie, and for a beat, she was sure he didn't believe it. That, angry or not, he was on her side. And then another beat passed, and she didn't deny it, and there was nothing she could say because she *had* designed it, and all she could do was to shake her head while he touched the back of his neck and stared at her in open shock.

He'd made himself her enemy, for years. He'd fought her, taunted her, distracted her, stolen from her.

He'd also believed in her.

"I did," she said, finding her voice. "I designed your implant, and the system that contains you to the tower. But I was really young when I made it, and I didn't know they'd use it on you. On any person. It was never supposed to—"

"Spare us, Francesca. If you'd given it five minutes of thought, you'd have known," Aya said, and it was true. It was all true. "Perhaps you did give it the five minutes. Perhaps you did know."

There wasn't time to deal with this now, with the devastation scrawled across Jord's face. She only hoped Reyche could prevent him from fainting off the roof.

Aya whirled around—whether to threaten the street with her arrows or show off her dance moves, Frankie couldn't say—and Frankie wrenched herself back into the fight, scanning the goddess for blemishes. If she were to build an android of this size, which she wouldn't, she'd be forced to place the control panel in the back. There was no other space large enough for so many circuits.

There wasn't much sign of water damage, unless it was hidden beneath the clothing. Frankie should have realized the goddess was only temporarily paused.

At the base of her neck, a minuscule protrusion poked out of the skin. To the Roguran eye, it probably looked like a bone.

To Frankie, it looked like a latch.

Given more time, she'd reprogram Aya to work for her. What the android needed was a remote control. With a mute button.

"Last chance, Francesca," Aya said, once more facing the inn. "Turn them over now, and I won't level this town."

It was smart of her to speak in Roguran. All the villagers would understand. They'd be afraid. Maybe even band together to give her what she wanted.

So Frankie did the least-safe thing she could think of.

"OK," she said. "I'd hate to see you ruin all this architecture. I'll get them."

Aya lowered her weapon. Frankie doubted the robot was rigged to smile, but the gesture felt triumphant all the same.

She stumbled around the ruined part of the patio, to where Reyche crouched behind a pile of debris. She could only hope it would block her from view, even for a few seconds. "Can you distract her?" she whispered. "Run across the street and wave your crossbow at her? Go for the knees. Maybe we'll get lucky."

If Aya fell, she might not be able to rise again.

Reyche nodded and sprinted across the roof, dropping out of sight behind the flowers. One of the arbors had come down with the arrow, but the rest still swayed in the breeze, unaffected and impossibly cheerful.

Frankie grabbed the stunner out of her pack, threw the bag over her shoulder, and returned to the edge of the roof.

Jord stayed with her. "What are you going to do?"

Surely he didn't think she really intended to turn Bex in. Though maybe now he didn't know what to think. Could she blame him?

Reyche had already reached the street. She couldn't hear what he was saying, but he stood on the porch across the way, acting his part as promised. Aya, however, remained facing the inn. Waiting for Frankie's return.

As Frankie watched, Reyche raised the crossbow and took a shot at Aya's knees. The arrow glanced off, but Aya turned to face him, swiping at his balcony with a huge palm. So the knees *were* vulnerable, then.

With Aya's attention diverted, Frankie climbed onto the half-ruined railing. Aya stood maybe three feet away. No farther than a jump across a city sidewalk. A little closer, even. Only instead of a curb, Frankie was preparing to leap onto an android's back. From three-stories high.

Jord grabbed hold of her pack from behind. "Francesca, this is not a good plan."

Aya raised an arm, presumably to goddess-smash Reyche. Frankie didn't have time to apologize, or explain herself. She shrugged off the pack, leaving it in his hands, then launched herself across the short space with so much force that she almost flew past the android. Still grasping the stunner in one hand, she threw her arms around Aya's neck, the quiver of arrows knocking her to the side as Aya whipped around.

How did her parents even know Frankie was up here? Cameras? Motion sensors? Weight monitors?

"I wish I had time to dissect you," Frankie said. With one arm still flung around the android's neck, she ripped away a layer of 'skin.'

There it was, in all its glory. Aya's control panel.

And Jord had so helpfully relieved her of her pack, and her screwdriver. She needed something to pry the door open. It wasn't exactly easy to survey her resources while spinning in midair like an amusement park ride. All she could see were arrows, and they were too big. She'd skewer herself before she managed to crack the panel.

If she were Aya—if she were Mom or Dad—she'd have backed the android into a building to knock Frankie's wind out.

Aya didn't do that. Either they weren't thinking, or they didn't want to risk accidentally crushing their daughter's lungs.

Frankie pulled herself higher onto Aya's shoulders, hooking her elbow around the android's neck so she could snatch hold of one of the round disks on her headband without letting go of the stunner in her other hand. The disk was nearly as wide as Frankie's palm, but razor-thin. A charger plate, a solar panel that routed power to the android's circuits. Clever.

Frankie wrenched the disc out of Aya's hair with a force

that practically sent her sprawling to the ground. She was starting to get dizzy, with Aya spinning in circles.

As she slipped the coin under the edge of the panel, Aya got smart. Or whatever, Frankie's parents got smart. It was hard to keep track. The goddess charged after Reyche.

But it was too late. He dodged, and Frankie buried the stunner in Aya's circuits.

Then she turned it on.

Aya lunged for Reyche a second before blue lightning zipped through her circuit board. She froze, stopping so suddenly that Frankie had to cling to her back to keep inertia from throwing her to the street. Sparks fizzled beneath the android's skin, chasing each other down her limbs.

Frankie had a feeling Aya wouldn't be reviving from this particular defeat. Her circuits smelled well and truly fried.

She climbed down carefully as Reyche picked himself up off the ground. "I'm weary of fighting gods," he said.

"They'll send more," Frankie said. "Or they'll come themselves."

Reyche nodded, stowing his own bolts as Jord emerged from the inn, blood trickling down his forehead from the cut above his eyebrow. "We need to disappear," Reyche said. "Find a place to regroup."

"We need to go to Caisrach," Frankie said.

"Because in person they'll suddenly embrace reason?" Jord said. "They'll apologize for treating people as poker chips?"

"That wasn't what I was going to say."

But Jord was already walking away. He'd never forgive her for this. He'd never understand.

"I believe I might be able to suggest a compromise," Reyche said, tugging his gloves off and stuffing them in his pockets. "A place to disappear that happens to be inside Caisrach. But first, has anyone seen the prince?"

THIRTY-TWO
FRANKIE

The palace clung to Caisrach's crater walls, like a metallic spider perched at the top of the cliff and reaching its legs over the edge, the haphazard buildings clustered in its shadow shabby and ill-fitting. Frankie couldn't decide whether it was ugly or beautiful.

If Lariasc was quiet, the streets of Caisrach were dead. No people. No vendors. Most buildings stood empty, doors and windows hanging wide. Every so often, a patrol of red-cloaked soldiers stomped by.

Once, Frankie caught sight of a black-clad figure moving stiffly among the early dawn patrols. She would have bet anything that it was made of wires and circuits.

Reyche led them to a box of a house on the outskirts of the city. When he knocked in an intricate pattern, an older woman opened the door and held a candle in their faces before ushering them in, her scowl deepening as Kol passed. They'd clearly dragged her out of bed; she was wearing a white night-gown and slippers.

With everyone inside, she lifted a rug to reveal a door in the floor, wedged her portly frame inside, and disappeared down the ladder.

"Excellent," Jord muttered. "This doesn't feel like a trap at all."

He hadn't said a word since Lariasc. The cut on his forehead was bright red against his pale skin. He didn't look much healthier than Kol, come to think of it.

Frankie didn't see another choice, and the prince had more to lose than she did, and Kol was already stepping inside—his odds of making it safely down a ladder had to be dismal—with Reyche behind him.

Sure enough, Kol was picking himself up off the floor when she got to the bottom. "Trick step," he said.

Frankie stepped around him while their hostess ambled about the room, touching her candle to lanterns that bathed the walls in warm light. Dirt floors aside, the room was pleasant enough. Dusty, but spacious, with a narrow hall leading to the left.

"Hello, Nessa," Kol said, when the door was shut.

Nessa finished her lantern lighting and joined them by the ladder.

And then, to Frankie's surprise, she slapped the prince across the face. Even more surprising? Reyche didn't attack. He folded his arms. Frankie thought he might laugh. "You said you might need my help. You did not say you would arrive plastered—"

Kol rubbed his cheek. "Is one to avoid drinking forever?"

"Yes," Reyche said.

"—and with those cursed gods going door-to-door, too. They're looking for Earthens, you know."

"That's why you have a secret basement."

"No, I have a secret basement for smuggling." She took off her slipper and shook it at him.

Next to Frankie, Jord swayed on his feet. She said, "I vote in favor of berating Kol more, but only after we get patched up."

For the first time, Nessa looked at the rest of the group, scanning past Audrey and Bex. When she saw Jord, her eyes widened. "There are *two* of him?"

"You're just that lucky," Kol slurred.

Nessa dropped the slipper, waving Frankie and Jord through the corridor and into a fully stocked pantry. For all her blustering, this room was definitely equipped for long-term hiding. The shelves were stuffed with sacks of flour, rice, and beans, plus a rainbow of preserves. Berries, mushrooms, pickles, squash.

The room smelled of oak, mixed with a tang of vinegar. When Nessa led them to the corner, Frankie could see why; the back wall was lined with barrels, each stamped with an image of a grapevine.

Jord sat on one of the barrels and rubbed his face while Nessa started sorting through a bin of bandages, needles, and glass bottles filled with herbs.

"What do you smuggle?" Frankie asked.

Nessa pointed to the bottom shelf, below all the medical supplies. "Between products. Not much of a market for dead magic these days."

Magic. The shelf was stacked with seeing stones like Kol's, along with screens made to look like hand mirrors. Even though none of the objects held a charge, Frankie tensed at the sight of the tech. Her fingers itched to drown it all.

She suspected Nessa would object, dead artifacts or not.

"Nessa," Reyche called from the main room, "Kol needs... assistance."

"Nature deliver us," Nessa said. She pulled a bottle out of the bin and gave it an approving sniff. Her knees popped as she straightened. She held the basket of supplies out to Frankie. "Can you manage?"

Jord snatched the basket before Frankie could, pulling it onto his lap. "It's nothing."

Nessa set a hand on her hip, lips puckered as though she wanted to take on that argument. But Reyche called to her again, and she sighed. "Take what you need."

Jord rifled through the box while Frankie hovered by the food. He'd been angry with her before. So why did she feel like there was an invisible forcefield preventing her from going to sit beside him?

"I'm sorry," she said.

It wasn't enough. It never would be.

Jord grimaced. He was in more pain than he admitted. "What do you need? To get this thing out of me?"

She shook her head. "I only ever installed it in animals. I can't try for the first time on you."

Jord ripped a strip of bandage off the roll, his hand shaking as he held it to the oozing cut. "You have to remove it."

"They can't trace it, if that's what you're worried about. They didn't have this tech last time they were here. I hadn't... I didn't invent it until after their last trip to Rogur."

He was just looking at her, eyes pinched and weary. She sighed. "I don't have anesthetic, or sterile instruments."

"In case you haven't noticed, I'm already ill. Infection is hardly on my list of concerns."

Ill. He did look sick, his hands trembling as he held the bandage to his cut. She wanted to protest, but she'd built this device. She'd tethered him to Pathbound Tower.

She owed him a choice.

She retrieved her toolkit and alcohol wipes from her pack, and a sharp knife from Nessa, then lined them up on one of the barrels beside a needle and thread for stitching the wound. She delayed as long as she dared, shifting her candle from one place to another for the best possible light—which still wasn't very good—while Jord waited in silence.

The cut of the wound was familiar, a half-inch scar bulging ever so slightly with evidence of the implant. They'd have used an applicator to punch it through the skin, where the device would have adhered to his spine within seconds. Frankie ran her fingertip over the scar, regretting everything.

She ran an alcohol pad along the skin. When she made the incision, Jord sucked in a breath.

"Why you?" she asked softly, staunching the trickle of blood from the cut. "Why did they take you out of Suhainn?"

His jaw worked as he gritted his teeth against the pain. "The King of Suhainn is as fake as Rogur's gods," he said. "I stumbled upon the truth, and they whisked me away. Even though I... I didn't realize what I'd seen, until you barged into my room at Pathbound Tower, with your holographic welcome presentation."

Frankie blinked, wiped at the blood. "There's no King of Suhainn?"

"He's a ghost. A hologram and, I assume, an android as well. Your parents rule Suhainn. I don't know if they're murderers, or the best con artists history has ever known."

Maybe both. Her brain tugged at the shadow of an answer, but there was a crucial piece missing. If she could only grasp hold of it, everything might fall into place.

Down the hall, a teapot whistled. The others murmured quietly, like an undercurrent of lava that might erupt at any moment. Every single one of them had been dragged through the mud by her family.

Frankie nudged his skin apart and located the device, so cleverly wrapped around the bone. God, she hated biology. She hated biology so much.

Using the tweezers, she unsnapped the first clamp, keeping her hands steady so the tiny needle wouldn't slip. Easier said than done, with everything coated in blood.

Better blood than spinal fluid.

She eased the clamp out, then dropped the evil thing on the barrel beside the wipes and set her attention to the next one. There were four in total, tiny stingers ready to mess with the nerve roots.

What a cruel piece of technology. And she'd created it. She hadn't thought twice. She made herself work without hesitation. Quickly. Safely. No overthinking it.

She found it hard to dredge up surprise at his story, that her parents controlled Suhainn. At this point, the hows and whys were less important than the escape route. If they made it back to Earth, they could help Suhainn, too.

With the clamps removed, Frankie let out a breath and began stitching Jord's skin back together, his knuckles whitening around the sides of the barrel.

When the wound was bandaged, the implant removed—if not the pain it had caused—Frankie just stood behind him for a moment, wondering what she could ever say to make up for what she'd done. What she'd nearly become.

"I'm sorry," she said. "I'm sorry I never asked what they were using it for. I'm sorry I never looked."

Jord braced his arms on the sides of the barrel and shifted his legs around to face her. His hands shook as he took hers, lacing their fingers together as she'd done on the roof. His were still cold. "Maybe none of us can start fresh until their secrets are locked up forever. Maybe we go in quietly. We extract Bex's father and the celebrities. And we go home without them."

She'd thought of it, too. But it was impossible. "If we do that, we damn Rogur right along with my parents."

Jord tipped his head back to look toward the ceiling. She

could practically see his veneer cracking, as if his story had been a chisel and Frankie was now playing the part of hammer. She still had his hands. What would he do, if she silenced his doubts by pulling him toward her, sharing her warmth? Would he push her away?

"You could traverse a thousand worlds in search of them," he said. "They'd only ask why you didn't try a thousand and one."

How could he still believe that this was about her place at Pathbound? About winning their esteem, their love? Frankie pulled her hands away. "You could visit a thousand worlds, and you'd still be afraid of them."

He took a measured breath before answering. "I am afraid of them, yes. Look at what they're capable of."

"Are you afraid of me? Is that why you spent years sabotaging my plans?"

"If you were to be fully inducted into the Hartiger Empire? Yes. I would be very afraid of you. Look at what you managed without even knowing it."

His voice was too calm, too measured. Frankie did her best to match it, though she wanted to scream. "You think I'm like them."

He waved a hand at the remains of the implant. Her handiwork. "Are you?"

She'd chased their love for so many years. If Mom were to embrace her now? Frankie wanted to believe she'd turn away. She wanted to trust herself. But Jord's doubt only increased her own.

"You can't shove your problems into another world and hope they go away," she said. "You'll never beat them unless you learn to defy them."

He held her gaze. "And you'll never earn their admiration until you no longer deserve it by any other standard. Don't expect me to take part in a plan to save them, Frankie. I won't do it."

Veneer shattered. His real feelings. She couldn't quite blame him for thinking so little of her, but she couldn't stand to spend another moment in his presence, either. She stumbled back, knocking a jar off the shelf with her elbow. It shattered, spilling blood-red guts into the dirt, but she didn't stop.

She made it all the way to the main room, and through the gauntlet of stares that greeted her there, before she realized he'd called her Frankie. Like Francesca had always been the lie, and she'd goaded him into the truth.

Instead of a triumph, it felt like an intrusion.

She dropped to the floor in the corner and wrapped her arms around her body. The others were all so pointedly avoiding her gaze that she had to wonder how much of the fight they'd overheard.

The air was hot in here. Thick. She could practically feel the mold spores oppressing her lungs with every breath. Reyche talked quietly with Nessa, his two soldiers lingering nearby. Kol lay at their feet, looking nearly as ill as Jord. Bex had her head in Audrey's lap, which would have been sweet if Frankie were not opposed to the idea that anything in this world could ever be sweet.

Jord thought she was like her parents. He was afraid of her.

"You're missing the obvious solution," Kol murmured, and for a moment, Frankie thought she'd spoken out loud. But he wasn't even looking at her; he had to be continuing some conversation they'd been having before. With Kol, it was diffi-cult to tell. "Nessa must have some palace livery tucked away. We put it on and pretend to be servants."

"There's no way to sneak in," Frankie said, welcoming the distraction. "Facial recognition is hard to trick, and you can bet they have it installed at every entrance."

Plans, she could do.

Kol shifted, stretching his hands up to pillow his head. "I've no idea what that means, darling. You do sound very certain."

"Can you even remember your name right now?"

"My goodness, but you're a charming girl. What in the world could your handsome companion ever find to fight with you about, I wonder?"

Frankie considered abandoning her corner for the sole purpose of smacking him across the face.

Audrey cleared her throat. "Nessa said she smuggles magic?"

"Used to," Nessa said. "Not many buyers these days."

Audrey nodded. She reached her hand halfway to her neck as though to feel for her locket, and Frankie realized with a jolt that her friend's precious necklace was missing. "The Hartigers want Bex, Frankie, and me, right? So we could charge one of the artifacts and let them track us. Make them think we got caught by accident. Frankie can figure out a way to get Reyche and his soldiers into the palace."

Silence.

"It won't work," Frankie said.

"Don't we still think she's a traitor?" Kol said.

She wasn't, but she'd never convince them of it. Audrey, who'd been so close to forgiving her. Bex... Well, she'd been right all along, in her eyes. Frankie would have expected her to gloat, but the marooned girl was suspiciously quiet.

When Frankie analyzed the situation from an objective angle, she *did* understand Jord, a little bit. He'd set himself against her to protect her from her parents. And, if he was truly afraid of her, to protect himself.

And yet when he'd been named head of Pathbound, Frankie had been his priority. He'd waited to talk to her. Which meant he'd believed in her before they'd ever left Earth.

Frankie couldn't agree with Jord's methods, then or now, but she thought she understood. Jord was ill—very. She needed to get him back to Earth. But she couldn't doom another world to her parents' tactics in the process. She wouldn't. If Audrey and the others let themselves get captured, they'd lose. Guaranteed.

Which meant that Frankie was going to need her own plan.

THIRTY-THREE

JORD

With Frankie in the room, Jord had felt overly warm, like the place was set to burn down about his ears. Now, chills wracked his body, and there was nothing he could do to keep his shoulders from shuddering against the barrel.

Eventually, he dreamed. Of lemons and Frankie, her cheek pressed against his in the darkness. Of calling her back, of saying what he'd never mustered the courage to admit.

Words, whispered into his ear; the rustle of leaves, the shifting of the stars in the planetarium.

He was sorry. He understood. He knew she'd never meant to hurt him.

He woke beside a cold cup of tea—Nessa's doing, if he had to guess—his fingers closed around an object he did not remember picking up.

When he opened his hand, a pill bottle rolled onto the floor. The painkillers Frankie had stolen from him on the day of the Pathbound Disaster. She'd kept them? Why?

Wrapped around the bottle was a slip of paper containing

four Suhainnan words, printed in Frankie's careful hand-writing.

Élein ghlad est uspil.
Take a chance on me.

THIRTY-FOUR

FRANKIE

The veins of Caisrach's streets twisted and squeezed, the frequent patrols hindering Frankie's progress like crimson clots. Whether the soldiers had been convinced or coerced to work for the gods, she could not have said.

She circled as close to the cliffs as she dared, counting her heartbeats in the shadows, checking every angle before darting through the streams of light. The insect-like palace shone with steady electric light, as inappropriate in Rogur as the digital watch Frankie once dropped into a careless historical re-enactor's butter churn.

Lies on top of conspiracies on top of murders, as tangled as Caisrach's streets. Frankie wedged herself into a corner across from the stone staircase that zigzagged up to the easternmost leg of the palace. Bricks pressed close on either side; based on the smell, someone had recently used these cobblestones as a bathroom.

Frankie waited. Patrols passed. The stars faded.

She wondered if Jord had seen her note.

She wondered what had possessed her to leave it.

Dawn grayed the sky, and the black-clad android prowled past Frankie's hiding spot. He was the only soldier she'd seen wearing anything but red, a hunk of charcoal among the flames. He didn't have Aya's three-story height, though his swelling biceps threatened to pop his sleeves open at any moment. Double rows of brass buttons blinked down his front, and he carried a cane. Probably to help him cover his almost-smooth movements.

Human movement was hard to duplicate.

Frankie didn't know his story or his supposed powers. But in a few minutes, he'd be on her side. And then, they'd get her parents. End this before Audrey called them herself. Before Jord got sicker.

The god paused at the stairwell, not three feet from her, and turned a circle. As if he could smell her. Which, unless his technology was more advanced than anything that was possible on Earth, he couldn't.

Or he wasn't a robot. Always a risk.

It was one she was willing to take. Frankie gripped her screwdriver. Ambush time.

A splash of water hit the android from behind, followed quickly by a second. Before he could return the attack, he'd frozen in place. Like Aya.

Bex swung around the first curve in the stairs and grimly dropped a pair of buckets to the cobblestones. How long had she been hiding there? How had Frankie missed her? And what in the worlds could have possessed her to follow? Out of mistrust, surely, but Frankie could hardly begrudge the help.

"Subtle," Frankie said, fighting the urge to lean against the bricks in relief. "I was hoping to use him, not deactivate him."

Bex kicked the buckets between the buildings where Frankie had been hiding. Had some stranger watched from a distance, they'd probably have assumed that Frankie and Bex were friends rather than near enemies. What had changed?

"You can't ride that thing to pry open its control box like you did with the big one," Bex said. "If he's the same, we can like... pop him in a bag of rice, right? He'll be fine."

"It's too late now," Frankie said, grabbing hold of the god's bulky arm. There'd be time later to address Bex's change of heart. "Help me get him out of sight."

Together, they dragged the android into the nearest doorway—an abandoned one, with a crisscross of boards nailed over the door—and Frankie forced the control panel open. So much easier when she'd actually brought her tool kit along with her.

She ought to be able to disconnect the android from his command center; if he was anything like the security bots at home, though, he might reset to defaults every so often. His tablet control screen should have the settings. Once she accessed them, she'd be able to make him her ally—and her guide to Mom and Dad.

Since the android was already awake, her parents should have no reason to track her through him. Provided that they didn't notice he'd gone dark. And that they didn't have security cameras to catch Bex giving him that little bath.

Frankie didn't like it. Too many variables.

Bex stood there watching, fists clenched at her sides. Fine, so maybe a stranger watching might have a *few* questions about their relationship.

"What are you doing here?" Frankie asked cautiously. "Decided to throw in with the traitor?"

"You're not a traitor," Bex said. "Are you?"

"No. But I'm surprised that you're the one who knows it."

Bex glanced around the corner, fidgeting with her hands. "I don't like their plan. Getting captured on purpose."

"Seems like you could have mentioned that during their meeting."

Bex rubbed her hands on her pants, obviously uneasy. "Like they'd have listened."

They might. Audrey would have.

"How did you figure out what I was doing?" Frankie asked.

"I followed you. Not hard to put it together. You're a Hartiger." She hesitated, finally meeting Frankie's eyes. "But you're a strange kind of Hartiger."

It was, Frankie supposed, Bex's version of an olive branch. She decided not to question it—or whether she deserved the gesture. Instead, she started to poke at the android's controls. The water hadn't made it all the way to the tablet, which was a good thing, but it meant her time was limited.

The tablet wasn't as old as the tech on the island, but it wasn't exactly new either. No pass code needed, luckily—thank hubris for that—but the interface felt like a foreign language. She tapped through the menus. The androids had to be controlled by a central processing unit. A mothership.

She might have been able to reroute this one's signal and control it from her smartwatch. Unfortunately, that option was buried beneath several inches of mud in Lariasc.

"You came here to get your parents out of Rogur?" Bex asked.

"I don't think we should leave them to cause more damage. Not when I can use the androids against them." She paused. "But I'm here because of Jord. He's sick."

Bex stepped forward, peering over Frankie's shoulder. "It's funny," she said, "about the plague."

Frankie scrolled through the advanced settings on the android. It was like programming her watch, right? Barely more complicated than the elevator. Her parents always installed failsafes. Always. "Plague doesn't seem that funny to me."

"I meant it's funny that it doesn't affect Earthens."

Frankie stopped working, the tablet suddenly icy against her fingertips. "I thought your whole team died here."

Bex was still looking at the android's innards, the cords that jutted out from the tablet like capillaries. "A couple fell from the cliff, when we tried to get out of the crater. Another two died of infections from injuries after our antibiotics ran out. One drowned. And so on."

She related the details clinically, mechanically, as if they hadn't happened to her. Nausea shuddered through Frankie's body, rearranging her insides into a hot whirlpool of dread. She steadied herself against the wall to keep it from winning and turned her attention to the control box. "But no one died from plague?"

As she talked, she scrolled through the god's settings, fingers trembling. Finally, there it was: the option to disconnect the android from the central processing unit. Her mother would have designed them that way so that if an enemy were to take over the control center—as Frankie planned to—the androids could be disconnected individually. And returned to Mom's control.

She was starting to understand them. Not a comforting thought. At least she could use it to her advantage.

"Not a single Earthen died from plague," Bex confirmed. "Weird, right?"

Weird. Though maybe Bex's friends had been shielded by their isolation.

Altered memories, android gods, plagues that only affected non-Earthens. What was she missing? Frankie pressed her fingerprint to the panel to indicate who should be controlling the android and straightened as the android lifted his head.

The false god stared at them for a beat, his marble eyes frozen as he recalibrated his soul.

Bex shifted her weight from left to right, hands locked around her elbows. "How do we know if it worked?"

"Of course it worked." Frankie looked at the android. "Bring us to the Hartigers."

"And don't let anyone kill us," Bex added.

The god swiveled, marching to the stairs without a word. His footsteps spilled waterfalls of pebbles and dirt as he started to climb.

Frankie and Bex exchanged a glance. But the android didn't pause.

They climbed. Frankie tucked her tools under her arm instead of replacing them in her pack. Risky, and potentially hazardous, but she couldn't help it. She wanted to keep them close.

"Bren is supposed to be the god of jealousy," Bex said softly, jutting her chin in their guide-god's direction. "He was so jealous of his lover's singing voice that he cut her throat open. That's why he doesn't speak."

"That's a lot less picturesque than a giantess who pinned the stars," Frankie said.

"The stars are the hearts of her enemies," Bex said.

Gruesome stories. Angry gods. Frankie's thighs burned, but she didn't slow. "How do you know all this, if you were hiding on the island?"

"We lived here for a couple months," Bex said. "The team would go off to study stuff, and Dad went along in case of emergency. I mostly stayed here. I went to Kol's lessons with him."

"That must have been delightful."

"He was different then."

"And you never thought gee, this palace sure is weird?"

Bex sniffed. "Of course I did. But we were in another world, and I was eight. My philosophy was, 'the weirder the better.'"

Frankie's lungs were working too hard to let her continue the conversation, so she nodded. Kol and Bex, attending tutoring sessions together. And people said they felt bad for Frankie's teachers.

By the time they reached the top of the stairs, Frankie thought she might collapse. She leaned one hand on the cliff while Bren pounded on the metal door that led into the center leg of the palace. From here, the other spider legs loomed like jumbo jets, pinned to the side of the cliff.

Frankie didn't share Jord's fear of heights, but she still didn't look down.

The door slid open, and a guard stepped aside. He didn't question the android's passage, or theirs—in fact, he seemed intent on avoiding Bren's gaze.

As they entered the steadier light, burning low and unquestionably electric, Frankie groaned.

Another staircase, this one forged into a giant metal spiral. Lungless, heartless, the android didn't slow.

"You could have warned me," Frankie muttered.

Bex grinned and smacked her on the back before following the android. "All the way up, Baby Hart," she said. "Let's find the supervillains."

THIRTY-FIVE

FRANKIE

By the time the stairs dumped them into a golf ball-shaped observatory, Frankie could barely draw oxygen. The toolkit under her arm was damp with sweat.

She really needed to hire a personal trainer before she barged into any more hostile worlds. And learn to rock climb. Maybe some martial arts.

Assuming she survived *this* hostile world first.

The observatory was like a tourist attraction, and maybe it was meant to be; the arched windows looked over Rogur's crater, where the rising light caught sparks off the lake in the distance and the cliffs rose from behind the same murky fog she'd seen hanging over the dead forest.

Gasping, Frankie followed Bren down a short corridor, the tapestry-lined walls alarmingly out of place in this spaceship of a palace. She barely had time to contemplate the golden depictions of the gods, or the suspiciously perfect stitching, before Bren stopped at the first door.

He didn't knock, or bash it in. He simply opened it.

The room made Frankie blink. It was a carbon copy of her

parents' apartment at Pathbound, down to the view of New York City. The sight of the urban farm twisted her stomach with homesickness.

They had the same lab-white furniture, the same kitchen to the right. Breakfast bar, chandelier, hanging wine glasses.

And, seated at the high top table before the fake windows, enjoying the fake sunrise reflecting off the fake skyscrapers, were Mom and Dad. Mom had her feet propped on the top support of her stool, a napkin on her knee. Back straight as ever, dark hair so sleek she must have flat-ironed it into submission. She certainly hadn't been falling from cliffs, dodging deathly pendulums, or fighting off light-snuffing birds.

Frankie might have opened a door that led her home. Except that home had elevators.

When Dad saw them, he actually grinned. He abandoned his eggs to cross the room, arms open. As though Frankie was going to hug him, after he'd sent a giantess to bash in buildings when she hadn't done what he'd wanted.

Frankie stepped back. Dad didn't break stride. Instead of hugging her, he brushed a hand behind her ear, producing a quarter. "Look what I found."

It was all she could do not to flinch. Before she could form words—the one part of this plan she hadn't solidified—Mom crossed the room and brushed Dad out of the way.

And then, before Frankie had any clue what was happening, Mom folded her into a tight, flowery hug. The fabric of her shirt was soft and clean. Her hair was like silk against Frankie's cheek, and there was a not-so-small part of her that wanted to bury her face in Mom's shoulder and sob. "You brought the doctor's daughter," Mom said. "Francesca. I was hoping you would."

After a long moment, Mom stepped back, staring at Frankie like she might be able to drink her in.

Bex's whole body was quivering. "She didn't—"

"Yeah, I brought her," Frankie said. And an android ally, too.

If she had to, she'd make up a wild story about why Audrey and Kol weren't with her. But Mom seemed pleased just to have Bex here, and Frankie knew better than to volunteer a lie.

What would be the prize, for delivering part of the package? When she'd presented the design that had ultimately become Jord's implant, she'd been rewarded with a meal. An actual dinner, in a restaurant, and a full conversation with Mom and Dad.

Now, the impression of her mother's arms lingered on her body, the same way the phantom dangers had lingered in the jungle. Only this time, Frankie ached for the real thing.

Mom began assessing Frankie's injuries, skimming light touches over her face and clicking her tongue. She didn't offer Bex a second look; the girl was breathing, which—apparently— was enough to get them home. "Rogur has been hard on you," she said. "Look at your hands. My goodness, Francesca. You're nothing if not tenacious."

A year ago—no, a *week* ago—Frankie would have triumphed at those words. At so much attention from her mother, from either of her parents. Even now, tears welled in her eyes. Traitors.

Mom noticed. Of course she did. "My mother was hard on me, too," she said, softly. "Michael's parents were desperate for a true scientific legacy in the family, someone to make up for their son's failings, and my mother sacrificed everything she had to grasp the opportunity. She understood that I had to be the best in order to gain their attention, and there were times when I hated her for it. But I didn't falter."

"I *am* a physicist," Dad said. He sounded tired.

Rather than pulling Frankie closer, Mom's story snapped

her back to reality. Was Frankie supposed to pity her mother, because her life and education had been aimed in pursuit of an arranged marriage? Oh, poor Cindy, marrying into one of the richest and most powerful families on Earth. What a shame. So she didn't see Dad as her equal. Maybe that was *her* failing.

Frankie would've felt bad for her, if Mom had done anything good with that power. Instead, she just felt sick.

Mom didn't grant Dad so much as a glance. "It's not enough to be brilliant, Francesca, or hard working. You've always been those things. But you have to be ruthless, too. Willing to do what it takes, for the sake of science. Your grandparents coddled your father, and you see how that turned out."

Cruelty as a ticket into the family. So they hadn't been ignoring Frankie all these years. They'd been grooming her. Lovely.

"She couldn't do this without me." Dad muttered. "Without anthropology. Linguistics."

Frankie found it difficult to dredge up any sympathy for him, either, though she suspected he was right. Skills might be hirable. Loyalty wasn't. Look what had happened when they'd brought a small handful of scientists to Rogur. They'd figured out the deception and threatened the company.

Frankie still had a feeling that something was missing, the final piece drifting just out of sight. The scientists had realized the transport was hurting Rogur. What else had they learned?

Mom flipped a switch on the counter. The floor in front of the couches opened with a hum, and a spiral staircase unfurled like a coiled escalator. As usual, Frankie didn't understand the need for theatrics.

At least these stairs were going down.

"Ooh, yay," Bex said behind them as the stairs glowed blue to light their way. "A secret lab. I'm sure there's some great philanthropic work being done here."

Mom led Frankie slowly down the steps. She wasn't wearing her usual heels, and Frankie thought she moved a little awkwardly, though she seemed to be trying to hide that. Maybe Rogur hadn't been as kind to her as Frankie had assumed.

The stairs gave off a coppery smell, with undertones of dampness—like the rock walls of Kol's cave at the fortress—and Frankie realized too late that they were descending. With the screens hiding the true view, she couldn't be completely sure of where they were, but she thought the stairs might be drilling down into the cliffs.

More tunnels. Hidden inside more cliffs. She was really starting to hate this world.

Dad started after them, his hand on Bex's arm, but Mom waved him away. "Michael," she said. "Stay upstairs with the doctor's daughter."

"She won't remember, anyway," Dad said. A tiny rebellion. Frankie wondered if it would be worthwhile to trick him into siding with her, then discarded the idea. He might pretend and then betray her.

Mom sighed. "Just keep her out of the way." As if Bex were a puppy. Or a daughter.

Mom leaned in to Frankie's ear, giving her arm a light squeeze. "You have no idea how lonely it's been, how many times I've wanted to step in. To guide you."

Frankie wanted to weep with the irony of it. And maybe she should. She needed to convince Mom she was at least somewhat interested in her good opinion. She needed answers, and she needed to gain control of the androids.

Mom guided her to the center of a darkened room, where she stepped up onto a kind of arched bridge—though what the bridge was meant to cross, Frankie couldn't see.

When the lights flared on, she actually gasped. The glass bridge stretched across a replica of Rogur's crater, allowing her a full view of the lake beneath her feet, the fortress straight ahead, Lariasc at the water's edge. Villages were scattered across the interior of the crater, which was bigger—so much bigger—than she'd imagined, even after scanning it with the oculars. There was the cell tower on Bex's island, crowned in red lights, and the laboratory.

"This is how you track your tech?" she asked. "In red?"

Mom nodded. Did she seem... She couldn't actually be nervous, could she?

When Frankie glanced at Caisrach, no cluster of red lights flared in the city below the palace. She hoped it meant Audrey was holding off on her get-caught-on-purpose plan.

Wherever buildings were clustered into villages, pinpoints of green light patrolled.

A spark of hope ignited in Frankie's chest. If red meant magical tech, green could mean androids. She glanced around the room, searching for a computer or panel. Her eyes skimmed over the ruins of a dam to her left, the lake spilling toward the edge of the crater, and she thought of what Audrey had said about the drowned village.

Just above it, at the top of the miniature cliffs, a tablet stood on a pedestal. They must have commanded Aya from that spot. She pictured them standing there, heads bent together—or perhaps just Mom, shoving Dad out of the way.

Frankie could do it, too.

Mom was gazing over the map with that eerie look of pride still etched across her face. Was she really this proud of a piece of tech? It was nice and all, but Pathbound was capable of more than a fancy model and some tricks with lights. This model might have been an interactive display in a kids' museum.

Frankie looked again.

Strange to see the crater, the world she'd been traveling through, laid out like a simulation. Such a deep impact—she knew that firsthand, after nearly tumbling from the walls—and covering such a large area. She and Jord had touched only a spare triangle of it. The island rose out of the lake like a domed mountain. Probably formed out of liquified rock, from the meteor strike.

"It's a young crater," Frankie said, almost to herself. Trying to recall facts from when she'd skimmed through geology, considering it a largely unimportant addendum to the sciences. "The cliffs haven't been worn away like Earth's big craters, even though Rogur obviously has weather and atmosphere... wind..."

Mom waited, quiet, the model's lights blinking silently beneath her feet. What was this, some kind of Hartiger initiation test? Frankie pressed her lips together, thinking. "I thought a crater this big would mean global impact, but..."

She trailed off, not quite wanting to believe what she was about to say.

"Global impact," Bex repeated. She was leaning over the edge of the railing, Dad still holding halfheartedly onto her arm. "Like the dinosaur-killing kind?"

Exactly like the dinosaur-killing kind. If there had been humans on Rogur when this meteor hit... Could anyone have survived? It would depend on a lot of factors. As always, Frankie needed more data. But the odds that Pathbound would shoot a transport onto a recently decimated planet and just happen to land in the center of a thriving civilization—which had been constructed in the heart of the disastrous impact crater? Geologically recent could mean hundreds, if not thousands of years—but it was still too many coincidences.

Frankie stared at the map, and the final piece in the Hartiger mystery snapped into place.

The plague that didn't affect Earthens. The people's

strange memories. The cardboard towns and vacant streets, and Kol's moniker of foundling prince.

When Frankie looked up, Mom was watching her with this smile on her face, like she could read her daughter's mind, and... Was that actual pride in her eyes? Were those *tears*?

Frankie took a breath and let it out slowly. "Grandma and Grandpa never found inhabited worlds," she said. "They manufactured them. Right? Jord and Kol aren't doppelgängers from alternate realities. They're clones."

THIRTY-SIX

FRANKIE

Bex's mouth dropped open, and Frankie felt her father go still. He was always moving, always fidgeting with coins or scarves. The absence of movement was almost unnerving.

Mom held her gaze. She actually looked like she might smile.

Equally unnerving.

Frankie said, "You must have sped up the aging process in some of them, to create a full society. Who started it? Grandpa? Or you?"

Her grandfather had written that searching for inhabited worlds was like digging for a beach ball that was buried in a haystack the size of eternity. If you happened upon one, it was nothing more than pure luck. Hitting Suhainn, he'd said, was luck enough for several generations.

Lies, lies. Forever lies.

"The quiet cities," Bex said. "The wasteland beyond the crater. It's—you—"

Dad looked equally shocked, like he never would have expected Frankie to piece it together on her own. He was staring at her as if he'd never seen her before. "Where did you get all this?"

"She figured it out, of course," Mom said. "She's my daughter."

And she'd earned her way here. Not just because Mom mistakenly thought she'd brought Bex as a prisoner, but because Mom had watched her daughter treat people like instruments for years. She'd watched Frankie become mean and judgmental, critical and unhelpful. Brilliant at science, and merciless in her quest to obtain what she wanted.

But something still must have given Mom pause, until now. Audrey's influence, maybe, though Mom always seemed thrilled at Audrey's interest in Pathbound. Maybe it was the implant design, impressive and yet not aimed toward the proper Hartiger-worthy purpose.

Frankie thought back to Jord's arrival on Earth, to the heat of Mom's fury when she'd learned of Frankie's attempt to make friends through that embarrassing welcome presentation. Frankie had wanted to learn from him, it was true. But she'd also thought to help someone who was all alone in a new world.

Mom had rarely showed Frankie anything other than indifference. And yet that day, she'd been unable to suppress her wrath when her daughter demonstrated actual compassion.

Her parents had set her up to be as callous as they were, and they'd very nearly won. But they weren't the only influences in her life. There was generous Audrey, and there was Liz—who risked everything to search for her missing brother and niece, and befriended her enemy's daughter in the process.

And there was Jord, too. Her hidden ally, who knew what her parents wanted for her, who had done everything in his deceptively limited power to keep her from them. She wanted to punch him for not telling her everything. She wanted to rescue him. She wanted to hold his hands like she had in Nessa's basement, and never let go again.

"Sunset Protocol," Frankie said, her voice shaking. "You tried to bring Jord to Earth on Sunset Protocol, and you let Dad change it to Meteorite when I learned he was there. What was supposed to happen?"

Mom laced her hands together. "You tell me."

Mom's full attention. It was all Frankie had ever wanted. She choked back a sob. She had to stay calm for a few more minutes, so she could get to the android console. She took a surreptitious step toward it, trying to mask the movement as a shift of weight. Bren still stood by the stairs, waiting for a command. Bex was staring at Frankie like she wasn't sure if she needed to run.

There was nowhere to go.

"You activate a plague in your clones," Frankie guessed. "You scrub the world clean so you can start again."

Dad sputtered in protest, but Mom held her gaze. "Close. Oh, don't look at me like that, Francesca. Are you ready to claim your spot at Pathbound? You'll need to get used to hard truths."

"Research comes at a cost," Dad put in, collecting himself. "Utopia. It's within our grasp. We needed a testing ground."

Whose utopia? Not Jord's. Not Kol's. Just Dad's, his pursuit of cheap fame, earned by way of a firm grasp on the coattails of his parents.

Mom leaned in, conspiratorial, and squeezed Frankie's wrist. "It was hard for us at first, too. I know what it's like to be disappointed in your predecessors."

"Because you had to clean up Grandma and Grandpa's mistakes?"

Mom nodded, as though someone finally understood her. In a twisted kind of way, Frankie did. "It took years," Mom said.

"They designed the specimens to shut down with the absence of a specific protein supplement. A failsafe. Unfortunately, the trait worked erratically. It wasn't passed on to children."

Which explained why kids weren't contracting the plague. And why Kol hadn't gotten sick yet. He was one of the ones in whom the trait worked erratically. Maybe not at all.

Frankie's vision doubled. She blinked, righting it, and tugged her hand away from her mother. This was not the time to let anger cloud her reactions. She needed to get Jord home. "Specimens."

"It's what they are, Francesca. Earthen restrictions on science are far too rigid. We had to think outside the universe."

Dad's interest might be utopia. Mom, though, talked about her fake society—*two* societies—like she'd set up a couple of ant farms. The enormity of it was dumbfounding.

"But you lost control," Bex said. "Is that why Kol is the foundling prince? You figured you'd start over?"

What, they dropped a baby on the King's doorstep to grow up as a prince? So they could leash him?

"We did not repeat our mistakes in Suhainn," Mom said. "Rogur was always an alpha test. The beta is proving much more stable."

"Alpha test," Bex repeated. "These are *people*."

"They're rats."

Dad set his coin on the rail that surrounded the map and gave it a spin. "Fascinating, though," he said, as though that helped.

"So then, Francesca, with that background," Mom said, continuing the lesson, "define Sunset Protocol."

Frankie thought of the day she'd tried to approach Jord as a friend, the hollow look in his eyes as he'd evaluated her in silence before calling her parents. She thought of how he'd lain unconscious on the control floor, the drop of blood across his throat. "Sunset Protocol eliminates a single threat. Jord learned Suhainn's king was a fake." She swallowed. "You were going to kill him."

Bex made a strangled sound, and Frankie actually glanced at her to make sure she wasn't about to keel over. Or attack someone. There were probably android vampire bats hidden in the ceiling or something. This had to be handled calmly. Carefully.

Frankie wished she could shoot the other girl a look, a wink. But it was too risky.

"How is Jord doing?" Mom said. "Not well, I take it. I'd be interested to see how the effects take place in a Suhainnan generational. He's well supplied with the supplement on Earth, but here..."

The smoothies. God, Frankie was stupid. She'd spent her life thinking she was the smartest person in the room, and she'd missed everything. She gripped the railing of the bridge, afraid she'd faint without its support. This was not the time to show weakness. She took a breath, steadied herself, and stepped toward the edge of the crater. She could feign interest. She could feign supervillain.

She needed to get to the control tablet. "So Meteorite Protocol is what... evacuation to Earth? Immigration?"

With neck implants for leashes. A mad scientist had to keep track of her creations, after all.

"You see, Michael," Mom said. "She's ready."

"He was your age," Dad said, as though picking up an age-old argument, well-worn words. As though Frankie might side with Mom, tell him he should have killed Jord after all. "I thought... I hadn't imagined enacting Sunset on someone so young."

Bex snorted.

"I'd have taken care of it, once we got to Earth," Mom said.

"But you were always there, Francesca. No matter how many restrictions we put in place, you kept interfering."

"And then the media found out we had an interworld immigrant," Dad said. "They swarmed."

Mom glared at Dad, like she suspected him of leaking the information.

Frankie almost wanted to smile. Jord had cornered them into sparing his life. He'd bought himself time to become indispensable to Pathbound. Smart.

"Jord was an interesting study," Mom said, "and he gave us someone to manage the company during long absences. Fan clubs are all well and good, but he had no legal rights on Earth. And now we have you, Francesca. You're ready."

Mom was already speaking of Jord in the past tense. A problem, removed.

"How is this even possible?" Bex whispered. Frankie had never heard her speak so quietly. "How—it's—you transport them here? Twelve clones at a time?"

"They have bigger vehicles," Frankie said, thinking of the garage at Pathbound where she'd spent so much time disassembling the old transport.

Mom waved a hand. "Logistics are so tiresome. We have labs here, too. Rebecca, isn't it? Your father's here. You can go home. I take it that's all you want."

Without her memories, though. Not that Mom would advertise it.

"You'd better not send me home," Bex said, through gritted teeth. "I'll take out a billboard in Times Square listing all your crimes."

The print would be too small to read.

"You won't remember a thing," Mom said. Right, so apparently she *would* advertise it. That was some serious hubris.

"We never planned to leave you here forever. It took longer to perfect the solution than we'd hoped."

"Removing memories is easy." Dad gave the quarter a toss. "It's crafting new ones that's tough. You have to get the details right. Bit different for each person. It's an art."

Like fake magic. Like myths, games, traditions, and language. His eyes were shining, excited. Mom might look down on Dad's particular skillset, but he was right. They wouldn't have managed any of this without him.

"What about Jord?" Frankie asked, stepping off the bridge and circling the crater, studying the way the lights moved.

Mom followed her at a saunter. "Jord is another matter."

"We'd bring him," Dad said. Placating, or guilty? "We would. But the memory procedure is... complicated."

"Translation," Bex said, "it doesn't work on clones."

"I'll solve that particular glitch eventually," Mom said.

Glitch. Like a badly behaving computer program. If Frankie let them see she cared, they'd alter her memories, too—and she might well spend the rest of her life repeating the false story of Jord's demise in interviews and memoirs.

Fake, fake, fake. Worlds, reputations, memories. It was all a shoddy piece of theater.

"It's time for you to take up your role at Pathbound," Mom said. "I know you have a lot to contribute. Your full-planet exploration ideas, to start."

You'll never earn their admiration until you no longer deserve it by any other standard.

Jord was right. He'd been right all along.

"And Rogur?" Bex asked. "What will happen here?"

"Kol can get us into his fortress without incident," Dad said. "The transport dock is there. After that, the gods will clean up."

Scrubbing the world, via android.

"It's a wrench to leave them," Mom said, and for a moment Frankie thought she meant the people. But no. She meant her precious machines. To Mom, this was a laboratory, and the people were science projects. No more worth crying over than a petri dish of bacteria.

Frankie reached the console and stopped. "If you feel that way, Mom, then you can hang out with them a little longer. Bren, shield me."

Mom's head jerked up in surprise, but there wasn't time to care. Frankie bent over the tablet and started typing, following the same steps she'd used to reroute Bren's loyalty. From here, it was easy.

The android peeled away from the door, his steps heavy as he marched toward Mom. Dad tried to dive for Frankie, but Bex caught his knees, and they both crashed to the floor.

Mom, on the other hand, seemed to have recovered from her shock. She didn't move, and she didn't seem worried. At all.

Well, she should be. Frankie *was* brilliant. And she could be ruthless—when it was deserved. The lights on the map paused and blinked yellow, awaiting further instruction.

"Enact Houston Protocol," Mom said, walking casually around the perimeter of the crater to offer Dad a hand. Frankie was surprised Mom cared enough about him to help.

A hiss of air brushed through the back of Frankie's hair. Bex called her name, and she started to spin, but something dug into her shoulders, vice-like, lifting her off the floor before she could turn. Like metal fingers. Aya fingers.

Frankie kicked, which only wrenched her shoulders painfully. As if her poor arms hadn't been through enough already, now they felt like they'd crack open.

Mom sighed. Back to disappointment. "They revert to their original programming at the sound of my voice."

Dad nodded. "Or mine."

Mom cast him a glance, and Frankie understood that it was true—unless Dad were to attempt bot-mutiny against Mom.

Failsafes upon failsafes. Frankie would never outrun them. She twisted, biting back a cry as tears of pain pooled in her eyes.

Bren took a firm hold of Bex's arm as Frankie's captor set her feet back on the floor, where her knees gave out in relief at the sudden absence of pain.

She dropped her head back, then wished she hadn't; the android had a giant's features. A bulbous nose and bulging eyes, pointy ears dotted with golden studs—solar panels, she assumed—and a club holstered at his side.

Not their most creative design, but certainly a frightening one.

Thirty seconds. That was all it had taken for her parents to best her.

"I won't leave without Jord," Frankie said. "Liz has control of the operations floor. You can't win this."

Dad tossed his quarter again, uncomfortable. Mom caught it and tucked it into her pocket. "Before you arrived, we recouped enough technology to patch communications and reach our security bots at Pathbound. Quite a wonderful accident. I had no idea there were still so many artifacts left in Rogur."

Frankie's mouth went dry. Audrey and the others had tried their plan after all.

Jord would have stayed hidden in the basement with Reyche, though. If Frankie could find a way to extract Bex's father and the other celebrities, she might be able to sneak back down here and try again. How long did Jord have?

"Bren," Mom said. "Retrieve my daughter's pack before we reunite her with her friends."

Frankie swallowed. How many had they caught?

"Yes, all of them," Mom said as though reading her thoughts. She followed Bren to a door, and Frankie pictured androids streaming out of these walls, unstoppable. "We have thermal scanners, Francesca. Hidden basements, what an idea. No wonder you abandoned them."

"I didn't—"

"Enough," Mom interrupted. "There will be no schemes. No plans. No reprogramming androids. You have one night to say goodbye, while we finalize our affairs."

Genocide required planning, after all. Frankie swallowed her nausea as the android lifted the pack from Frankie's shoulders. And then, without instruction or preamble, Mom tugged the tools out from under Frankie's arm. "You won't be needing these, either."

The wrench was almost physically painful. Her tools, her safety, back in her mother's hands. It was almost too perfect.

"We'll get to Pathbound and you'll see," Mom said. "There are more opportunities for a brain like yours than you could possibly hope for."

THIRTY-SEVEN

FRANKIE

Bex kept a steady stream of expletives running under her breath as the android led them through a system of identical passages. The metal tubes were no better than Kol's dank cave; worse, Frankie could practically taste the rust. Nothing like questioning the structural integrity of a clifftop palace to calm the nerves.

For once in her life, Frankie had no schemes, no solutions, no plans. Every single one of her backups had been spent, and everyone who mattered to her was in danger.

What was she supposed to tell Jord?

Hey, so, have we ever talked about the process of transferring DNA into egg cells for the purpose of duplicating an animal? Like, say, a human? Because, funny story...

Or maybe he already knew. Maybe he'd been keeping that secret, too, and he wouldn't be surprised.

Too soon, Bren stopped and deposited them into a doorway. No ceremony, no expression, just another routine task.

"They forgot to activate that one's charm button," Bex muttered.

Given the unforgiving starkness of the hallways, Frankie had expected a bare cell, everyone huddled together in the middle of a cold floor. Instead, she found herself in a parlor with a circle of sofas and chairs, a coffee table. Dizzyingly normal. A spiral staircase—Frankie's knees protested the thought—led up to a loft, and there was a balcony at the end of the hall.

Imprisoned, Hartiger style.

And occupied, too.

Before Frankie could register the faces of the people seated before her, one of the men launched himself at Bex, who hugged a person Frankie could only assume was her father with all the fierceness she'd come to recognize as love.

The VR-TV star from *Mars Colony*, Wendy, nodded to Frankie, red curls bobbing. The celebrity chef looked at her with eyes narrowed in suspicion—Frankie didn't blame him— though his husband gave her a small smile. All in this together.

"Where's Audrey?" Bex asked. Her face was shining with tears, but she was smiling.

Her father's face sobered. He wore a gray T-shirt, and glasses with frayed string at the hinges. Seven years on a single pair of glasses. It was probably the least of the troubles he'd endured here. If Frankie got them out of this, Pathbound would make it right with Bex and her dad. They had to. "She's with the prince's twin," he said.

Frankie stomach flipped. A part of her, she realized, had feared he might not wake up at all. "Is he... I mean, the fever?"

"He's not comfortable, but he seemed lucid enough. I take it you're Frankie?"

She nodded.

"Hartiger?"

"Yes."

He shook his head. "This gets weirder and weirder. But if

you're Frankie, he's been asking for you. He's in the infirmary. End of the hall, before the balcony."

The whole space was so strange, open and meticulously perfect. It reminded her of *Mars Colony*, actually; too many people stuffed into a small space, under trying circumstances. Maybe VR-TV was meant to be Pathbound's next big endeavor. Would they vote people out of the world? What would they call that protocol?

At first glance into the infirmary, Frankie questioned the lucidity analysis. Jord sat hunched over a desk in the far corner. He'd shoved a pile of medical supplies to the side, and was writing on what looked like a strip of cloth. Audrey stood to his right, watching over his shoulder with a somber expression.

Jord's skin might have been made of wax, he was so impossibly pale. She could tell by the deliberate way he placed the pen that he was working hard to keep his hand steady.

Her family had done this to him.

He finished writing and handed the cloth to Audrey. A quick glance around the room showed it was a piece of the bedsheet. He'd ripped up his sheets, to write on.

"What's going on?" Frankie said.

Jord rubbed his fingers together and looked up at Audrey. "Thank you."

Audrey rolled up the sheet and put it in her pocket. "I've got good lawyers."

"Hello?" Frankie said. "Shouldn't you be resting, or have you stopped dying?"

Audrey lay a hand on Jord's shoulder. "I'll let you talk."

Jord nodded, and Audrey stepped past Frankie. "Our plan didn't work," she said.

"I figured. Neither did mine."

Audrey gave her a sympathetic smile, which should have been a good sign—one of forgiveness, maybe. Instead, it made

Frankie's stomach hurt even more. It felt like the bile was rising to thread its way around her throat and choke her.

When the door closed, Frankie made herself cross the room. Jord was cleaning up the ink, setting everything in place. "They can't know I was writing," he said. "Not that Michael would notice. I could tip a jar of ink over in front of him. He'd make some joke about clumsy Suhainnans and watch me clean it up. Cindy's another matter."

He knew them well. "Jord," Frankie said. "What are you—"

"I've signed Pathbound over to you," he said. "Audrey's my witness. I may get Russ to sign as well. Bex's father. I know it's not official, but under the circumstances..."

He crossed to the wash basin in the corner, moving with a feverish intensity that scared Frankie more than his listlessness at Nessa's had. He dipped his hands into the water and rubbed his fingers together, scrubbing the ink away.

"That's stupid," Frankie said, "because I'm getting you to Earth."

Jord finished his washing and turned to face her. "I don't know how well bedsheets will hold up in court, but I already indicated verbally to the lawyers that I wanted you as a partner. The transition ought to be natural enough."

"Will you shut up?"

"Never. I refuse to exit this life without proper last words." He said it without so much as a hint of a smile, yet Frankie refused to take it as anything other than a joke. A dark, black-humored, horrifying joke.

"Stop," she said, more emphatically than she meant to. "No one is exiting life."

He came toward her, his brown eyes shining with fever. She was almost surprised she couldn't see shimmers of heat radiating off his body. She could certainly feel it. "You asked me to take a chance on you," he said. "This is what it looks like."

Frankie had no idea what to say. So she did the only thing she could think of. She twined one hand around his neck, skimming carefully around the bandage she'd put there, and she kissed him.

He inhaled sharply as their lips met, as if it was the last thing he expected from any version of Frankie, in any world. For the barest instant, he leaned in.

But he broke away almost immediately, like a slap. "The plague," he said. "We don't know how it's contracted."

The choking feeling intensified, trying to silence her. This was all her fault. If it wasn't for Frankie, he'd be at home with his smoothies and his supplements. Her parents wouldn't be second guessing their decision to save him. He'd be safe.

She lifted her hand to his face, drawing him back to her. "It isn't... Earthens can't catch it."

He was so close, their breath mingled between them. "You'll save the worlds one day," he said.

He didn't demand explanations, or proof. He believed her when she told him Earthens were safe, because he knew her.

This time, he kissed her. Gently at first, as though he feared she might evaporate, and when she didn't, with more certainty. His lips were too hot, his skin burning against hers. She let her hands slide into his hair as he pulled her close, his arm around her waist.

He kissed her the way he'd always fought her. Like he had attention for nothing else.

And he wiped away her tears before she knew she was crying.

Frankie stayed with him until he fell asleep, because he asked her to.

Because she wanted to.

When he'd no longer had the energy to stand, Frankie helped him to bed. And because she didn't know what else to do, because she didn't know how to fix this, she slid her shoes off and lay down beside him. He was still so warm, but shivers wracked his body. She wrapped her arms around him, like she might be able to hold him here.

"You really made me hate you," she said.

She wasn't expecting a reply, so when she heard his voice, rough from fever and dehydration, she startled. "It was just so damn easy. Francesca."

For a while, she stayed tucked against his side, feeling the breath come in and out of his chest. When she'd convinced herself he wouldn't slip away in the next few minutes, she slid off the bed, careful not to wake him, and tiptoed out of the room.

She found Bex's father on the balcony, watching the day

wane. The balcony was arranged with chairs and a little table, as if this were a beach house rather than a pretty prison cell. Clearly, her parents were confident enough in their security systems to allow balconies. They were surrounded by walls of sheer rock. No scaling those, unless you happened to be a spider.

Kol was there, too, standing by the rail with a mug in his hand and flicking shards of glass into the crater. It hurt to look at him. "How are the parents?" he asked. "Did they applaud your plan to save Rogur from the brink of destruction?"

Frankie ignored him and sat down next to Russ. "They're going to bring us back. Tomorrow."

Russ looked at her steadily for a long moment. "You look like you're going into battle, not going home."

They weren't soldiers, or guards. A bunch of kids. A handful of celebrities. This world might have toughened them up, but they had no weapons. Jord might be able to throw a few punches—she made a mental note to ask him where he'd acquired that particular skill, as a page—but he wasn't exactly in good form at the moment.

Frankie took a deep breath. "Did you know?" she asked, glancing at Kol. "That they're clones?"

"I didn't *know*," Russ said slowly.

"But you suspected."

Russ sighed. "Your parents were careful, Frankie. No one on our team ever set foot in Suhainn. No chance of running across a doppelgänger. But this illness... It's bizarre. After your parents left, I made a study of it. There was never a single victim younger than seven years old, and very few between seven and twenty. It wiped out older adults, your grandparents' generation, without exception. But in the in-between years... It was wildly inconsistent."

"How is this even possible?" Frankie said. "This conspiracy... It's massive. They started work on Suhainn before they'd even left Rogur."

"Long before. They didn't work alone. They have all of Pathbound at their disposal. Half the people there don't know what they're working on. I didn't, when I signed up. It seemed like a good opportunity, and the compartmentalization, well... Your parents are extremely convincing."

"Russ. We have to save him."

Russ stood and headed for the door, an abrupt movement that reminded her of Bex. "There's no cure."

"There is. On Earth. All we need to do is get him there. Convince my parents."

Russ paused, hand on the door. "I want to help you, Frankie. But I have no idea how to do that."

Frankie tried to muster a thread of anger, or even indignation, but she couldn't. It wasn't as if Russ was concealing information from her. He didn't know how to save Jord. And besides, he had his own daughter to take care of, his sister to defend when they returned to Earth.

Frankie stayed put, watching Kol. He leaned on the rail, looking out at the crater. Not that there was far to see, in the darkness. Spots of light burned in the distance, reminding her of her mom's map.

Kol held up his mug and examined it for a moment before tipping back its contents.

"You didn't tell me Jord was sick," Frankie said.

She'd spoken in Roguran, but he answered in English. As if to remind her that he could. "He asked me not to."

"And you're so reliable?"

"That's all right, darling. Take it out on me, if you need to." It was the kind of statement the prince usually dashed off sarcastically. This time, though, he sounded sincere.

"I don't want him to die, either, incidentally," Kol added. "We're so evenly matched at *cluichur*."

And back to not-so-sincere. Frankie wrapped her arms around herself, the cold biting through her thin layers. She should go to Jord. She should be with him, not Kol. "What *do* you want?"

"Another drink."

Frankie waited. Kol ran a hand through his hair, gripping it like he might pull it out. "I want my world back."

"I'm sorry."

"Yes, well. You should be. You're entirely responsible for the actions of people who share your name."

"I should warn you," Frankie said. "They're going to leave the gods when they go."

"A fitting end for a rotten world," Kol said.

Frankie had no idea how to respond. It wasn't a fitting end for anyone. What would the androids do, when their task was completed, when the last human life was extinguished? Would they continue to patrol, or would they freeze in place, as Aya had in Lariasc, leaving the dust to sweep them into oblivion?

They sat in silence for a long time, until Frankie couldn't stand the cold any longer. She got up, somehow reluctant to leave him. "It's freezing out here," she said. "Don't get so drunk you lose your balance."

THIRTY-NINE

KOL

Kol stayed on the balcony long after the cold had driven Frankie inside, her words ringing in his head like an invitation.

If only she knew how the wind tempted him, curling up out of the depths. Beckoning. He could throw glass into the crater all night, as if he hoped to sever that siren's vocal cords, but still she would call. A man didn't need war in his ears and *afan* in his veins to hear death's song. But war and murder, alcohol and despair, those things fueled her.

He'd been here before. He knew how easy it was to lift his body to sit on the rail, or perhaps—if he wanted to prevent his captain's interference this time—to simply vault over it.

How long would he fall? How long would Rogur miss him?

He ought to find Reyche. Instead, he stayed, and he thought about Frankie Hartiger. Even after her talk with the Earthen doctor, a conversation Kol only half understood, the light of hope lingered in her eyes.

Kol didn't want to care. If she could be believed, his world was about to be extinguished. Not with the agony of famine, but with the flames of a war his people did not even know they should resist. These gods were like the *afan* in that way. Tricky. Insidious.

He didn't want to care about Frankie Hartiger and her Hartiger problems.

He sighed and pressed his forehead against the rail. There was something so profoundly unsatisfying about tossing glass into a canyon like this. For all he could tell, the shards might dissolve like snowflakes as soon as they winked out of his line of sight. They might never hit the ground.

He could heave a boulder, and he doubted anyone would hear it land.

Don't get so drunk you lose your balance.

No. He had a better idea.

Kol launched his empty mug against the rail. It shattered, sending a wave of *afan* splashing into the crater. He knelt, feeling around until he found a chunk of clay with a particularly jagged edge.

He slipped it into his sleeve, and swept the rest away.

When Jord woke, the room felt wrong.

To start with, it was so hot that it might have been transported to the inside of a volcano while he'd slept. A blurry, spinning volcano. And when he tried to kick off his blankets, something prevented him. Some*one*, sitting at the foot of the bed.

The last few hours rushed into Jord's head. How he'd arranged his affairs, however haphazardly. And Frankie. Her lips against his, the dizzying taste of citrus and honey. Her head, tucked between his chin and shoulder.

He could easily have dreamed it. Jord sat up. "Frankie?"

"Even better."

Jord fell back. It was just Kol. Though bereft of his usual accompanying cloud of alcohol fumes. "Where is she?"

Kol got up and paced to the desk, where Jord had so carefully rearranged the medical supplies. The prince moved casually, hands in his pockets, shoulders rounded. And yet, there was something deliberate about the movement that suggested he knew what he wanted. Perhaps it was that, for once, he was steady on his feet. "Hounding everyone who will listen, and some who refuse, about a plan to save your life. It's quite annoying."

Of course, she would still be trying. Jord wanted her here. He wanted his arms around her. Too late. It was all too late. "She can't save me."

Kol surveyed the items on the table. The light was dim, and it was hard to guess what he might be looking for. He ran his hand over the supplies, then plucked up a roll of bandages and a hand mirror. A real mirror, not a screen, unless the Hartigers had changed up their designs. "Little known fact. Should she manage to get you to Earth, she can save you. The group leaves at first light, in fact. But Mama and Papa Hartiger prefer to let you die."

Jord didn't ask why. He didn't care. "She has to stop."

Kol passed the bandages back and forth from one hand to the other. "Ah. I was under the impression you'd met her before."

She would never stop fighting. Frankie knew failure, which meant she knew persistence. But this time, it would keep her from him. "How long would you say I have?"

Kol returned to the bed, seating himself at Jord's side. "I think you know the answer to that."

Jord's world blinked. Hours. "Would you get her for me?"

"Afraid not."

"Last request?"

Kol shrugged. "I've seen quite a few people die. It's nothing new. And I'm idealistically opposed to the concept of a last request. Too maudlin."

Jord could have pointed out the numerous contradictions in that statement, but there wasn't any point. He struggled to sit up in bed. "Then I'll get her myself. I want to see her, before she goes."

Kol held him down easily with a fist to the chest. "A moment, if you will."

Right. Frankie would have anticipated this. "She sent you here to prevent me from interfering, didn't she?"

Kol laughed. "Oh, she has no idea I'm here."

What scheme would keep her from him, in his dying hours? It was too late. He could feel it. They wouldn't even be able to reach the transport before... No. She had to come. "When she runs out of other options, she'll go to her parents," Jord said. "She'll beg for my life."

"You're concerned they'll demand a heavy price."

"She's not exactly a cold negotiator. They could get anything out of her, if they see she wants it badly enough."

And they would not keep their word. His knowledge was too dangerous.

"So this is a noble death, then," Kol said. "Good. I like it. Chin up, and all that."

"It's the only way I have to beat them."

"Mm. By running away."

As if he had a choice. He closed his eyes and found it took several seconds to force them open again. "If you don't mind, I'm trying to think of it as an act of defiance."

Kol sat back beside Jord, propping his feet up on the bed. He hadn't bothered to remove his shoes. "Sure, dying can be radical. Though sometimes the best way to fuck them all over is to live."

It was not the kind of sentence Jord expected to hear from his twin. The opposite, perhaps. "And how do you propose I do that?"

Kol handed him the mirror. "Hold this up, if you will."

Jord complied, confused. It was still strange, it would never stop being strange, to see their faces side by side. Not that he had very long to contemplate it. Twins, but not brothers.

Before he knew what was happening, Kol shook a jagged sliver of clay out of his sleeve and applied it to his own forehead. The clay parted his flesh like a zipper, a wound to match Jord's.

Jord let the mirror fall, but it was too late. Kol held a bandage to his forehead. He sat up, eyes burning with intense focus. "They need me if they hope to get into the fortress, and they know it. I've arranged it so that my soldiers will only open the doors for me. Not for Reyche, or any of the others. I realize they could muster their robot army, but they're looking for an easy path out. And I'm it."

"How did you—"

Kol held up his hand. "If you are strong enough to hold on, to play a part for a few hours, my face will get you to the transport. The rest..."

The rest would be up to Jord, and the others. Something like hope stirred in Jord's chest. But he shook his head, tamping the feeling down hard. Hope had only ever led him astray. "If you stay here, you'll die."

"Perhaps."

"I can't let you die for me."

Kol smiled. He actually looked excited. Almost giddy with it. "Let me handle that little situation, if you please."

Little situation. More like a fuse set to blow open a powder keg. But Kol was already unbuttoning his shirt, preparing to trade clothing. Maybe he had a plan, and maybe not—but clearly Jord's acquiescence was as essential to Kol as it was to Jord.

If Jord could make it to Earth, he might live.

"I can barely stand," Jord said. "How will I convince them?"

"Excellent. That's the attitude I was hoping for." Kol slipped a flask out of his pocket. "You are in luck, my friend.

Because most of the time, I can barely stand myself. A bite of *afan* on your breath, a dab on the neck and wrists, and they'll assume I've been in my cups. I always knew my drunkenness would amount to something."

However lightly he said it, he wasn't drunk now. His eyes were clear as he helped Jord ease out of the bed. "There's one thing I need you to translate for me, if you don't mind," he said. "An English term. I'm afraid I can't quite grasp its meaning."

Jord nodded.

"What in all the worlds is a *clone*?"

FORTY-ONE
FRANKIE

Hartigers didn't do horses, wagons, or caravans. They certainly didn't walk.

No, Hartigers brought driverless cars to their fabricated worlds, the better to frighten the poor magic-fearing subjects with.

This one was more like a military-grade bus, with huge wheels and a hulking body. Frankie tipped her head back and watched the sky float across the sunroof, the corner of a bright red flag whipping in and out of the frame.

They had everyone. The celebrities. Russ, Bex, Audrey, Kol. Everyone but Jord.

He'd been asleep, when she went to say goodbye. She'd stood there for a long moment, watching him. Considering whether to interrupt his dreams. She'd lingered in the doorway, reciting excuses, then settled for brushing her lips on his forehead and hurrying out of the room.

He hadn't stirred. It was better that way. He knew her well enough to know that. She sucked at goodbyes.

When Mom and Dad showed up, the only thing she could

think to do was to sit on the floor and refuse to budge. Dad called it a whim. Mom called it a fit. As if Frankie were a person who experienced whims and fits.

They'd directed one of their android gods—not Bren—to carry her onto the bus, slung over its shoulder. It was probably the least dignified way to be hauled down the side of a cliff.

Frankie was well acquainted with the thoughts, feelings, and particular stomachache that accompanied failure. She'd always assumed that eventually, she'd achieve her goals. She'd win. Now, the pain drove up through her chest, threatening to open her throat from the inside. For the first time, it occurred to her that she might not win. She might not be able to save anyone.

She could hardly breathe.

Worse, she was stuck next to Kol. Mainly because she'd wanted to be as far from Mom and Dad as the bus would allow, and Kol was sitting in the front, presumably for similar reasons. He was so drunk, it was clear that the seat belt alone kept him from sliding to the floor. A mess of curls had fallen across his forehead, and he wove in and out of consciousness as they bumped along the road.

An hour into the trip, they reached the dead forest. The trees stretched out for her, skeletal and accusing, as if hoping to breach the sunroof.

"Tell me something," Kol said, and Frankie jumped.

"No," she said.

"You don't know what it is."

Frankie couldn't face him. It wasn't his fault he looked like Jord, but it didn't matter. "Don't care."

"What kind of enchantment causes a carriage to run on its own?"

That, she couldn't resist. "An electric engine."

"Electric. It's like... fire?"

"No, it's currents of energy that interact with a magnetic field to produce motion."

Kol leaned back. "I'm going to keep thinking it's like fire."

"You do that."

The bus careened through the woods, and she could feel the others craning their necks to look out the windows. This world was sliding into death, faster than anyone could control it. As soon as they were gone, Pathbound's androids would finish the job.

Regardless of what happened here, the Hartigers were never going to stop their interworld exploration. Rogur could become a husk. They'd use it as a bridge until it ceased to function.

And yet, Frankie couldn't entirely wish to stop interworld travel, either. They needed to continue delivering the antidote to Suhainn, or everyone there would die. Jord had a brother there. Friends, or so she assumed.

She couldn't save him. Maybe she could save them.

Mom wanted her on the team. There might even be a way to placate her enough that she'd choose to let Frankie remember.

Placating the Hartigers. That was Jord's specialty, not Frankie's. She squeezed her eyes shut, but her treacherous body allowed a tear to squeeze out and run down her face.

"He'll be OK," Kol said, his voice low.

Frankie dragged her sleeve across her face. Of course he had to be watching her right at that moment. "Don't lie."

"Want to talk about it?"

"Nope."

"Want to tell me how a magic mirror works?"

Now that he was talking, he didn't seem drunk at all. He smelled like alcohol, and he looked like death, but he wasn't slurring his words.

When Frankie didn't bother answering, Kol leaned toward her. "I'm trying to help," he said. "Truly."

"What do you care?"

He shrugged. He'd experienced trauma, too, his parents dead of the Pathbound Plague, his world trampled by gods. Maybe Frankie had been unfair to him. Maybe he did care.

She glanced around the carriage. Her parents sat in the last row, heads together. Everyone else looked scared. "I left him alone."

"What choice did you have?"

In some other world, somewhere, another version of Frankie had found a solution. Some version of Jord would live.

Rogur and Suhainn didn't prove the alternate world theory. So what? Alternate worlds could still exist. Frankie found herself wanting to believe that they did.

There could be versions of her parents who had done good.

"Reyche is there," Kol said. "I asked him to watch over your friend, until... I asked him to help."

That was actually nice. Didn't make it easier to look him in the eye, but it was nice. "He came here because of me," she said. "I killed him."

Kol leaned his head back and gazed out of the skylight. When he reached across the seat to take her hand, she didn't pull away.

Too soon, the car reached the fortress gates. What would the soldiers think, to see this monstrosity lumbering toward the walls? Her parents had gone to the trouble of creating magic-mirror screens, an army of robots to match their fabricated mythologies, and they couldn't bother with cars that fit in.

If you were going to accept a part like this, the least you could do was commit to the role.

"All right, your highness," Mom said. "I'll open the roof, and you'll show your face."

"I hope you don't plan to murder me as soon as we're inside," Kol said, fumbling with his seat belt. "That would be unpleasant."

Of course, Mom wouldn't see it as murder; murder was reserved for humans. She saw Kol and Jord as vermin, and vermin required extermination.

Kol climbed onto the seat, swaying slightly, as if it was an effort to keep his balance. Drunk or not drunk? The Prince Kol story.

Frankie looked up, mostly to make sure he wasn't about to fall on top of her. If she'd blinked, she wouldn't have caught it before he stuck his head out: stitches, raw and heeling, right at the base of his neck.

Not Kol. Jord.

Hope bloomed through the pain in her chest, warm release mixed with renewed fear. It was all she could do to keep it from slipping onto her face.

Frankie unbuckled her seat belt. "I'll stand with him."

"That's not necessary, Francesca," Mom said.

"You know, Mom," Frankie said, "I think it is."

She didn't give her mother a chance to argue. She jumped up onto the seat and stuck her head and shoulders out of the skylight next to Jord. This place smelled like stale fire, and mildew. She gripped the edges of the sunroof, unable to take her eyes off of him. How could she have missed it?

He shouldn't be out of bed. He shouldn't even be able to stand. But he was still here, grinning at her. They still had a chance.

It took a concerted effort not to throw her arms around him in relief. "Electric, it's like fire? Really?"

Jord held up a hand to shield his eyes from the light. "As glad as I am to hear I'm a convincing actor, it took you entirely too long to put that together. Please tell me you did not kiss him goodbye."

"I didn't."

"You didn't kiss me goodbye? Are you a monster?"

"Aren't you supposed to be dead right now?"

He set a hand on top of hers, and she could feel him shaking. No wonder he was so warm. She twined her fingers with his. "This is a last ditch move, Frankie," he said.

No. It was a plan. And it was going to work. He was here, and that meant she could get him onto the transport.

Kol had switched places with Jord. Voluntarily. She'd told him what was going to happen, that Rogur was about to ignite. Caisrach first, no doubt. He'd stayed anyway.

A figure on the ramparts peeled away from the watchtower and lifted a hand in greeting. Jord returned the wave. "I hope I didn't signal for them to shoot at us."

The gate shuddered, then eased open. The car rolled forward.

Frankie started to help Jord into the car, and something behind them clicked. Dad stood balanced against the back of the skylight. He had a gun aimed at Jord.

The car was still moving, but the world froze. Dad had told her it was different, killing someone in person, but he didn't look like a man with a moral dilemma. Two hands on the weapon, comfortable and solid. Like a cop at a shooting range on TV. His eyes were cold.

Frankie didn't think. She threw her body in front of Jord, just as Dad pulled the trigger.

The blow struck before her feet landed, throwing her off balance. Jord's hand brushed by hers as the world screamed.

And then she was falling.

For an instant, Jord thought he had her.

His fingers closed around air, too slow. Too weak to haul her up, even if he'd caught her.

The car lurched to a stop. Michael stared at Frankie's crumpled form, his eyes wide and glassy, mouth frozen in a horrified O as Russ darted outside.

Jord dropped to the seat, his body heavy and scarcely under his control. He scrambled to the ground, landing on his knees with a jolt that jammed his teeth together. He tasted blood.

He crawled, scraping his body through the dirt to get to Frankie. He was vaguely aware that a smattering of soldiers had assembled around the car. Kol's soldiers; his soldiers. They were probably waiting on instruction, but Jord could only focus on Frankie.

She groaned and tried to lift her hand to her head—and Jord could breathe again because it meant she was alive—but Russ held her arm down. A red stain bloomed across her shoulder.

They were in great shape for a showdown, clearly.

Russ ripped a strip of cloth from his shirt and shoved it against the wound. He looked as if he'd had a lot of practice doing that. "What happened up there? Michael shot his own daughter?"

Jord swallowed a wave of nausea. "He was aiming at me."

"He shouldn't have missed."

Cindy. In his peripheral vision, the soldiers raised their swords. As if that would save anyone.

Jord wrenched his eyes from Frankie to look up at her mother. She had a gun aimed at his face, a situation that was beginning to feel disturbingly familiar. Unlike Bex's firearm, Cindy's had been recently oiled, and he had no doubt it was loaded.

The gun was aimed at Jord, but Cindy's eyes were on her daughter. Jord had seen her angry, firing employees for minor offenses and cowing everyone in a three-mile radius. He'd never seen her look shaken, of all things. Surely she didn't actually care that her daughter was in danger? Now, of all times? "Help the doctor, Michael," she said. "We need her."

"Since when? Since today, when you decided I'm the only one who gets you?" Frankie asked, brushing her father's attentions aside with her unrestrained hand. "Get him away from me."

Russ shushed her, but he didn't push. Michael sat back, looking stricken and sorry. It made Jord want to hit him.

"You don't give us enough credit, Francesca," Cindy said. "We've always appreciated your mind."

Jord couldn't help it. He laughed.

Cindy glared at him, like she might glare at a scorpion before extinguishing it beneath her shoe. Disgust. Disdain. What, because of the clone thing? Kol's question had slid the truth into place clearly enough. But it seemed like a less-than-valid reason to hate someone.

Kol might think the best way to defeat them would be to live on. Right now, Jord would settle for standing. He pulled himself to all fours and then slowly, methodically, pushed to his feet. Cindy allowed it, probably because it was the most pathetic example of a man trying to stand that anyone had ever seen, in any world.

Dizziness pulled at his ears in a roar of heat.

Somehow, Jord kept his body squarely in front of the gun.

"It's you," she said. "You switched places with the prince. That was clever."

"Are you still going to shoot me, Cindy?"

She treated him to a little smile. Nice. "I suppose I don't need to. Can you see the light of death from here, Jord? Or does your kind see something else?"

The only thing Jord needed to do was get Frankie to that transport. Spots of red were already leaking through the T-shirt bandages, even as Russ tied her arm into a sling. She had to get home.

Jord held up his hands. "No need to shoot me in front of your daughter," he said. "I'll die here, like a good little clone. Just go, before I tell these soldiers to make your journey as difficult as possible."

Cindy didn't respond. Frankie did.

"No."

The girl had been shot, and thrown from the roof of a car, yet she was struggling to her feet. She inserted herself between Jord and Cindy. "I won't leave without him. I don't see any of your androids here. You can't drag me to the transport. I'll bleed to death."

He loved her for saying it, but it was a mistake.

Cindy's gaze traveled between Frankie and Jord, and back again. "Ah," she said. "I've been misunderstanding the situation. I thought Francesca was merely showing misguided kindness. An unfortunate quality. Michael's genes. But it's more than that, yes?"

He didn't even rank as high as a scorpion. To Cindy, he was mold-riddled bread. A black spot on the shower curtain.

Michael, on the other hand, looked at Jord as he would a mouse that was stuck on a glue trap. With a certain amount of pity, maybe even a wish that things could be different. Jord could see why Frankie often looked to her father to be the reasonable one.

But Frankie had given Cindy all the tools she needed to win. Cindy might not bend to sentimentality herself, but she knew how to manipulate it in others. "Michael," she said, "escort Mr. Mathison to the transport. If Francesca fights? Shoot him."

"And what if I fight?" Jord said, an ounce of rebellion welling up through his purpose. "What if my soldiers fight?"

Cindy lowered the gun. She was completely comfortable here. No wonder she was certain getting back to Pathbound would be no trouble. "Then I'll shoot her. Remember, Mr. Mathison. I can always make a copy."

A copy she would despise. Frankie didn't even react. She stared at her mother with steel in her eyes.

"It would be regrettable," Cindy added, "considering the resources we've put into her education, and how well it's worked out. But if it can't be helped, it can't."

Michael took hold of Jord's arm. "She doesn't mean that."

"She absolutely means it," Jord said. "If you don't think so, you're fooling yourself."

Russ offered Frankie an arm for support, while Jord looked to the soldiers. He didn't see another choice. "Stand down," he said, in Roguran. Suhainnan. Whatever it was. "Lead us to the Earthen carriage."

They lowered their weapons, exchanging glances here and

there. He could practically hear their thoughts. Their prince wasn't drunk? Their captain wasn't with him?

Get Frankie to the transport. Get her to Earth.

He nodded to the soldiers, trying to look official, and they fell into line. Two in front, with Frankie and Russ behind them, followed by Cindy and the others.

"This is all a misunderstanding, you know," Michael said jovially, as if they were at Pathbound exchanging anecdotes after a party. Jord stumbled, and Michael caught him. "Cindy wants to test the limits of science. I had something else in mind."

Jord clamped his lips shut and kept his eyes on Frankie's back as Audrey, Bex, and the others fell into step. Frankie's posture was slumped, her shoulder drooping awkwardly.

"Utopia," Michael said. "A real one. Think about it. The chance to test utopian theories in other worlds. Tweak where necessary. Return to Earth with the answers to all our problems. We'd be heroes."

"So far all you've managed to create is a world at war."

Michael shook his head. "Not in Suhainn."

"Suhainn thrives under a false monarchy," Jord said. "They think they're living under a good, fair king. He never leads them into war, because there's no one to war with. He doesn't overtax. They're well fed and happy."

"So, then," Michael said, "what's the problem?"

Words shriveled on Jord's tongue. Michael didn't truly want a utopian society. He wanted to play with Pathbound puppets, and Cindy used that to control him. If he didn't understand the difference, Jord wasn't going to make him see it during a five minute walk. Especially not with the world flashing black every few steps, waves of heat radiating up the sides of his face.

Get Frankie to the transport. Get her to Earth.

After that, she would have to find a way to fight this. They could erase her memories, but she was still Frankie Hartiger. She'd figure it out again. Eventually, she might even remember.

She might remember him, too.

When they got to the hatch, Cindy swung the door open. "I'll go first," she said. "The rest of you, follow me. And don't try anything."

She directed that last comment to Frankie. She knew a little about her daughter, after all.

Jord slid down the ladder more than he climbed. His hands were numb against the rungs, his feet like blocks of concrete. He could feel his body shutting down, his blood slowing.

He landed next to Frankie. She looped her uninjured arm around his waist and helped him around to the side of the transport where the operations panel glowed orange in the wall. Cindy was already there, beckoning to Bex to tell Liz that all was well.

"I won't let them take my memories," Frankie whispered.

"Perhaps have them erase the ones where you hated me."

"Those are probably the ones they'll let me keep."

He wanted to tighten his grip around her shoulders, pull her closer, but she drifted out of reach. His head fell back, like an unintentional doze, and it was difficult to right it again.

He wasn't supposed to die until after she'd gone. He wasn't supposed to let her go without... without what? He fumbled in his pocket for the one thing he could give her that actually belonged to him. It wasn't there.

His stone. His anchor. Where had it gone?

The wall met his back, cold metal against his palms. The rush of the ocean drowned the voices—all but one. Calling his name.

It was funny, the sound of those waves. He didn't

remember traveling to Suhainn. The water sounded wrong somehow. Mechanical. Whirring, more than rushing.

A silhouette, solid. The click of a firearm, the cold tang of metal. Voices, arguing. Falling away.

A hand on his cheek, warm. Her lips against his, salty, too brief, and then against his ear. "I will send them to the farthest reaches of the universe. I promise."

"No," he heard himself say. "I was wrong. You're not like them."

Her warmth pulled away.

Her father's hands guided her into the transport. Firmly, though gently, as if he didn't want to be unkind. As if that were anything more than a show, when Mom stood over Jord with a gun in his face.

He was dying, anyway. If she didn't get in the transport? He'd die now.

Dad strapped her in behind Bex, whose eyes were locked on Jord. Frankie hissed as Dad arranged the strap around her injured shoulder, and he had the audacity to give her a sympathetic smile. But he didn't stop. He didn't apologize.

Frankie half expected Mom to kill Jord, anyway. But once Frankie was secured, Mom stepped away from him and pocketed the weapon. As if he were nothing more than an insect, struggling to crawl out of a flooded bathtub.

Not that he was struggling. She wasn't even sure he was breathing, the light too dim to see. He was a few feet away, propped against the wall, head tucked against his chest.

He had to be alive.

"Dad," Frankie said. "We can't leave him."

"There's nothing we can do for him, Francesca," Dad said. "It's better this way."

And then he was gone, leaving no buffer between Frankie and Jord. The burning pain in her shoulder might have been a minor inconvenience, compared to the sight of him, lying there. Alone.

He'd come after her. He'd tried to live.

Dad buckled himself in on the far side, behind Mom, and the transport doors started to ease closed.

Liz's voice crackled over the com. "Everything copacetic?"

In front of Frankie, Bex drew in a deep breath. Frankie wanted to tell her the trip would be short, that it was smoother than it had been the last time she traveled.

The words drowned in her throat. She had no power to comfort anyone else. She had no power to comfort herself.

And then, Bex threw herself across the seat and pressed her lips to Audrey's. Before Frankie understood what was happening, Bex dropped the com into Audrey's lap, rolled out of her seat, and squeezed under the closing door. She landed on the floor and hauled Jord's limp form across the short distance to stuff him onto the transport. She stepped back, hands lifted in an exaggerated shrug, a smile playing on her lips.

Frankie had no idea whether Audrey was in on the plan, but her friend didn't hesitate. She dove across the seat and grabbed Jord's legs, yanking them all the way inside before securing the restraints around his body.

Mom watched the doors click shut, nostrils flared, and Dad just looked shocked. But neither of them spoke, and Frankie could practically read their thoughts: if they protested, if they shot at Bex—or Jord—Liz would hear through Audrey's com. She'd stop the launch.

Bex met Frankie's eyes. "Yeah," she said to the control box. "We're all here."

Frankie knew what Bex was sacrificing, the family reunion she was putting on hold. Potentially forever. Seven years in this world, stuck on that island, and she'd just let go of the girl she loved so Jord could live. The weight of it stuck in Frankie's throat as she put a hand to the glass. *We'll come back for you,* she thought.

Some treacherous corner of her brain added, *If we win.*

They had to win.

The transport shuddered. Bex faded to an outline, then disappeared.

Frankie didn't care if it was unsafe. She leaned forward as far as she could, and stretched her left arm to touch Jord's shoulder. Alive, for now. Here.

During the thirty seconds of inky blackness that encompassed the transport, his words echoed through her head.

You're not like them.

Well. It wasn't too likely she'd get the option to shoot them off to some remote world, anyway. As much as she wanted to picture them battling alien snakes and dinosaurs—no, dinosaur-sized snakes—Cindy and Michael had the guns. They had the security bots, waiting at Pathbound. In all likelihood, Frankie's memories would be gone by dinnertime.

But Jord had made it onto the transport. She could still save him.

Too soon, threads of light knit their way through the darkness.

The dock materialized in a hurricane of chaos. Security bots formed a ring around the transport, dozens of them, weapons protruding from their utility domes.

They were shooting at each other.

Blue stunner rounds screamed around the transport, mixed with the unmistakable blood red of shots that were meant to injure or kill. That wasn't legal, but Frankie couldn't summon an ounce of surprise.

Mom was out of the transport before it stopped shuddering. The killer security bots backed off, their bolts arranging a zone of safety around her, but Mom still had to dodge a few of the icy blasts. She wasn't heading for the door; she was headed for Jord, her weapon drawn. His memories threatened Pathbound so much that he was her first priority.

Finally, something they had in common. Frankie ripped off her restraints and dove.

Audrey got there first, and Frankie joined her a second later, the two of them shielding his body with theirs.

"Try to replace me with a clone," Audrey said. "I've been training my voice since I was five years old. Can you speed up that growth process?"

She couldn't. Frankie saw it in her eyes. Frankie expected to feel a twinge of regret that the opposite was true of her, that her mother had no hesitation about the idea of replacing her own daughter. But for the first time, she honestly didn't care. She'd spent her life trying to overcome some imaginary failing, when Mom and Dad were the ones who'd failed her.

A stunner bolt zipped past Mom's protective bot-circle, catching her in the ankle. She dropped, lunging into a crawl as Frankie tried to locate her father. Russ and the others hit the floor of the transport, unable to escape the crisscrossing stunner rounds.

"Come on," Frankie said. Together, she and Audrey dropped to the ground and dragged Jord toward the door.

The last time she'd crawled across this floor, Jord had been the one dragging her as the transport belched fire and smoke.

Not so different, then.

They made it through the doors. Her bandage was soaked, the blood loss already making her lightheaded. Frankie dropped Jord's arm and dashed for the manual panel, sliding the doors shut.

A storm of laser rounds assaulted the metal doors like hail, and Audrey gave them a dubious look. "That's not going to hold."

Frankie held a hand to Jord's wrist. He had a pulse. Faint. Stuttering. But a pulse.

Liz stood on the control deck, switching frantically from one screen to another, bending to type, switching again.

Frankie had to shout over the noise of bolts hitting the door. "What's going on? Why are the bots shooting at each other?"

"I opened the elevator to send Jamie upstairs for Jord's protein shot," Liz said. "The bots were waiting."

"My parents activated them from Rogur."

"Yeah, well, I reprogrammed them for a hot second, but it's not sticking. And now they're at war."

How had Liz known they'd need a protein shot? *Not the time for questions.* "I can shut down the bots, but I need to keep those doors closed as long as possible," Frankie said.

"And what are you going to do when your parents get free?" Audrey hissed. "They're armed. You have to turn the bots to your side, not shut them down."

Liz slid a tablet across the floor to Frankie. "They can't be overridden without direct input to the hardware," Frankie explained. Not without her watch, and the party-crashing software she'd installed on it so long ago. "By the time these doors open, they'll all be on my parents' side."

"So what are we going to do?"

The screen felt odd under her fingertips. Strange, to work on tech that looked like what it was, without being a million years old. Strange, to watch the security coding flip by like water over rocks.

Comfortable.

"The doors are opening," Liz said. "You need to take cover."

"The supply room," Frankie said, slipping the tablet under her injured arm and grabbing Jord's hand. Her shoulder fought her, sending tremors of pain down her arm.

She ignored it.

The streaks were more red than blue as Frankie and Audrey dragged Jord into the room where Frankie had spent long hours hiding, listening to her parents' voices and imagining their heroic adventures.

She set the tablet onto a bench and kept working.

"We need to drive them into the transport," Audrey said. "Liz can send them to a place that's never even been seen."

"That's not possible."

"Then send them to one of the places without people. We have to do something."

Frankie hit enter. The rounds stopped.

After the shrieking blasts, the silence burrowed into Frankie's ears like a thing with claws. She knelt beside Jord, leaned her cheek down to feel his breath. Shallow. Infrequent. But there.

Her father's voice broke the silence, from the other side of the door. "Francesca."

Audrey threw herself against the door. As if that would stop them for long.

"If you come out, we can get Jord the protein shot," Dad said. "If you stay, he'll die."

Audrey met Frankie's gaze and shook her head. *No kidding,* Frankie thought.

"Mom's waiting to finish him off," Frankie called back. As if Dad hadn't already tried to do the same.

"We can negotiate that. But only if you come out."

"You can't wipe his memory. I'm not stupid."

Dad let out that deep, fake laugh she'd always used to find him in a room. She was supposed to have inherited his fatal ethical streak? Really? "He could have revealed our secrets on television any number of times," Dad said. "Maybe we've been unfair."

Audrey raised her eyebrows and mouthed, "Do something."

"There aren't any weapons in here," Frankie whispered. "They'll find a way in eventually."

End of the line. She brushed a curl out of Jord's eyes.

And then she realized. There *were* weapons here.

She jumped up and ran to the locker of protocol boxes. They stood at attention like soldiers awaiting active duty. NEBULA, DWARF, STARDUST, ORBIT.

METEORITE.

Frankie ripped the cylinder open and grabbed two of the applicators she knew she'd find there. They were like syringes, only instead of a needle they had nickel-sized openings at the end. The push of a button would puncture the skin, insert the chip with a puff of air, and seal the wound.

A beautiful design, if she said so herself.

"Francesca?" Dad said. "What do you say?"

Frankie shoved one of the applicators into Audrey's hand. "Straight to the base of the neck," she whispered. "Push this button. You get him. I'll get her."

Audrey nodded. "I hope you know what you're doing."

Frankie slid the applicator into her sleeve. And then she opened the door a crack. As if she were tentative. Unsure.

She was a terrible actress, and a terrible liar. No better than Dad, when it came down to it.

She had to do this fast.

"Dad?" she said. "He's not—he isn't breathing."

Her father's face crumpled, his display of sympathy as

amateurish as his sleight of hand. Frankie affected her best sob as she threw herself forward.

Instead of landing in his embrace, Frankie ducked under his shoulder toward her mother, and Audrey leapt out of the storage room, all grace as she took advantage of Dad's turned head, his surprise, to press the applicator to his neck.

Dad gasped as his body went rigid. He fell.

Frankie didn't pause. She only had eyes for her mother.

Mom was favoring the ankle where the bot had zapped her, standing with her weight tipped to the side. Her face was smudged, her hair erupting into a tangle not unlike Frankie's usual mess of curls.

"Clever, Francesca," she said, staring at her husband. "What will you do now?"

"Now we give Jord the protein shot."

Mom shook her head. "I should have burned that world to a cinder, with all of you in it."

"Secret's not worth the trouble after all?" Frankie asked.

"One day, Francesca, you'll see what I mean. You can't win this."

Frankie maneuvered closer, her sore hands protesting as she gripped the applicator, her shoulder screaming like it was on fire. "You've already won," she said.

Mom actually paused at that. Like maybe they'd zapped Dad to help *her* somehow. Like maybe Frankie understood her after all.

It was all the hesitation Frankie needed, and all she would get. She lunged for Mom's injured side, with none of Audrey's grace—but she didn't need it. Mom was off balance, favoring that zapped leg. When she tried a step to ward off Frankie's attack, the ankle gave way, slamming her knee into the transport floor.

Mom twisted to grab Frankie's wrist, not finished yet. One

handed, Frankie used Mom's grip as a pivot and jammed the applicator to the back of her neck.

"You were right," Frankie said. "I do understand you. And you raised me to be ruthless. Didn't you?"

Mom's eyes were wide as she fell.

It was exceedingly kind of the Hartigers to leave so much magic for Kol to play with.

With the villains fled, every door of the palace yawned wide. To make it easier for their soldiers, no doubt. Why would they care whether Kol—or Jord, or whoever they thought he was—escaped the suite, if the gods were set to kill everyone, anyway?

And so, plagued by Reyche's protestations, he made his way to the top of the palace and helped himself to a tour of the Hartigers' rooms. Their suite was alive with magic, pinpricks of fairy dust that blinked and beeped in the dark.

When one's world was already scheduled to burn, one had no cares about flipping as many switches as he pleased, until he discovered how to reach the Earthen imposter Elandria. So she might ready the protein his twin needed.

His brother, in truth. He'd left his *cluichur* token in his clothes, like a reminder.

Standing in the Hartigers' apartment, Kol gave the stone a

toss. Perhaps he'd live to return it one day. Learn what the markings said.

"This vista," Reyche said, standing before the window, "can it be a portal to Earth?"

Kol pocketed the pebble and moved to examine the wall beside the window. He selected the prettiest button, an enchanting turquoise. The towers melted into a sea view, with reedy trees decorating a strip of sand. The red button shifted the sea to a fire-spitting mountain, ash collecting in a cloud above. He'd never seen its like in Rogur.

"I wonder why the Hartigers did not choose this view," Kol said. "It fits them. There's a latch on the window. Shall we try that?"

"I don't think—"

But Kol was already opening the door.

Another balcony. His life was strewn with them. This view was entirely less pleasing than the metal teeth of the Earthen skyline. He'd have preferred the flaming mountain, truly.

In his own world, smaller spots of fire bloomed through the city, his people dying at the mechanical hands of the gods. "We have to help them," he said.

"There are android patrols on the floor," Reyche said, testing the Earthen word for the gods. It was all the same to Kol, but he liked the way English sounded on his captain's tongue. "We won't be able to escape."

"So this is our last stand, is it? How appropriate." Kol stretched over the side of the balcony, the wind tugging at his too-short hair.

The long way down, then. Excellent.

He started over the rail.

But Reyche caught hold of Kol's hands and drew them to his chest, dragging him back so abruptly that Kol fell with him, knees hitting the steel balcony with a crack.

"Do not do this," Reyche said. "I beg you."

Kol could feel his captain's panicked heartbeat against the back of his hand, and for a moment, he did not understand. He'd been so caught in his own heroics, he'd assumed his intentions must be obvious.

He should have anticipated Reyche's response. The poor man must think himself caught in an eternal loop. Kol should have spared him this moment of pain, and every threat of pain, forever. If he wanted to help his people, he should start with the one who had never abandoned him.

He gripped Reyche's fingers and edged toward the captain until their arms were flush against each other. "How is it that after all the trouble I have heaped upon you, I somehow still have your love?"

Reyche dropped his chin to his chest with what might have been a laugh, or a sob, and Kol could bear it no longer. He took Reyche's chin between his fingers and kissed him. He would make no empty promises; he was not certain he had the ability to accomplish anything useful. He was not even certain they would live out this day.

It seemed likely they would not.

For the first time in a long while, he wanted to. Reyche clutched his hands, returning his kiss with a hunger that was at once familiar and thrilling. A beginning, at the end.

"The darkness has fled," Kol said. "I will not leave you."

Reyche still held onto him, as though he could not entirely believe it. "The darkness will come again."

It did have that tendency, had even before the false gods. But perhaps Kol was not so alone as he'd always assumed. Perhaps if he could remember that, and keep the *afan* at arm's length, he would stand a fighting chance against it. "Then we will face it down. I have people to help, after all."

Kol considered postponing the mission until they'd had a

chance to make up properly. The prospect of getting interrupted by murderous gods was somewhat more distasteful than waiting.

But as they prepared to climb, a bell rang from the Hartigers' suite, an insidious kind of a whine. Kol looked at Reyche, who shrugged.

On the outside of the balcony doors, a woman's face materialized. Elandria. She'd shed her hood. And she was smiling.

"Prince Kol," she said, "I know how to deactivate the gods."

FORTY-FIVE

JORD

When consciousness threaded its way into Jord's mind, his first thought was that the world no longer sounded like Rogur. It sounded like air conditioning, wheels rattling on linoleum, the rhythmic beeping of some machine. It smelled like alcohol, and green Jello.

And citrus. He opened his eyes.

Frankie was asleep in a chair, her chin propped on her left hand. She'd pushed the chair so close to the bed that if Jord were to reach out, he'd be able to touch her hand. Her right arm was bound in a clean sling, no blood showing. Jord felt a pang of fresh anger at her parents for having put her through this.

How had she managed to defeat them?

Beyond her, daylight streamed in through a window packed with skyscrapers. He recognized the globe of the urban farm, the spires of the old brick towers, all surrounded by highways of darting drones. They looked like bees on a mission.

And, off to the corner, the lacy titanium of a building he'd never thought he'd see from the outside.

His first visit beyond Pathbound Tower, and it was to a hospital. That was... well, sad.

His head didn't hurt, but the back of his neck did. He touched it tentatively, dragging a strand of IV tubing along with his hand. There was a wound at the base of his skull, and tightly woven stitches. No bump. No implant.

Right. He recalled his demand for its removal, Frankie's attempt to dissuade him. Her fingertips on his skin, trying to be gentle.

Jord cleared his throat. It felt dry. Cracked. "Looks like I missed some fun."

Frankie startled awake, sitting up so fast that he regretted having spoken. Still in survival mode, clearly. He could hardly blame her for that. She stared at him, eyes wide.

And then she threw herself into his arms. "You're not dead."

"I think someone erased your memories," he said into her hair. "You don't seem to know who I am. It's been too long since I sabotaged one of your—"

Her lips found his, cutting him off. After everything that had happened, after everything he'd said to her, she still wanted him.

He didn't deserve it. He didn't deserve her hands in his hair or her legs tangled with his as she kissed him like she needed him to live.

"You're only rewarding me for bad behavior when you do that, you know," he told her, trailing his lips along her jaw.

"Try sabotaging one of my plans again someday. See what happens."

He pulled away, with an effort, and tucked a strand of hair behind her ear. "I'm sorry," he said. "I thought I was protecting you."

"And yourself?"

He nodded, words catching in his throat. She'd see it now, how afraid he'd been.

This time, though, he'd let her go.

But she dipped her head, closing the short gap between them to brush her lips against his again. "Aren't we past that by now?"

The fear in his throat dissolved into relief, such a strong wave that he had to blink a wave of tears away. He'd spent years deliberately stacking the odds against himself, as if building a wall between them could save him from the Hartigers.

A few days traipsing around another world, and Frankie saw through it all. "I'm sorry," he said, "but my brain has ceased to function. What are we past?"

Frankie smacked him on the back of the head.

At least she didn't stop kissing him.

FORTY-SIX

FRANKIE

Security bots moved aside now, when Frankie presented her credentials. Doors parted, and elevators stopped on any floor she wanted—even the hidden ones. No fancy tricks, no loopholes, just facial scans and fingerprints and run-of-the-mill ID checks.

All the access she'd ever begged for, yet Frankie stood outside the glass doors of the transport operations center and watched as Jord, Audrey, and Bex worked together to turn Frankie's plans—the first virtual-reality orientation experience for interworld immigrants—into reality. They knew better than anyone what newcomers to Earth would need help with.

And one way or another, immigration was coming. Interworld travel didn't have regulations. Not really. Not yet. While politicians argued over what to call this little situation—reintegration, since the people were Earthen clones? But they'd never been integrated in the first place!—Rogur slipped deeper into chaos by the day. Frankie couldn't keep delivering supplements, which Suhainn would need soon, too, when reports from Kol confirmed that every trip wrenched the planet further apart.

Frankie didn't have a solution. The people would need a place to go.

So she'd stripped the operations floor of its faux-spaceship feel, swapping metal walls for wooden panels, harsh overhead lighting for softly glowing sconces. She removed the gaudy travel vids and replaced them with calming scenes from Earth. She added carpets and chairs, tasting stations and vaccination booths, and games designed to make interworld immigration as smooth as possible.

Audrey had volunteered to write the music.

Today, Jord was out of the hospital. Free, after a week of tests and healing, and already throwing his energy into making Frankie's plan work.

Even though she'd spent many of her waking hours down here since returning, she found herself hesitating to join them. They were all on the same side now, all working together. Still, nerves sliced between her ribs, freezing her at the threshold. What did she have to add to this, really? A few ideas. A bit of mechanics.

Maybe she ought to give them their space.

Frankie had spent so much of her time working alone, on schemes that never quite gelled. Teamwork wasn't exactly a familiar approach.

After a while, Liz joined her at the doors. They hadn't talked since Frankie's return, except to exchange essential information, but Liz was still here. She'd worked her contacts to find the best VR coders to build the orientation. And she'd saved Kol's life by shutting down the androids. That had to count for something.

They watched together as Bex plucked Audrey's pencil from her hands, and Frankie almost feared for Bex's survival, interrupting the great songwriter at her work. But when Bex ran away, taunting her girlfriend with the pencil, Audrey threw the notepad down to chase after her, laughing.

"Last time I saw Bex, she was a little kid," Liz said. "She wore pigtails. She played princess. Now, she's... a warrior. She's in love. She's a young woman."

Audrey caught up with Bex, pulling her into a kiss. They looked so happy.

"Luckily, she's an awesome one." Frankie hesitated. "But Rogur was hard on her. She still needs you."

Liz nodded. Clenched her fists. Nodded again.

"You rescued them," Frankie said. "You fulfilled your mission. Why are you still here? At Pathbound?"

"I hear there's a world full of people to save. And who knows what's happening in Suhainn?"

They were still strategizing that particular diplomatic mission. She'd suggested, tentatively, that Jord might go with them. See his brother. He'd replied that he wasn't sure he could face it.

His whole life, a fabrication. But real, nonetheless. She wouldn't push him on it. He'd go to Suhainn when he was ready, or he wouldn't.

Interworld travel might not have regulations. The world was certainly at a loss for what to call the Hartiger manipulation—and what kind of charges they could possibly face as a result.

Clone science, though? That did have regulations. Many. Which meant whole sections of Pathbound Tower were currently roped off as authorities worked out solutions for the hundreds of incubation tanks—some occupied and already connected to speed-growth drugs. Every day, the police took more Pathbound scientists into custody, while Frankie's parents were held without bail.

It wasn't enough. It was a start.

"I'm still mad at you for stranding us," Frankie said.

Liz sighed. "I know. I'm still a little mad at you for *being* mad." She set a hand on Frankie's shoulder and gave it a squeeze. "But we're family. We'll get through it."

And with that, she opened the doors and headed for the console.

Family. Liz saw them as family.

Frankie could work with that.

Join my mailing list to read deleted scenes from *Bypass the Stars*—and gain access to my exclusive VIP reader library!

Sign up here: https://www.subscribepage.com/bypassthestars

Also by Kate Sheeran Swed

League of Independent Operatives

Alter Ego

Anti-Hero

Mastermind

Nemesis

Defender - *coming soon!*

Pathbound Enterprises

Bypass the Stars

Toccata System Novella Trilogy

Parting Shadows

Phantom Song

Prodigal Storm

Complete Trilogy Box Set

(*includes bonus short story*)

Short Stories

Don't Look Back (And Other Stories)

ABOUT THE AUTHOR

Kate Sheeran Swed loves hot chocolate, plastic dinosaurs, and airplane tickets. She has trekked along the Inca Trail to Macchu Picchu, hiked on the Mýrdalsjökull glacier in Iceland, and climbed the ruins of Masada to watch the sunrise over the Dead Sea. Kate currently lives in New York's capital region with her husband and two kids, and a pair of cats who were named after movie dogs (Benji and Beethoven). She holds an MFA in Fiction from Pacific University.

You can find more of Kate's work, and pick up a free novella, at katesheeranswed.com.

 facebook.com/katesheeranswed
 instagram.com/katesheeranswed